Knowledge is power, and keeping knowledge away from people shifts the balance of that power to the few who are in control. Then it is time to be afraid--to be very afraid.

Gary Petras, author of *Memories End,*
The Sisters Hood and the *Thorndancer,*
Small Heroes And Farrow And Blackstorm Trilogies

With the rapturously pulpy *5 Clones,* Bonilla envisions the combustible screwball future of a not-so-United States, where dark folklore mixes with intercepted email transmissions, groundbreaking scientific advances brush up against the promise of religious salvation, border walls are erected to keep people in, and everybody's got a gun. It's probably the best thing Johnny Depp has appeared in in a decade.

Christopher Clancy
author of *We Take Care of Our Own*

Ed Bonilla's novel, *5 Clones,* is a chilling tale in which our present day political divisions and technology trends project to a frightening future collision. A fun and thought provoking read!

Chuck Brown, author of *The Lake Hayes Regatta,*
Letters from the Attic & The Forgotten Lake Secession

If you want to take a peek into a possible future of The United States of America, definitely give *5 Clones* a read, but be careful because once you peek, you may find yourself completely sucked in until the last word of the last page!

Jonathan R. Rose, author of *Carrion, Gato y Lobo*
and *The Spirit of Laughter*

5 CLONES

Montag Press
ISBN: 978-1-940233-71-0
Cover art © 2020 Sean Gregory Miller
Design © 2020 Rick Febré
Author photo © 2020 Greg Mettler

Montag Press Team:
Project Editor – John Rak
Managing Director – Charlie Franco

A Montag Press Book
www.montagpress.com
Montag Press
777 Morton Street, Unit B
San Francisco CA 94129 USA

Printed & Digitally Originated in the United States of America
10 9 8 7 6 5 4 3 2 1

Interactive 5 Clones Playlist:

This playlist is available on Spotify. Simply search: "5 Clones by Ed Bonilla" and have a listen. Thank you to Jocelyn, Dan, and Scar for choosing the songs. This is simply what they are listening to, singing, and bands they are watching as the story progresses around them. More information available at www.5Clones.com.

Track list:

Jocelyn's Songs:
1. *The Whole of the Moon*- The Waterboys
2. *This Charming Man*- The Smiths
3. *Blister In The Sun*- Violent Femmes
4. *Heroes*- Hollywood Vampires
5. *Please, Please, Please Let me Get what I Want*- The Smiths
6. *Positively Lost Me*- The Rave-Ups
7. *Tomorrow*- Morrissey
8. *Save It For Later*- The English Beat
9. *Tenderness*- General Public

Dan and Scar's Songs:
1. *Hyena* Rancid
2. *California Uber Alles*- Dead Kennedys
3. *Apocalypse Redux*- The Old Firm Casuals
4. *Funky Kingston*- Toots and The Maytals
5. *Red Lights Flash*- Year of the Fist
6. *Clones (We're All)*- Alice Cooper
7. *Skinhead Moonstomp*- Symarip
8. *Don't Count Me Out*- Screaming Bloody Marys
9. *No Eager Men*- Swingin' Utters
10. *5 Clones*- Radical Times
11. *Victim*- Charger

For Herb and Linda Bonilla.

5 CLONES

EDWARD BONILLA

MONTAG

Suppose that every prospective parent in the world stopped having children naturally, and instead produced clones of themselves. What would the world be like in another 20 or 30 years? The answer is: much like today. Cloning would only copy the genetic aspects of people who are already here.

-Nathan Myhrvold

I'm all alone, so are we all
We're all clones
All are one and one are all
All are one and one are all

-Alice Cooper

ONE

HE WAS ALMOST TO RENO but the truck was making gasping sounds and just begging to be pulled over to join the other decaying abandoned vehicles that littered the sides of the freeway. The sun was going down and sand and dust swirled in orange eddies of wind that raced across the pavement in front of and behind him. His cargo sat in silence, heads covered, crouched in the bed of the old vehicle wrapped in blankets and burlap.

Mentally Dan urged the truck on. It was an old Chevy that had served him well for years, but he could feel the tired engine succumbing to the dry sands of the Nevada desert. Dan considered his mental map. Maybe 20 miles to Reno, but finding any water there he could afford would be a long shot, and finding gas would be nearly impossible. Then there were the Sierra Nevada mountains to cross before he could reach California. He wouldn't even bother with Sacramento, which by all accounts was a burned black wasteland without a building standing. Dan's destination was about 50 miles south of Sacramento. The city of Stockton was a rumored green paradise where fresh water still flowed in the old delta as fires flickered and scorched over the rest of California.

A dust devil hit the truck from the left with nearly enough velocity to force them from the road. Dan swerved the truck back through both lanes and kept it rolling on the black asphalt, just barely. The old engine sputtered but soldiered on. The speedometer read 20 miles an hour. They were hardly moving at all now. Dan's knuckles were white as his calloused hands gripped the steering wheel; visibility through the smoky sandstorm was about 10 or 15 feet. He could see that much road ahead. Everything else was a haze of orange swirling around him.

He had been having dreams about Stockton lately, the last Eden of the once Golden State. A traveling trader had told Dan that people still had vegetable gardens in Stockton. The San Joaquin Valley soil was so rich that everything grew there whether the sun was frosted with smoke or not. Residents were able to keep wildfires at bay by pumping water from the delta canals, and the delta was indefatigable.

The truck's crawl through the heat and the sand and the smoke continued as Dan rubbed his eyes, expecting the mirage that suddenly appeared before him would go away. Standing just to the side of the road immersed in the swirling eddies of sand stood a scarfed figure in a leather jacket. A gas mask completely covered the hitchhiker's face, but a long shank of chestnut hair blew vigorously over the glass of the mask. Both feet had been firmly planted in the dust long enough for them to have become completely buried. One arm shot straight at Dan's truck holding out a gloved fist with its thumb up and pointed directly at Reno.

Dan slowed and then stopped the truck, cursing himself for an idiot the minute he did it. That chestnut hair. Despite the gas mask and the leather jacket, he could see that the figure was slender and feminine.

In the back of the truck his cargo murmured. They were incapable of speech but Dan understood the emotions they expressed through their wordless mumbles, much the way a shepherd would read the bleating of his flock when a wolf was near. They hadn't been happy for days (if anyone besides Dan would have ever considered them happy in the first place), but they were now making known to Dan their discomfort at stopping in the middle of a sand storm.

Before Dan could give thought to the fact that a hitchhiker

should not be here, or that he knew not to ever pick up hitchhikers in the first place, the passenger door swung open and dust and smoke blew in, as the woman in the gas mask sprang quickly into the cab and slammed the door behind her. The orange illumination of a small fire burning out of control nearby lit the movements of her thin figure, making the realization all the clearer to Dan that this was indeed a young woman.

The truck choked, almost died. Dan gently pressed the gas to get her moving again. Once they were back up to 15 miles per hour, she started running a bit more smoothly, and Dan glanced back and forth from the road to his new passenger.

Content to be moving again, the cargo cooed to each other soothingly and hunkered down more deeply together under their blankets in the back.

Dan hadn't seen a woman in months. He remembered what it was like to be around a woman. A man acted differently, said things differently when a woman was present. A woman brought out the kinder, gentler side of a man. He did remember. Maybe that is why he had stopped the truck. If she killed him and stole his unquiet cargo it would be his own damn fault now. But, when he had set out on this trip, he had said he had nothing to lose. *Nothing to lose.*

The truck was slowly passing another smoldering field alive with raging fire. The wind attacked the truck again with a wave of ashes and sand. Everything that could burn out here was burning. It was a bad one. Dan said a silent Hail Mary that today would not be the day the engine quit on him.

She was taking off her mask.

He glanced over again and saw her pale face for the first time. Dan's mouth fell open a bit. She was filthy and looked exhausted but she was a young and beautiful woman. He could see grime caked about her neck and ears as she tucked her dark, stray locks up into a black cap and hood that covered her head. Shivering, she tucked her hands into the armpits of her old fashioned brown leather bomber jacket. There was a patch of an upside down American flag at the shoulder. She did not look at Dan, only straight ahead at the sand and the road and the flames and the wrecks that stretched on in front of them. There was no horizon to see.

"Look, I'm not a thief and I'm not a prostitute." Her voice was rough and grainy like the wind hammering the truck. "I don't want to hurt you or steal from you, and most of all I don't want to fuck you. Is that cool? Because if not, you can let me back out."

Dan didn't say anything as he considered her words silently. He stared straight ahead at the road and checked his rearview mirror. No running lights ahead and no headlights behind. His was probably the only running vehicle for miles and miles. They drove on in silence for several seconds.

His young passenger continued, "I had an... an accident back there and I got stranded. I was stranded out there for almost an hour before you came by. All my shit burned up. I really don't want to go back out there, so I really hope you can just be cool." Her voice wavered a bit and for a moment Dan thought she might cry. She didn't.

Instead, for the first time now, she glanced over at Dan. He kept his dark eyes on the tattered road but did not miss her calculating glance. Dan knew what she saw with those analytical eyes. He was tall and lean and did not smile. His shoulders were broad and thick with muscle. His skin was dark.

"It's cool," Dan mouthed the words but nothing came out. He cleared his throat and tried again. Still nothing. He nodded. She seemed to understand.

TWO

Listening to: *The Whole Of The Moon*
by The Waterboys
(On your dad's old turntable)

Dearest Sarah Joy,   365 days today since you were born!

Happy birthday my one-year-old girl! Today we had the sweetest party for you. Your Uncle Russel and Daddy and Johnny Depp were all there. Johnny even baked a cake for you! He said it was the first cake he had ever baked because he used to have two personal chefs that would cook him whatever he wanted. It was a little lopsided, but it tasted great. Strawberry icing! So sweet of him.

I wanted to take a picture of you stuffing your sweet little face with Johnny Depp's cake, but taking pictures has become a thing of the past for us. Your daddy and I haven't had cell phones since we left California and I haven't seen a film camera since I was a kid. We just don't take pictures anymore. The other day your daddy said, "Jocelyn, I'm going to get you an old Polaroid camera," but who knows where he would find one of those, let alone the film for it? You were so sweet and good today and Daddy got you a big stuffed giraffe from the mercantile in town. Gosh, I wish I could have taken a picture.

What is a mother to do? Life's so different here in Colorado. I want to record it all. I want to post it all to Instagram like my friends with babies did back in the day, but the internet is gone for us now. Johnny has access to the NFUNet on an old desktop computer at his place, but it's not like it was. He told me, "Social media is completely dead! The information and news are so heavily censored by the Union now they're not even worth reading."

That's what I was thinking about when I saw this journal at the mercantile the other day. Facebook was just a big journal that people shared with their friends online, right? So, I figured I would start writing everything down for you. This journal is Facebook for my daughter! I love you so much, Sweetie! I want to write all about the long drive out here with you in the back of the car. You were so good! You didn't even cry when we were held up at the border crossing for two days trying to get out of California. We had to sleep in Daddy's truck and eat Cup O' Noodles for breakfast lunch and dinner, but...

Wait, that's not what I want to write about right now. I want to tell you about meeting Johnny Depp and what it's like to have someone who used to be famous as our neighbor. He really loves you too, Sweetie, especially since his own family is...

Wait, that's not what I want to write about either. I want to tell you all about what life was like when we had cell phones and the World Wide Web and what it was like growing up in the State of California before California left the United States and became the California Independent Republic. Those were interesting years! I want to tell you about how I met your daddy and what a beautiful, strong man he is. He loves you so much! I want to tell you about your Uncle Russel and what it is like living and working out here in the middle of nowhere on his farm with all the animals. We grow a lot of... well, I don't think I can tell you about that until you are older! Ha-ha. I guess by the time you are reading this you will know. You will understand.

There is so much I want to write to you! My beautiful one-year-old girl. Most of all I want to tell you how beautiful you are while you are taking a nap. You get really sweaty when you sleep, Sweetheart, like a nap is a work out for your body. It must be because you are growing. Your hair is so fine and light. It's just like a spider web of gold. Your breath is so warm and sweet. It's just like the steam coming off of a bath with rose petals in it. Your little feet are so soft and wrinkled and pink. I just love every inch of you so much!

So, where do I start, Sarah Joy? Where does my story begin? When I met your daddy? When Calexit actually became a thing? When I was born? Where I grew up? When we moved to Colorado so we could start all over again? There is so much to tell. My hand is already cramping just from writing these few pages! Oh, I hear you waking up from your nap, Sweetie! I will be back!

-Love Mommy

OK. I'm back. What a day. Your birthday, Sweetheart. After your nap we went out and saw the horses, then I finished making dinner and cleaned up from your party. Daddy and Russel came in and ate with us. Not Johnny though, he went back up the hill to his place. Maybe we will see him tomorrow.

Now it's all dark outside. You are back asleep in your little room. Daddy and Russel are out tonight with their rifles looking for coyotes. Daddy said we lost a lamb last night and we can't have that.

Here I am again in this quiet old house, listening to one of my old records on your daddy's old record player. No more phone apps or MP3s anymore. No more streaming songs from the cloud. Just old fashioned vinyl records. Just a journal I am writing for you. Sarah, someday you will know what life was like when you were a baby. And even before you were a baby...

I was born in a place called Stockton, California. It's near

San Francisco. Daddy says we will go back there someday. I was going to write "I hope so!" but I don't know if that's true. When I was a kid, Stockton was a pretty rough place. Back then, California was a state in a much larger country. It's not anymore. That's why we had a tough time getting out. We had to become citizens of the New Federal Union of 48 states. But that's getting back to what I don't want to write about now...

My parents, your Grandma Cindy and Grandpa Mark, had a nice house on the North Side of town when I was little. Things were much better on the North Side than they were on East Side where your daddy grew up. It was really rough over there.

I used to walk to school every day with the other neighborhood kids to Colonial Heights Elementary School. It was a clean little school and the teachers were all really very nice and friendly. I hope you can go to school someday, although right now it looks like I will be your teacher for a few years. The closest schoolhouse to us right now is up in Fort Collins and it is a long drive.

We also had a big supermarket near our house where we could go and buy whatever we wanted to eat: candy, chips, soda, whatever you wanted. Of course, now we can buy and trade things at the mercantile but it's not the same. Someday, I'm going to take you to a big city in California, little girl. I will take you inside a supermarket in the summer when it is so hot outside you have to walk barefoot on the white lines in the parking lot because the asphalt will burn your feet. Then, you can't wait to get in that air-conditioned market to look at all the things waiting there for you to buy. The linoleum floors are so cold on your feet and it always smells like fresh fruit and plastic wrapping. It's the smell of new stuff. I haven't smelled anything like it since we left California. Someday you will see.

Until then, Sweetheart… Life is good here. Your daddy is so sweet and kind now. He's a different person than he used to be. I think it is important for you to understand that. When you are older you will understand. Things are better now.

And you! You are perfect! Someday soon we are going to make a little brother or sister for you. And even if California and the New Federal Union go to war, we are going to be safe here in Colorado. Everything is going to turn out just fine. Your daddy is going to protect us and take care of us and we don't need to worry about a thing.

-Love Mommy

THREE

The following emails were retrieved from the computer of Dr. Derek Timm: Professor of Robotics and Engineering UC Berkeley, without his permission.

Three messages were sent by Dr. Abraha Tadese: Professor of Nanosciences and Nanoengineering UC Berkeley, Reassigned to Army Research Lab Nano Technology Division (ARLNTD), Adelphi Maryland.

Directive: Find Dr. Abraha Tadese at any cost.

—Department Homeland Security NFUS

From: Tadese@arlntd.army.mil
Date: Tuesday, March ▇▇ 2:17 p.m.
To: DTimm@berkeley.edu
Subject: The Team

Derek,

Greetings from Maryland! It has been a while my dear friend. How I miss beautiful California, and the fishing trips we would take out into the bay. Sailing past Alcatraz leaving all appurtenances behind, no thoughts of the laboratory, just the gulls calling as they floated an arm's length from the deck and the taste of salty fog in our mouths... I also miss our late night debates with graduate students. Where do the days go?

Maryland is a complete and utter change. Of course, I moved here expecting profound exploits. Teaming up with the Federal Government, with the Army for crying out loud, is not something that one does lightly. The intellectual team was my impetus for making the change, and, that is the reason that I am staying now, despite some early, shall I say challenges?

At Berkeley when I walked into the lab, I was confident that I was working with some of the most perspicacious minds in the field and doing important work. I am not trying to make you jealous buddy, but here at Adelphi our team has far surpassed my wildest dreams. Frank Turner the polymath from Carnegie Melon? He's here and now one of my closest associates. Shin Ha Kyo, the brilliant prodigy from North Korea whose research we had only read about? I don't know how the Army did it, but he is domiciled four doors down the hall from me. He has a new BOLT (Broad Operational Language Translation) prototype robot following him around everywhere like a shiny C-3PO on wheels translating (and recording) his every word and making him hot Korean tea whenever he wants it. The list goes on and on. This is the think tank to end all think tanks. The only astute mind that we are missing is yours, Derek. I wish you were here.

The effluence of ideas is beyond my reckoning. Just sitting around talking about what we could do is a process almost paramount to actually doing anything. There is no end to ideas. We still have our struggles and disagreements but they are easily eclipsed by the abundance of pure zeal for what could be.

In my mind there are always the moral questions and objections that must be raised before an idea should even be allowed to take shape. Of course, ethical dilemmas always bring you to mind, wondering what you would think or say...

Do you remember the discussion we had when you bought your first Tesla? We joked about Elon Musk offering an option for a "sticky hood," which would save a pedestrian's life by not throwing him away from the vehicle when said pedestrian was struck by the car while in self-driving autonomous mode. I can still picture an old grandma driving around town mindless of the various people glued to the hood of her car. I would have taken that option!

In any event, the ethical dilemmas raised by private ownership of self-driving vehicles is exactly the type of debate I have now with my new colleagues. Say your Tesla is driving you to campus in autonomous mode and a group of school children suddenly jump out in front of the car. You are not driving, and the car must make the flash decision of either running over the children, or swerving and sending itself and you, it's esteemed passenger, into the frigid bay.

Of course, the Tesla would be perfectly capable of making such a decision, but only if it is programmed ahead of time to do so. Therefore, morally, how do we program our autonomous vehicles? With the greater good in mind? To protect the greatest number of lives? What if you have your beautiful daughters, Sofia and Marisa, in the back seat and are taking them to school when a group of drug addled vagrants jumps out in front of the car? Who should your machine decide to kill and maim? Should we be programing our automatons to weigh not just the value of human life in quantity, but also in quality? Is that coldhearted?

When I was young, I must have read Isaac Asimov's I, Robot a hundred times. This novel is what inspired me to study robotic engineering and nanotechnology. The three laws of robotics were of course the wave of the future. They seemed so literate and so real. They are engrained in my memory:

1. A robot may not injure a human being or, through inaction, allow a human being to come to harm.

2. A robot must obey orders given it by human beings except where such orders would conflict with the First Law.

3. A robot must protect its own existence as long as such protection does not conflict with the First or Second Law.

Where are these laws today? Drone strikes kill thousands of men, women, and children in Iraq, Iran and Saudi Arabia on a daily basis. Automated machine guns protect our borders. The modern goal for robot programming is not to calculate which lives have the greatest value in order to best preserve humanity, but to reckon which lives are of the least value in order to best destroy them and keep them from crossing our borders. 75% of our robots today are made for killing under the pretense of protecting and defending.

I'm afraid the same is becoming true today with the field of Nanoinformatics. Where is Isaac Asimov when you need him, Derek? What good can we claim to do with our brilliant creations if they only leave human blood on our hands?

Sorry buddy, this started out as a friendly email. I do miss the times when we would stay up all night debating such moral hypotheticals. Sadly, these ethical dilemmas are no longer hypothetical for me.

My love to Tricia and the girls.
As always,
Ab

FOUR

DAN AND HIS ENIGMATIC PASSENGER traveled on through the storm quietly for a while. Dan wondered if she was armed. She would have to be crazy not to be. His own pistol, an older model Colt 45, was stashed within easy reach but he wasn't sensing any threat from the pale, lovely, young woman. Not yet anyway. She stared out the window of the truck for a long time, motionless, eyes fixed upon nothing. She seemed to be in shock. Finally, from her loosened jacket, she produced a nearly empty plastic water bottle which she absentmindedly drained. Her thirst seemed to bring her back to reality.

"Do you have any water?"

Dan passed her a half empty water bottle without a word. She drained the bottle and wiped her mouth with the back of her hand as the old truck rolled on through the smoke and the dust.

The storm seemed to be dying around them, at least Dan hoped it was. In the back of the truck someone farted loudly and loosely enough to be heard over the wind. A muttered nonverbal argument and hissing broke out. Dan rapped on the glass behind his head. "Knock it off," he called over his shoulder. His voice was soft yet rough and thick, reflecting no emotion.

The mysterious passenger quickly pivoted in her seat to peer into the bed of the truck. Her right hand disappeared into her thick leather aviator jacket and her body tightened. She had not expected anyone to be back there. Seeing that the road was clear in front of them, Dan took this opportunity to turn and give her a measured look over for a full three or four seconds. Her face was ashen and fine lined in the amber light that filled the cab. Her skin nearly translucent. Dan's eyes widened in recognition. *I know that angelic face!* It was a gentle yet strong face that he had seen many times before. Her quick eyes flashed back at him, alive with a quick thinking intelligence, fierce and strong.

She looked back into the truck, hand now tightly gripping what could only be a weapon beneath her coat. There was nothing to see in the back of the vehicle besides a large tarp, covering several large lumps and a 100 gallon plastic IBC tote tank that appeared to have a few inches of water remaining in the bottom.

That face. *Ave Maria, Gratia plena…*

"Who the fuck is in the back of the truck?" she asked slowly and carefully. She did not look back at the road nor at Dan. Her eyes were glued on the cargo buried under the blankets and tarps. She had probably seen it move. Dan could feel his heart beat in his temples. Once. Twice. Three times. The road was clearing ahead of them. Were those city lights in the distance? Dan accelerated the truck.

"They're harmless." Dan heard his voice crack dryly as he tried to speak. It may have been weeks since he had spoken this much. *No one to really talk to except for them.* He tried to clear his dry throat without sounding too disgusting. His mind found it strange that he was suddenly conscious of such things. He sickly swallowed the thick ashy rheum he cleared from his gullet with a slight hacking cough. He wasn't going to roll down the window and he didn't want to spit in the Chevy. A man did act differently around a woman.

His passenger kept her eyes glued on the bed of the truck. Her voice was a mix of curiosity and distrust as she slowly asked, "Who are they?"

Dan considered her question and his reply carefully before simply saying, "They're my clones." His voice implied a shrug of the shoulders but he didn't actually move. "I'm gonna sell them in California." His voice was deep and clear again. He sounded very much like himself. More so than he had in a long time.

"Clones…" she murmured thoughtfully as she turned her head to look at Dan again. Having his passenger's eyes on him made Dan nervous, so he reflexively glanced at himself in the rearview mirror. Dan's hair was thick and black, his heavy cheekbones jutted out below his eyes like the cutwater of a powerful tugboat. He was Mexican, but his features were very hard and sharp and mean like a Native American warrior. When he was a child the Gente in the hood had called him, "Indio." The nickname had been based on more than simple appearance. Dan spoke like an ancient indigenous American as well. His words, when they came, always came slowly and clearly. Dan liked to think that his voice was heavy and thick with the wisdom and the long suffering of his ancestors.

The distant lights of Reno could now be seen a bit more clearly through the fading storm. The fires they passed became smaller and less frequent in the cold Nevada desert that stretched on for miles around them. He could almost make out a hazy horizon line to the west. It had seemed like night in the sandstorm, but the sun was just setting on Reno, and the fading light was crimson pink like wine spilled on a dirty tablecloth.

Dan thought she had taken her hand out of her jacket, maybe. He couldn't really tell without looking over. He kept his eyes on the road.

"They can't hurt nobody," Dan sounded like he was talking to himself. His deep baritone voice now almost too soft to hear. "They have slow brains. No real thoughts of their own.

They only take orders." He stole a glance. Hand still in jacket. "They're harmless."

"Can you take me to California? I can pay you. Either in New Fed or California Republic dollars."

Dan frowned as he considered the offer. He was close to broke. Gas and water were going to be expensive in Reno. *Nothing to lose.* A few more miles rolled by. More smoke in the air but less sand. The truck seemed to be running better.

He looked back over at the hard, pale beauty next to him. Her eyes were lost again, looking out into the fading desert. She wiped away a solitary tear. Her right hand was still in her jacket close to whatever weapon she hid there, but no longer grasping it firmly.

That face is unforgettable. The same milky marbled countenance of the Holy Virgin had looked down on Dan lovingly from paintings in the Annunciation Cathedral when he was a child.

Ave Maria, Gratia plena…

They passed another fire, very close to the highway this time. The dull light created a coppery halo around her head. She was glowing. She slowly turned, and then her eyes suddenly flashed open and met his. They were the deep brown of seasoned and polished wood.

The truck's tires skipped dangerously as it glided off the road and into the shoulder. Dan jerked his head suddenly bringing his eyes back to bear onto the hazy highway ahead of them, and turned the wheel bringing the Chevy back straight.

"My name is Mary," she said.

"I…" Dan's voice cracked again before he had the chance to say, *I know.* He cleared his throat again and thought better of it.

"I'm Dan."

He looked back out to the road before them as it was being swallowed into the gathering darkness. The truck was running strong and moving well, bearing them into the future.

Those eyes.

Ave Maria

Gratia Plena

Dominus Tecum

Benedictus...

They would be in Reno soon.

FIVE

Currently listening to: *This Charming Man*
by The Smiths

Dear Sarah Joy,   413 days since you were born!

These quiet afternoons during your nap time are a great time to add to this old journal. I have to remind myself to write in here more often. Let's see, I was going to tell you about...

I decided I want to tell you the story about how I met your daddy, and in order to tell you that story, I have to tell you the story about this crazy guy named Jack that I fell in love with when I was just a teenager. It is really because of Jack that I met your daddy. When I met Jack, I was just 17 years old. We went to the same high school and we had Spanish together. He was from a completely different side of town than me and we had nothing in common. He was tall and he was handsome, but he was rough and kinda mean! I wasn't interested in him at all. For one thing, I had a nice boyfriend who I went to church with. My parents raised me in the Baha'i faith (I haven't taught you much about that yet but I will). Baha'i teaches us the oneness of humanity. All people are leaves and fruit from the same tree.

Anyway, that's probably why I didn't like Jack at first. I mean that, and the fact that he was a skinhead. That pretty much went against everything I believed in. He stalked into Spanish every day in his tight bleach-spotted jeans and oxblood Doc Marten boots with this angry look on his face. He looked like what he wanted most in the world was for someone to say the wrong thing to him. Scary dude. He had a real chip on his shoulder. Most of the other kids just stayed out of his way. He was the only skinhead at our school.

Meanwhile, on the other side of the classroom, I was wearing long flowery skirts to school every day and talking to my friends about peace and love. The Baha'u'llah tells us, "The earth is but one country, and mankind its citizens." What did I want with an angry skinhead? Nothing.

But at some point, the teacher rearranged our seating chart and Jack was assigned to sit right behind me. I did my best to avoid contact with him for at least a day or two, but we got partnered up to have conversations by the teacher. "Quieres ir a la playa?" That's how we got to know each other a little bit. The other kids must have thought we made a pretty interesting pair actually. The skinny, pale, little red headed hippy girl and the big tall Mexican skinhead striking up a friendship.

I really liked Jack on a friendly level right away. Especially when I learned that he wasn't a racist skinhead. I didn't understand anything about that at first, but he brought in the "Skinhead Bible" and a bunch of other anti-racist literature to teach me about the history of skinhead. He showed me pictures of the original skinheads. They were black boys from Jamaica. He told me, "There was even an entire skinhead movement called Two Tone that was all about the unity between black people and white people. It has its own dance music called ska." Pretty interesting right?

So, in return I started teaching him a little bit about my Baha'i faith. The Baha'i also value the importance of unity and brotherhood (kinda like skinheads!) in bringing about world peace and tranquility (less like skinheads I guess). The ultimate wish of our faith is that all of mankind will dwell together as one family. The funny thing was, he found that interesting as well. Turns out he was raised a good Catholic boy and went to Mass every Sunday with his mom. We are taught that the Baha'u'llah wrote, "Consort with the followers of all religions in a spirit of friendliness and fellowship."

We had a lot in common but, I still wasn't interested in dating him. I had my nice Baha'i boyfriend after all, and who wants to date a skinhead? It was definitely a strange lifestyle choice.

But that changed, Sweetheart. Jack and I become close. This was before your daddy.

I think it all kind of changed in one night. That was the night that my nice hippy Baha'i boyfriend (geez, I can't even remember his name now) took me to see a punk rock show in Sacramento.

Maybe that's where my story really starts.

There was a skate park in Sacramento called... The Cube? The Square? Something like that, and one Saturday night this great punk band Rancid (I know Daddy's played you his Rancid records) played right in the middle of all the ramps and rails and everything else. I think that's why we went because Good Ol' Whathisname (my nice Baha'i boyfriend) was really into skateboarding at that point.

The place was like this huge warehouse and everything was spray-painted with graffiti, crazy colors everywhere. A band called Screaming Bloody Marys opened up and were rad, and when Rancid started to play, the floor was just packed. Everyone was in leather jackets covered in patches and foul words and spikes. All the kids looked absolutely crazy and danced even crazier! When everybody shows up looking crazy, I guess the whole point is to be crazier than everyone else. They had to stand out. To be different.

I wonder if you will be like that when you are a teenager?

Anyway, there was I, little hippy Jocelyn doing my little hippy dance in the back of it all. It was a pretty new experience for me. We didn't have punk shows that big back in Stockton.

I remember dancing all on my own, far away from the "pit" where everyone was slam dancing. Rancid was great, everyone said their heyday had come and gone, but for old guys (older than me anyway) they were still kicking butt. I lost my boyfriend right away. He ditched me for some friends, the jerk, so that was that. I was on my own. And then I saw Jack from Spanish class.

He was in the middle of the pit, dressed in his best skinhead gear and drenched in sweat. His breathing was really heavy, because he was dancing so hard, but other than that he wasn't moving at all. Just standing in the middle of the pit and staring right at me. The kids were going crazy dancing all around him, but no one bumped into him. The look on his face was so intense and his muscles were just bulging out of his wet collared shirt. We locked eyes for just a few seconds with all the madness going on around us.

Then he gave me a little wave, mouthed the word, "Hi" and dove face first back into the pit swinging his arms and dancing. I lost track of him for a while after that, but I remember I was looking for him.

Anyway, what I really remember, and I will never forget, is what happened after the show.

It wasn't until after Rancid was done that I started to notice just how many skinheads were there. They were walking around in their gangs or crews with their braces down and their chins stickin' out just like they knew something bad was going to happen. And who was in the middle of the pack? My sweet Spanish partner, Jack.

I never would've known the difference between a Nazi

skinhead and a Traditional or Anti-Racist Skinhead if Jack hadn't taught me about it. I mean, it's still kind of confusing right? Why be an Anti-Racist Skinhead? It seems like you would have to explain yourself all the time to everyone. Like, "No, I'm not a racist. No, I'm not a Nazi. I'm just really into skinhead for the sake of skinhead..." What a drag right? But at the time, there were all these marches happening, and people shouting "Go back where you came from!" at immigrants on the T.V. because ever since the Red Hats had taken over the white house, suddenly it was OK to be racist or something. The president had given the Nazis back their place in our society, so it became OK to stand up and shout out loud how much they hated Mexicans and Muslims or whatever. How is that ever OK?

Anyway, after the show I went out into the parking lot, only nobody was really leaving. Everyone was out there, drinking beer and just hanging out. I bumped into this goth girl I knew from my freshman year named Aurora and she offered me a smoke (yes, I know, Sweetheart, smoking is a terrible habit and it is really bad for you and you should never ever do it, just please don't judge your mommy, I was only sixteen years old).

So, Aurora and I were leaning on the back of her car and we were smoking and watching all the crazy people swarming around us. I was sitting there and Aurora started telling me, "These skinhead boys are really kinda sexy..."

Ha. I still remember just wrinkling my nose at that one because, of course I was thinking about Jack and I in Spanish class. I had never thought he was sexy, had I?

But Aurora kept on about it, saying, "I mean punk rockers are cool, but they stink. Literally stink. They don't bathe, they sleep wherever they pass out. They're cool for sure but who wants a punk rock boyfriend? Skinheads are where it's at. I'm gonna get me a skinhead boy!" She was eyeballing Jack and his friends across the parking lot. I thought she was mostly looking at Jack. Maybe that piqued my interest a little.

"Look at these boys!" That girl could talk. I didn't have to say a word; she could carry a conversation on all by herself. "These are kids who actually polish their boots! And they can't be just any old boots, they have to be Doc Martens from England." Then she looked me in the eyes and her voice got kinda soft and velvety and I could tell she had actually given all this a lot of thought before. "And they lace their boots in a special way. And they have their jeans all tailored in a really tight taper to accentuate how big their boots are. And they all wear those sharp British shirts too. Either football jerseys for English teams or Fred Perrys, and Ben Shermans..." she sounded like she was taking notes for an erotic skinhead Harlequin romance.

She was looking at me sideways through all her gothic Siouxsie Sioux eyeliner, "Wouldn't you like to date a skinhead boy, Joc? They're so fashionable in an old-fashioned way and they look so nice, even though everyone knows they're crazy."

I couldn't even say yes or no to her after that. Ha-ha. Can you picture that moment, Sweetheart? Maybe when you are sixteen, like I was then, you will feel the same. At my first ever punk show sitting on the bumper of this old Datsun with this total goth chick dressed all in black with crazy eye make-up, catching a midnight smoke in the parking lot of this crazy old skate park while she explained her skinhead fetish to me...

And it made perfect sense.

And we suddenly realized we were actually caught right in the middle of two rival gangs of thugs, edging up to each other, getting ready to fight this crazy street battle right there in the parking lot of the Cube or the Square or whatever.

I think I noticed first. There was a crazy group of ten or

fifteen bald heads creeping up to the right of us, and there was a crazy group of ten or fifteen bald heads stalking up to the left of us. And the mood in the whole parking lot just got super tense and scary. Aurora and I couldn't even move.

Then someone shouted, "Sieg Heil!" and threw up a straight right arm, and the whole place exploded. Just went nuts. I had never seen a brawl like that before and, even with all the madness in the world now, I haven't seen anything like it since...

Whoa. Getting late, and man my hand is cramping from writing so much! Gotta go make dinner now. I will tell you the rest later. I hope this isn't too scary for you! I probably won't be able to give you this journal until you are 21! Ha-ha. You know it will all end well. Love you, Sweetheart!

-XXOOXX- Mommy

5IH

From: Tadese@arlntd.army.mil
Date: Tuesday, March 20 ■ 1:35 a.m.
To: DTimm@berkeley.edu
Subject: RE: Hollywood's burning

Derek,

I was so sorry to hear about your parents' house in SoCal. How many wildfires are raging out of control as we speak? Federalnews.nfsu.gov claims 14, but I am never sure if the news they post about California is real or fake. I did see a satellite feed that made Southern California look like Hades on earth.

Opening my tablet this morning to read that Hollywood is all but gone was heart-wrenching. Thousands of dead. Tens of thousands evacuated with no homes to return to. People afraid to go near each other because of contagion. Without any Federal assistance, I don't know how you will make it. A lot of people are saying that the California Independent Republic can't help but fail at this point. Many are predicting that they will beg their way back into the union. I try and stay out of the politics. You know I will always want what is best for California. California is my homeland! My heart! In any event, I am glad your parents got out. Where will they go now?

Here the floods just get worse and worse each year. They

have opened a refugee camp on the high ground next to the base and there is a line of tents out in front full of people trying to get in. They called the Virginia/Maryland floods of 2016 "historic," but this year we have already far surpassed the number of homes destroyed by that deluge.

How is it possible that the Red Hats still blindly follow their old president who refused to acknowledge global warming? They are so focused on keeping our borders closed that they are blind to everything else. They can't see the forest because of the trees.

Here we are on the cusp of  he wants to

From the gate surrounding our base, I can see the profusion of poor souls with nowhere to go as they line up for bowls of soup or to shit and shower in the makeshift portable bathroom tents the Feds have set up. I wonder what makes our refugees so different from those fleeing from Mexico, Syria, and Afghanistan? A lighter shade of skin? The good fortune to be born in an English speaking country that claims to be Christian? Displacement by floods and fires created by humankind's destruction of our natural environment as opposed to displacement by wars created by humankind's differing views on religion?

Last night I watched a video on my tablet. A completely automated 50 caliber machine gun on the South Korean border simply mowing down 30 or 40 North Koreans trying to flee their own country. Who pulled the trigger? There was no soldier controlling the gun. The automaton was programmed to fire on the unarmed group of civilians (mostly women and children) without the benefit of any human conscience. A preprogrammed reaction to a stimulus. The South Korean government says these weapons are sending a black and white message to would be immigrants: Cross the line and you die. There is no margin for bargaining. No room for discussion about the value of human life. Decision made. Order given. Machine programmed to destroy any hint of movement. Done.

So, who pulled the trigger? The officer in charge? The South Korean president? What about the engineer who originally created the software for the drone gun and made it possible to mow down 40 humans over and over again without a breathing human lifting a finger or considering any possible consequences? Didn't that engineer hand South Korea the ability to destroy other human beings in the most guilt-free manner possible?

That engineer is me, Derek. In any event, I developed a major piece of the technology that is now used in these autonomous drones and weapons. Unmonitored machines of death. I pulled the trigger on those 40 innocent refugees. Who knows on how many more tomorrow?

And here is  How will I sleep at night?

Now we are directed  but it hasn't

I must again apologize for the depressing email. Black thoughts overwhelm me as of late. I must believe that the direction my actions take are on the road of righteousness. Surely, I am doing some good in the world? More soon.

As always,
Ab

From: Tadese@arlntd.army.mil
Date: Tuesday, March 27 ▆ 4:40 p.m.
To: DTimm@berkeley.edu
Subject: RE: Censored email

Derek,

Why am I not surprised that they are censoring my emails

at this point? Everything has changed since the attack in El Paso last week. We now have hundreds of armed U.S. drones patrolling the Mexican American border and the killing continues. Most of those drones are automated with the same code I developed so many years ago. No man or woman is directing those drones. Where is the human element? How good is the intel that guides their automated decisions? Who lives and who dies? The machines decide.

I know now that it is only a matter of time before they are making strikes on suspected insurgents and terrorists within our own nation. How will the citizens of our new nation react when the first NFU citizen is killed by one of our own self-regulating drones? Here I am acting like it hasn't already happened. Just because it hasn't been reported on the web doesn't mean it hasn't. ███████████████

███████████████████████████████████████

███████████████████████████

Now, the pressure upon us to complete our project is fiercer than ever. I won't even bother to tell you the new direction our work has taken or the astounding measures being put into effect here on the base. Expectations run high. As the world crumbles around us the balm to cure all our ills seems to be within a finger's reach. I cannot believe how far we have come in such a short amount of time. There is nothing I want more than to be able to sit down with you and tell you all about it over a good cup of coffee. I pray that day is not far off.

I'm sure you read in the papers about the refugee camp in ██

███████████████████████████████████████

I am praying for you and your family, Derek. So far it seems like the Bay Area and Central California have avoided a lot of the disasters happening elsewhere. Are you overrun with refugees in the East Bay? I hope the Republic of California is not taking the drastic measures there that we are seeing here in Maryland. I still dream of California as a bastion of safety and freedom.

I need to finish up. One last thought: As California's secession from the Union moves forward, I am left with an awkward choice. At least I would like to think I am. Perhaps there will be no choice available to me at all. I love my home state, and at this point I completely support California's quest to move forward as its own independent nation (I read today that Canada, Denmark, and Germany are already fully willing to recognize the Republic of California). I would of course want to come back and do whatever I can to protect my friends and family there.

On the other hand, the work we are doing here in the NFU is so important to what is left of humanity on such a grand scale that I don't see how I could leave Adelphi. How does one walk away from ██████████████████████████

██████████ I am sure you will think I am aggrandizing the gravity of our project, but being on the brink of ██████████ ██████████ would mean immediate change for a sick and possibly dying world.

Still, if I tell the Army that I am quitting the team and requesting a travel visa back home to California, what would their reaction be? I ask it again here in an email they are sure to read, because ████████████████████████████████████ I believe the lack of a direct answer from them is the only answer I need.

I hope this email (at least a good chunk of it) finds you and your family well, Derek. Know that I am safe and healthy and immersed in a work that breaks the very boundaries of science and technology. I continue to pray for peace. I hope to see you again.

As always,
Ab

SEVEN

DAN SLOWED THE TRUCK WHEN he saw the stark spotlights cutting through the smoky night ahead of them. They were illuminating a New Federal Union checkpoint that blocked the freeway on the way into Reno, Nevada. The chain link fencing that barred their path was 20 feet high and topped with rounds and rounds of razor wire. The gate set over the road was securely framed by steel beams and bolstered by several concrete barriers. Circular towers stood on either side topped with glass observation posts. Above these, the spotlight arrays shot down cold white reality through the darkness and onto the heavily armed soldiers that awaited traffic there.

Just on the other side of the barrier Dan could see rows of white tents. *That must be the FEMA camp*, he thought. Two dusty cars waited to pass through ahead of them and Dan joined the queue. Personal travel by car had really become scarce once cash money became mandatory again. Gas and cash were scarce enough, but credit cards and bank accounts, those kinds of ideas didn't seem to exist at all anymore to the average citizen. Too many banks had failed after Calexit. Gasoline and water could only be purchased with cold hard New Federal Currency now, at least here in the New Federal Union.

The needle on the old Chevy's gas gauge was reading close to empty. Dan realized if he hadn't happened into Mary, this might have been his final stop. Stuck in Reno with a truckload of clones.

The first car at the gate was being waved through the brightly lit checkpoint and the dirty old station wagon behind it rolled up. There was power here, which might mean network, which would mean internet. At least access to what was left of the internet. Dan had an old iPhone in the glove compartment of the truck. He hadn't even tried to connect to the web in quite some time. The news online was seldom true, and never good. Why pay attention? Dan had no control over the various tragedies that were unfurling across the world. Tragedy had already hit him hard in the face. He didn't need to read about the sorrows of others.

Still, that old grasping desire for information gnawed quietly at him. What was going on in the rest of the world? How were people surviving in other places? How bad was the violence out there? Would he find the road through the mountains clear? Could he even get through? Was Stockton even still there?

Mary had a handheld device out and was silently making use of it somehow as Dan tensely waited their turn, gripping hard on the steering wheel. Checkpoints always made Dan nervous. *There should be no problem*, he told himself wiping his sweaty palms on his jeans. His passenger seemed to be keeping her composure just fine. Not in the least bit worried, or was that an act? She didn't even look up from her device as the Chevy finally rolled slowly forward directly under the harsh glare of the light.

The three heavily equipped soldiers waved the station wagon through the gate and into the Reno night. Dan eased the truck up to the barrier. Beyond the gate in front of him the wagon was edging its way through a thick crowd of people begging for food, cash, anything. The Reno FEMA camp was drastically underequipped for the swarms of people who had nowhere else to go.

The young sergeant that Dan pulled up to looked tired and annoyed. His uniform was food stained and not fastened up properly. He leaned in close to Dan's window. Beneath his paper sanitary mask, Dan could see that he hadn't had a shave in days. The smell of cheap coffee on his breath came through the surgical mask just fine. "Where you headed?" he asked robotically as his eyes roamed over Dan and Mary. His equipment looked deadly, but well used, dusty and worn. There was a short black assault rifle strapped to the body armor at his chest and an automatic pistol at his hip.

Mary did not look up from her device.

"California," croaked Dan.

"And how do you intend to gain entry to the California Independent Republic?"

"I'm a native. I was born there."

"Cargo?"

"My clones."

A look of doubtful curiosity lit a spark in the soldier's eyes. "Clones huh? Like on those commercials online a few years back? I never heard about anyone who actually did it."

Dan just nodded. Ahead of him a hundred desperate eyes were searching from faces pressed up against the metal fence. Dull, lifeless faces with white masks covering noses and mouths. Eyes bathed in want. Five hundred fingers grasped the wire barrier without pulling or pushing. Just waiting. Beyond the crowd Dan could make out nothing but darkness.

"I will need to take a look."

Dan shifted nervously in his seat as the soldier moved toward the back of the truck and pulled back the thick tarp.

EIGHT

The following is a copy of a non-electronic paper letter intercepted at the office of Ralph Willis: Army Colonel, New Federal Union of States, Washington D.C.

It is believed that another copy of the same letter did reach Colonel Willis in Virginia. The letter arrived via an underground private courier paid for by Dr. Derek Timm: Professor of Robotics and Engineering UC Berkeley.

Directive: Begin electronic surveillance of Dr. Derek Timm and an internal investigation into Colonel Ralph Willis– NFA.

—Department Homeland Security NFUS

Ralph,

Hello old friend. I am attempting to send multiple copies of this letter to different addresses where I believe you can be reached. With the creation of the New Federal Union's Great Firewall, our internet communications with any non-allied countries are completely disrupted and that includes emails coming out of California and into the New Union. I have no idea if this letter will find you, but I hope that it will.

Times are tough here in California, but not as bad as

in many parts of the New Union I am sure. When last I heard from you, you and Lois were living in Virginia and you were working directly with the Pentagon as a CIA liaison with the United States Army, but that was long before California and Texas voted for secession and left the U.S.A. California news media reports that the New Federal Union of States is now in a state of economic collapse and defaulting on all of the old United States' foreign debts. I am not sure if that is really the case or just more fake news.

Since the NFU's consolidation of the Great Firewall they are able to control citizens' use of the internet, and block information sharing with Texas and CA. Lately, it has been very hard to get current news about what is actually going on over there. We are spoon-fed only whatever "news" the New Feds release on NFUNet.

California's borders are tightly closed now. Even citizens originally born in California are having a tough time obtaining visas when they want to repatriate. And I am sure you know the mobs of immigrants trying to get into California grow by the thousands every day.

You were born in California, which means you may have repatriated back here at some point. If you were here in the Bay Area, I would have found you by now. So, I deduce that you have chosen the side of honor and loyalty and stayed with the CIA in the old U.S. and found your place with the New Federal Union. Either way I only wish you the best. There may be many Californians that bear a strict grudge against New Feds, but I hope that you and Lois are safe and well somewhere. May we always be friends.

With all the upheaval and lack of communication

between the New Union and the independent nations of California and Texas, I know that a lot of people are struggling to maintain contact with friends and family. I have been very lucky. The girls are all well. Marisa and Sofia are safe and well here in Northern California. The UC system is still plugging away, although in a very different existence than it maintained a few years ago. Sofia is here at UC Berkeley and Marisa is attending Stanford. Tricia has been working hard in San Francisco with the relief effort. Food and water are in high demand in the city after the earthquake collapsed both the Golden Gate and the Bay Bridge.

If this letter reaches you, I am hoping we can catch up better in the near future. Maybe we will be meeting for coffee next week. Nothing would delight me more.

I almost hate to get to the point, but I am writing to ask for a favor. Like thousands of others here on the continent, I am missing someone.

Dr. Abraha Tadese was a fellow professor and close friend of mine from Berkeley. Two years ago, he was recruited to join a brain trust in Adelphi, Maryland at the request of the United Sates Army. This was just before the U.S. split. I am not sure if you are familiar with the Army Research Lab Nano Technology Division (ARLNTD) in Adelphi Maryland or not. In any event, I have not heard from Abraha in more than six months. He was emailing regularly when he first moved to Adelphi, but as Calexit became a reality, his emails started to arrive censored of information. Then, they stopped coming altogether after the Great Firewall was implemented. I guess whatever he was working on was top secret and of great importance to the New Fed Army.

He claimed that his team was on the brink of an amazing breakthrough that was going to change the entire world. I could not ascertain what he was working on because the army was editing information from his correspondence, although they did let most of it through. Bizarre.

Abraha has now disappeared into the quagmire that was the old United States Army, and is now the New Federal Union Army. I have no idea if he is still in Maryland, or if he is even still alive. I know the flooding in that region had been out of control and there were thousands of dead and displaced. The deadly virus still lingers as well here as I am sure it does there. However, with a lack of any reliable news coming out of the New Union, I do not know if this is still the case or not.

Dr. Tadese is one of the most brilliant minds of our generation, as well as a close friend. The loss of such an intelligent man would be an unbelievable tragedy, not just for the California Independent Republic or for the New Federal Union, but for humanity as a whole.

If you can obtain any information on the whereabouts or the wellbeing of Dr. Abraha Tadese, please reach out to me.

I hope this letter finds you and your family well.

Your Old Friend,
Derek Timm

NINE

THE SOLDIER MOVED TO THE BACK of the truck and pulled back the thick tarp that covered Dan's five clones. With their cover gone, the Five shifted nervously in the bed of the truck. They sat up slowly, blinking their dark brown eyes at the sharp electric light pouring down from the towers and poles all around them. Five pairs of dull eyes darted around looking for Dan. Five pairs of sore legs and arms stretched and squirmed restlessly.

Dan watched attentively. "Gotta stop for the night soon. Get them fed," Dan said distractedly out the window. His voice rumbled out softly from deep in his chest, his eyes fixated on the crowd at the fence where a little blonde girl in a dirty dress gazed back at him.

The army sergeant shifted his rifle and pulled a small flashlight from somewhere. He held the bright beam over the clones to better examine them. The Five stared out at nothing, insipid eyes avoiding the bright light. They were still half asleep.

Dan's clones were thick and brown and muscled just like him. Their black hair was shaved close to the scalp. The thick black eyebrows beneath were knitted together and their lips pursed, in a caveman-like look of confusion that never really went away. After stretching and straightening, the Five sat silently, very still, emotionless, waiting for instructions from Dan. All five faces the same as Dan's, only different. They lacked any sign of the human intelligence and purpose that was somehow obvious in Dan's own face.

Two more soldiers stepped up close to the truck to gaze at the dim-witted quintuplets in the back, murmuring to each other in mild curiosity. Their shoulders slouched over the deadly weapons they grasped at their chests. Their fingers caressed the triggers.

"What do they do?" asked one.

Dan could sense without even looking that these soldiers were sloppy. They lacked the diligence and commitment that their post should require. They hadn't asked for any identification, or about the pretty passenger on the bench seat next to him. Some of their surgical masks were smudged with dirt. They were easily distracted by his cargo and were not paying attention to their immediate environment. *The army sure isn't what it used to be.*

Dan cleared his throat again. Outwardly, he didn't seem to be paying attention to the soldiers' movements and actions around him. His eyes remained fixed on the caged crowd in front of him. It made him nervous that he didn't have a mask when everyone else was wearing one. The little blonde girl in the dirty white dress was carefully placing white flowers on the razor wire. Her eyes were so familiar... "They're trained farm hands." He nearly whispered to no one in particular. "I'm gonna sell them in California."

Since leaving Colorado the clones had lived in a constant state of bewilderment at the ruination of their daily routine. In Colorado every day had been the same for the Five. They had eaten the same meals each day, accomplished the same chores. They had lived a simple quiet existence of hard work, all of their basic needs provided for by Dan. Now, with the routine gone, they had no idea where they were going or what they were doing. The only constant in their existence now was Dan.

One of the clones looked over his shoulder to see Dan through the rear window of the truck cab. He stood out from the others because of a large shiny scar that ran down the right side of his face. It split the thick eyebrow then disappeared at his eye only to start again on his sharp cheekbone and then down to the corner of his mouth. For a brief moment, Dan thought he noticed a splash of awareness in those eyes that was lacking in the features of the others. But no, he was mistaken. All five faces were complete blanks.

"Soldier! Are you pulling that truck aside for inspection or passing it through?" called an officious voice from the watch tower above the truck. Dan tried squinting up in that direction but could see nothing through the white electric brilliance of the spotlights.

The curious soldiers backed away from the truck again gripping their rifles and tightening their shoulders, but only barely. *Sloppy. No discipline.*

"Passing it through sir," shouted the sergeant. He threw the tarp back over the Five who gladly crouched beneath it in one large huddled mass once again.

The sergeant returned to the cab of the truck, "Now listen here Mister, we have no problem letting you through into Reno, but there is zero chance of you passing on into California. You understand me? Zero. The border is closed. I-80 is barricaded on the other side of the city and no one gets into or out of the mountains. You are welcome to sell your Clones here in Reno, but you are a citizen of the New Federal Union of States now despite wherever you were born. There is no repatriating back into California. Is that clear?"

Dan gave him a short silent nod and the unkempt sergeant waved Dan's truck through as he backed away already looking for the next vehicle.

Dan accelerated slowly through the gate as he scanned the dense crowd of desperate humanity on the other side. He thought the soldier's apathetic wave was equivalent to a rolling of the eyes at the authority above him in the tower. *These "sol-diers" would drop their guns and run at the first sign of real trouble. No one wants to die for this government.*

Dan edged the car slowly toward the crowd as it parted for him. Hungry eyes probed the truck, empty hands stretched out. Dan rolled up his window to the repeated calls:

"Do you have anything to eat?"

"Any water?"

"Please sir, I have hungry children." He drove on searching the crowd for the dirty little blonde girl. *Where did she go? Where the hell did she get those flowers in the middle of the desert?*

Mary looked up from her device for the first time. She had seemed to completely ignore all interaction with the soldiers, but Dan was sure she had heard every word.

"What are you looking for?" she asked.

The truck was surrounded. Dan kept her rolling slowly.

"Please mister, water!"

"Any food? We need food."

Dan shook his head in stoic resignation, "Nothing."

"Do you know where you're headed?" Mary had put the device away and suddenly seemed very attentive.

Dan shook his head still focused on the dirty and poor around them. He didn't want to run anyone over. "Not really."

The crowd was beginning to thin around them as the lights from the checkpoint faded behind. The old Chevy carried them on, down the highway. A full moon had broken through the clouds and smoke. Ahead of them, Dan could see the old casinos and hotels looming dark and deserted in the moonlight. Here and there they passed tents with campfires lit in front of them. Everywhere hungry eyes watched them pass. Mary had her little black tablet out again and was silently tapping away at it.

"Almost outta gas," Dan said. "You say something about money?"

"Take the third exit we come to," Mary told him without looking up from her device. "I know a safe place where we can spend the night and tomorrow, we can…" her words were cut off by gunshots. Dan ducked his head and pressed the gas hard. *Ping ping ping*, the bullets hit the side of the truck. *Small caliber. No more than a .22.*

"They're aiming for the tires!" Mary shouted ducking down low. The truck lurched forward, the tired engine revving high and loud with the effort.

The tires were not hit and the truck carried them on down the empty freeway and past the attempted ambush. Dan never even saw where the shots came from.

"Damn it, I'm shot," Mary said, exasperated. She started breathing heavily.

Dan looked over to where Mary was holding her leg tightly at the thigh next to him and cursing softly. He pushed the old truck on, getting up to 60 then to 65 miles an hour.

"Damn. Damn. Damn." Mary was chanting softly to herself. Her breathing became ragged. Suddenly she shouted, "Here! Turn off here!"

Dan redirected the truck toward the dark freeway exit she indicated without slowing down.

Ø Ø Ø

A tall thin figure emerged from the side of the road and watched the battered Chevy barrel away. He wore a dusty flat brimmed cattlemen's hat, and a heavy duster over dark fatigues. Andrew Eldritch's grin revealed an even row of perfect white teeth which glinted through the dark night in the rays of the moon.

Keep moving, Sister Mary, keep going. His adept fingers clicked away at the tiny device he held in one hand and a high humming tone grew louder and louder until a small black helicopter drone buzzed over his head and then slowly lowered itself to the ground beside him. The four rotors at the top of the ugly little machine halted their spinning suddenly and Eldritch bent down to release the .22 caliber Ruger pistol mounted to the drone's side railing.

Deftly tapping at a few keys, Eldritch brought the drone back to life and sent it straight up into the night sky. He set it to autonomous mode, with direction to follow and survey the truck it had just peppered with bullets. *I'm right behind you, Sister. Right behind you.* He gazed out into the desert night still grinning.

TEN

Currently listening to: *Tomorrow* by Morrissey

Dear Sarah Joy,   435 days old big girl!

We have had a busy couple of weeks on the farm. Harvest season is always that way. I haven't added to your journal in a while. Let's see, I was writing to you about that story of the big fight at the skatepark. Where did I leave off? The big fight? The big fight.

Aurora and I were smack in the middle of a race riot. It was like her Datsun was a shark cage or something because nobody even ever touched Aurora and I or even noticed that we were there. It's a good thing too, because when the fighting broke out, I started to run for it, but for some reason Aurora reached out and grabbed my jacket and said, "Don't move!" So, I didn't. And then, there were three or four really brutal fist fights going on just a few yards away from me. And I just sat there frozen because I had really never witnessed violence like that in my life. Boy, was I scared.

I could tell that some of the skinheads were older and some were younger. I didn't know until after that a lot of the Nazis were older guys in their late 30s and 40s. Some bigwig member of their crew had just gotten out of jail or something and they were celebrating by going to the punk rock show, but of course Jack and all of his buddies were there. They all called themselves Traditional Skins or SHARP Skins, which is an acronym for "Skin Heads Against Racial Prejudice."

After the punk show, of course, everyone was all riled up

on adrenaline and cheap beer and all it would have taken was one dirty look to get set some of them off, not to even mention someone yelling, "Sieg Heil!" at them. I mean you'd have to be an idiot.

Most of Jack's friends were in their early 20s and maybe there were a couple more teenagers there like Jack. I remember Little Mikey was there (he was just a kid then) and Big Mike, and your Uncle Ty had just graduated high school, and Jack's handsome friend Cormac... Pickles was there and Spanky, I think. Toothless Chris and Ninja. Nazi Bob was there (who wasn't really a Nazi anymore, but had been when he was younger so the nickname just stuck). I didn't know really know any of them well at that point, but most of Jack's friends became my friends sooner or later (including your daddy).

So, there I was, Baby, an innocent 17-year-old hippy girl who was mostly oblivious to what was going on in the great wide world around me at the time. I was sitting there on the bumper of this old car smoking and there were these incredible fist fights going on all around the car. I mean I could have reached out and touched these guys. We could have been attacked or splattered in blood at any minute!

There was this one guy who was older and didn't look like a skinhead because he had long black hair and he was wearing a leather biker vest with a swastika on it. He was definitely winning his fight because he was fighting this young skinhead I didn't know who was much smaller than him. The skinhead kid was holding his own, but I saw him glance over his shoulder wondering where all his friends were because this big biker was pretty much wailing on him.

When the biker connected a hard right straight into the kid's nose with a crunching noise. The kid went down on one knee, shaky. I almost jumped up to try and stop it, but Aurora grabbed me again and held me back. Then this biker dude was just lining up this great big kick at the kid's face. I could see it coming. I wanted to look away, but it was like trying not to look at a car wreck you are passing on the freeway. It was just horribly captivating.

And then suddenly there was this hugely loud SMACK! and there was splintered wood flying all over the place.

I hadn't even seen Jack come up behind the guy. He was carrying this piece of fence board in both hands. I have no idea where he got it, but he smashed it with all his 17-year-old might right against the back of this biker dude's head. SMACK! I'm not kidding you, like slapping water. The plank just exploded as it came in full contact with the back of this guy's noggin and splinters went flying everywhere.

The biker guy went down hard, and then Jack was just kicking him and kicking him, and the young skin the Nazi biker had been fighting was up and kicking him too, and the biker dude was trying to crawl away but a couple of other guys joined in to stomp on him. Finally, some other Nazi busted through the mess and grabbed him and pulled him up and then they ran for it out across the parking lot. Then they were starting their cars and all the Nazis were getting the heck out of there.

And there was Jack, no shirt, just a wife-beater with his sweaty arms around that little skin with the broken nose, and some of his other buddies and they start chanting, "Nazi punks, Nazi punks, Nazi punks, FUCK OFF!" And then they were laughing and hugging each other and they looked happier and more excited than anyone I had ever seen before in my entire life. They didn't even need drugs, these kids, they just got high off whooping on Nazis.

Whoo. I need to take a break from writing for a minute or

two. I'm going to go in and see if you are awake.

Sarah Joy, it feels good to be writing all this down for you, because I haven't thought about it in a long time but I do want to tell you the story of how I met your daddy. I am getting to that, I swear. I also want you to understand that I would never condone all that violence. We are a peaceful people. That night was just... It was out of my control.

Jack from Spanish class though, I respected him because Jack had a purpose. He was fighting for a cause. He was dead set against racism and that's how he handled things. I'm not saying it was right. It just... It just was. He grew up dealing with racism, and his parents and grandparents dealt with prejudice their whole lives. When he was young, this was just how he dealt with people who wanted to flaunt bigotry and make it socially acceptable.

So, I might as well finish the story of that night...

There was some confusion for a while. Someone kept shouting, "Cops are on the way!" and more and more cars were tearing out of there.

Aurora tried to grab my arm again, but this time she couldn't stop me because I was running until I found Jack. He was sweating like a madman, still in nothing but a wife-beater and jeans. The heat and the sweat were just pouring off of him. He wasn't surprised to see me. He was a good foot taller than me and he was looking down at me all dark and serious. His hair was cut so short it looked like a shadow. His friends unhooked their arms from him and ran off chasing somebody, friend or foe I wasn't sure, but Jack just stood there for a moment looking at me.

"You OK Joc?"

It was a magical moment like out of a movie. I mean here was this hero, out fighting Nazis, and I just wanted to care for him. I wanted to take him in my arms and bandage his wounds and take him home with me and sit with him on my couch and make him hot cocoa and watch T.V. with him.

"I'm fine, what about you?" His face was swollen. He had taken a few punches at some point.

"I'm fine, I'm fine." he said. "No sweat, but can you help me find a white Toyota truck?"

Then we walked around in the thinning crowd until we found the truck he was looking for. He stuck his torso in and came back out with a bright white Fred Perry shirt. He had taken it off and thrown it in the random truck when the fight started so it wouldn't get blood on it. "I only have two real Freds," he told me, and then I could tell he was embarrassed that he had said that.

"Come on Jocelyn! We gotta go!" My boyfriend (who I already knew was not going to be my boyfriend for much longer) was calling at me from the window of his dad's VW. He was already putting toward the parking lot's exit. He probably would have left me there, the jerk.

"I'm glad you're OK," I told Jack.

And all he said was, "Adios muchacha! I'll see you in Spanish." And then he ran off with his friends.

And the whole ride home I couldn't stop thinking about him. And I woke up thinking about him the next day. They say opposites attract. I have asked myself many times over the years, could it ever have gotten more opposite than Jack and I?

Love you, Sweetie. More soon.

-Mommy

ELEVEN

"RIGHT AT THE BOTTOM," Mary indicated, pointing with a finger tinged in her own blood.

Dan ignored the stop sign at the bottom of the freeway exit and did not slow the truck as it screeched around a corner and to the right. There were no other car lights visible to him on the street. They passed a gas station and a strip mall, both completely dark with boards nailed over the windows. Here and there small fires burned in metal barrels. One lane of the road was clear but the sides of the road were littered with the ruins of cars, piles of trash, and ash. Dan blew through two more stop signs without slowing. They were speeding through a residential area now. Small flat-roofed houses lined the streets. Some were boarded up. Some were burned out shells. There was no electricity in this area. The only light came from Dan's headlights and the white moon above. There were fewer fires here.

"Left," Mary directed. "Right. Left. Stop here. That one on the left. Kill the lights and pull down the driveway. You should be able to park in the backyard." Her voice had become a whisper. She was still holding her leg, but her posture was slack.

Dan solemnly did as he was directed. He knew they had to stop and give some attention to her wound soon. His headlights passed over the small house as he turned into the drive just before he killed them. The front yard was a mass of tall dried weeds and dead brown bushes. The structure looked intact, but the windows and front door were mostly boarded over and the boards had strange markings spray painted on them in bright orange.

Then, Dan was idling the Chevy down the side of the house along a gravel driveway and into the tall crackling weeds of the backyard. Dan's eyes quickly adjusted to the dark, but he could not make out their surroundings at all. He killed the engine and they were left in absolute silence, save for Mary's heavy breathing next to him.

"Damn. Damn. Damn," she continued to whisper to herself. She had both hands clamped tightly around her wounded thigh. The clones rustled nervously at the back of the truck but remained silent.

"I'll come 'round and get you," Dan whispered opening his door and stepping out into the waist-high weeds surrounding the truck.

"I don't need you..." Mary broke off and tried to straighten up a bit. There was still strength in her voice, but a quiver of fear and uncertainty crowded her words now.

Dan moved quickly around the truck's backside, pulling the tarp back as he went. Ten eyes reflected moonlight, gazing expectantly and obediently out at him from the darkness. He grabbed a flashlight from a box in the truck bed and stuck it in his back pocket without lighting it up.

"Stay still!" Dan hissed quietly at the still figures there. He was sure they were thirsty and would need to relieve themselves, but they would have to wait for now.

Dan made his way around to the passenger door moving surely and quietly. The door creaked open with a push from Mary and she tried to swing her legs out of the cab but groaned quietly with the effort. Dan thought she might be crying again. He couldn't tell, nor could he see the damage to her leg. Her hands were both bloody from holding the wound, but her right hand now firmly held an automatic pistol in its slippery red grip.

Without asking for permission he gathered her up in his arms, cradled her slender frame like a baby, and lifted her easily out of the truck. She bit into the flannel of his shirt at the shoulder stifling a small quiet scream. Her right leg was slick and sticky.

"What now?" Dan whispered.

Mary waved weakly into the darkness and toward the back of the house with the gun. "Back porch. Door's supposed to be unlocked," she whispered into his ear. Her breath was warm and quick.

Dan stepped carefully through the darkness and the tall weeds towards where she had pointed. She seemed to him to weigh nothing at all. "Hold onto me," he whispered and she wrapped her arms around his neck allowing him to move his right hand back and grab the flashlight. His hands were now sticky with blood as well.

They both blinked as he switched on the light. She was right. There was a cracked cement patio at the rear of the house with a heavy metal security door that appeared to lead inside. Dan moved onward and found it unlocked. The door swung open, outward toward them with a slight pull, and then they were inside a small musty kitchen with a table and counters covered in a thick layer of dust. Dan flashed his light around quickly as he carried his slender companion through the kitchen into what appeared to be an empty living room with dirty hardwood floors. Then, he headed back down a short hallway where he found a small bedroom with a mattress in the corner. The mattress was covered by a cheaply woven Indian blanket that appeared to be new and clean.

Dan gently lowered Mary down onto the mattress where she sprawled with a heavy sigh. He unbuttoned and removed his own flannel shirt which was now soaked in blood. He sat next to her on the mattress to wrap the shirt around Mary's thigh, "Keep pressure on the wound," he told her. She dropped her heavy weapon down on the bed between them and grabbed his arm tightly. Her grip was strong as steel despite the loss of blood. Mary looked deeply into Dan's black eyes. "I need to know if I can trust you. I have no idea who you are or where you came from, but I need to know."

Dan returned her intense stare for a heartbeat. Two heartbeats. Then he whispered, "You can trust me." He didn't know what else to say. The thin woman continued to stare into his eyes for a moment as if she was trying to read what was in his heart. Then she finally lay back, one hand pressing his shirt against the wound, the other tightly gripping her weapon.

Dan left her and silently moved on through the house flashing his light into each corner of each dark room until he was satisfied that the house was empty. There were two more small bedrooms similar to the one where he had left Mary. The house appeared strangely well kept for something that obviously hadn't been lived in for years. It appeared as if someone had prepared it for their arrival. Dan found a battery-powered lantern in the kitchen that filled the room with an electric glow when he pushed the button.

Tend to the girl and then to the boys. Dan peered through the back door into the darkness where his clones were still quietly waiting in the truck. "Shh, Shh, Shh," he whispered to them comfortingly. Then, he shut and locked the door before returning to where Mary lay on the small bed. Her breath came quick and shallow. She had passed out.

Dan placed the lamp on the wood floor by the bed and flipped open his pocket knife. He quickly sliced through the fabric of the black cargo pants Mary was wearing and pulled them off of her. Her legs were slender, pale, and muscular. She came to, wincing a bit with the pain as he moved her right leg up to cut away at the cloth before returning it to the bed.

He carefully left her black underwear intact, and though the sight of her form-fitting skivvies titillated Dan somewhere in the back of his mind, he modestly avoided looking at anything but the wound.

He held her thin ropey thigh in his hand and examined it in the bright light of the lantern. The small caliber bullet had amazingly passed through the car door, and then cleanly into and out of Mary's thigh. There were two small holes on either side of her leg that were still leaking thick dark blood, though it appeared to Dan that the bleeding was slowing. The muscle was fine, alabaster, and hairless. It did not appear that an artery had been hit. The bullet was probably still in the bench seat of the truck.

"You're lucky," he murmured. "Gonna be OK" Her eyes fluttered half open and half closed. He flashed his light into them checking for signs of shock. He then tore the sleeves from his already ruined flannel and tied them tightly around her leg covering both wounds.

"Don't move and keep pressure on it. I got to see to my boys and find something to disinfect it with." He looked into her eyes, "You're gonna be OK. I want you to keep telling yourself that alright? *I'm gonna be ok.* Cause it's true." Dan's voice was little more than a hoarse whisper.

"I'm gonna be OK," she whispered back at him.

"I'll find you some water."

"Listen, I have got to tell you something very important…"

"Shush now," Dan warned her softly. "You can tell me in the morning. You need to rest now."

Mary's eyes slowly closed.

Dan left the lantern with her and moved back into the kitchen. He was about to open the back door again when he heard a rustling movement in the weeds by the truck. He peered through a crack in the boards barricading a rear window and he could see the beam of a flashlight flooding over the truck bed and into the five identical faces now agitated with fear.

Someone was in the backyard.

TWELVE

The following is a non-electronic paper letter
intercepted leaving the office of Ralph Willis: Army
Colonel, New Federal Union of States, Washington
D.C. This is not a copy. It is important to note
that this letter never reached Dr. Timm in
California.

Colonel Willis is guilty of treason against the
New Federal Union for the attempted leak of
classified information to citizens of the California
Independent Republic.

Willis's Security clearance has been revoked.

Directive: Arrest and execute Colonel Ralph Willis
immediately.

Directive: Continue Surveillance
of Dr. Derek Timm.

                    —Department Homeland Security NFUS

Derek Timm,
    It was good to hear from you, old friend. However,
once again you have stuck your nose into a beehive
looking for honey. How did you get yourself mixed up

in this mess? You probably don't even know what you are into at this point.

I am sending this paper letter (snail mail) via a reliable courier and I hope that it reaches you. I am sticking my neck out for you for old time's sake, buddy. If this message is intercepted, we are both in for a world of hurt. You are in grave danger, Derek. Are you aware that you are currently under 24-hour surveillance by the New Feds? You either have agents, or long range drones keeping track of your movements at all times right now. This is due to your correspondence with Dr. Tadese.

I'm not sure what life is really like in the California Republic these days, but by most trustworthy reports, the economy is improving and things are calming down since the secession. I hope you are well; however, you need to take immediate precautions to protect yourself and your family.

Just the mention of the name Dr. Abraha Tadese sets off alarm bells on several military fronts. His dossier is highly classified. I had to call in a favor to access it. I am sorry to tell you that by all accounts your friend Dr. Tadese is dead.

I'm not sure how to explain his death to you. I went through the documents three times, and I will attempt to explain it thusly:

The Army Research Lab Nano Technology Division (ARLNTD), Adelphi, Maryland, where he worked, was a top secret facility. A top secret facility that completely disappeared a few weeks ago. I have been able to access some of the files regarding the base, but most of them are over my pay grade. There was some heavy

duty spook action going on there my friend. Heavy
duty, and then one day, it was just gone, and there is a
lake where the base used to be.

It appears Dr. Tadese may no longer have been a willing participant in the work going on there. According
to his dossier, Tadese requested several times to be repatriated back to California. Request repeatedly denied.
There is also a note that he was reprimanded by base
security on at least three different occasions, although
I'm not clear on why or exactly how the New Federal
Army would "reprimand" a scientist working for them.

In any event, on the morning of May 1st of this year,
just one month ago, all was business as usual at ARL-
NTD. 569 personnel were on base that day, including
you friend Dr. Tadese. Then at exactly 10:38 A.M. all
contact was lost with the base. It was silently, completely destroyed without any warning.

How is that possible, you may ask? The Army Research Laboratory was flooded with an estimated 6,000
hectares of water (that's 60 million cubic feet). The entire base drowned. The valley in Adelphi containing the
base is a huge lake now with ARLNTD at the bottom
of it. According to reports from the only two survivors,
this occurred in a matter of two or three minutes.

You might not be surprised, since there had been
heavy flooding in Virginia and Maryland the year before, which destroyed entire neighborhoods. But here's
the kicker Derek, there was absolutely no weather in
the area at the time, or in the weeks before this incident occurred. The night of June 30, before the incident, was a clear night. There was no rain. In fact,
there was not a cloud in the sky. There were no rivers,

streams, or creeks in close proximity to ARLNTD capable of producing that much water. The closest body of water containing anything near an amount of aqua that huge is the Potomac River near Washington, D.C. over 50 miles away.

In short, no one has a clue how an entire valley containing a top secret laboratory suddenly flooded with water in a matter of minutes. 573 casualties have been estimated. A multitude of bodies were found floating, although most are still unaccounted for, including several civilians who lived nearby but outside the base. Looks like the New Feds sent in diving teams. I have no access to information on what they found.

I also have not been able to access the survivors' statements.

As fantastic as it sounds, your friend Dr. Abraha Tadese drowned with 573 souls in the bottom of a lake that inexplicably appeared out of nowhere and should not exist. Again, my condolences.

Not sure if they reached you in CA or not, but the official media reports here are that the area was contaminated by radiation after natural flooding. A tragic accident. The entire area is now quarantined. There is a strict no-fly zone being enforced as well. An order stands to shoot down any aircraft that come within 50 miles of the area. That includes private, business, and consumer aircraft. I am willing to bet the entire area is patrolled by armed drones. Those suckers are deadly as hell and they can be programmed to instantly vaporize anything that moves without wasting time by asking for human approval.

For what it's worth, it would appear that Tadese's

work in the field of Nanoinformatics was groundbreaking. I have his dossier open here, and even with my high level of clearance; I can't see the classified portions that detail exactly what he was working on. The guy was obviously a genius. I read here that Nanoinformatics is the use of microscopic robots to change the very scope and substance of matter? That's beyond me. It appears that Tadese was completely reimagining the entire field of study. He was doing things that no one has ever done before. No one could.

Be warned that multiple agencies are aware of your correspondence with Dr. Tadese, Derek. That is why you are being surveilled.

I wish I could help you further, but I can't. Sending this letter is dangerous enough, but I wanted to warn you. As strange as it sounds, we are citizens of different countries now. No need to mention that your country and mine are on the verge of taking military action against each other at any time. I truly hope it doesn't come to that.

When you do receive this letter, please burn it immediately. As soon as I send it, I will be doing my best to cover my tracks and destroy any electronic evidence that I even looked into the Tadese or Adelphi files. I don't need any attention coming my way over your friend and his mysterious disappearance.

I will not be contacting you again, Derek. Sadly, I don't see how our paths will ever cross again. Please hug Tricia and the girls for me and send them my love. May God bless and keep you and yours.

-R.W.

THIRTEEN

Currently listening to: *California Uber Alles*
by Dead Kennedys

Dear Sarah Joy,   1 year and 137 days old today

You slept cradled in my arms last night. You giggled in
your sleep and I wondered, what could be so funny to a sleeping one-year-old? The aura of peace around you is astounding.
I love you so much, Baby Girl. Sorry I haven't added to the
journal here in a bit.

Now I feel like a have a story to finish for you. I want you
to understand how we ended up moving here to the farm in
Colorado with Uncle Russel, and how we became friends with
Johnny Depp. I think it's important that you learn our true
history. I do hope you will be able to read this someday. I keep
worrying that I may not be there for you when you are growing
older. I have this recurring dream that you are looking for me.
You need me, but I can't be there. I can't help you. It's scary.
Anything can happen in these troubled times. If something
should happen to me, at least you will have this journal, this
piece of me. Hopefully, this will tell you who I am.

So where am I in my story? Oh, I know...

How can I explain Calexit to you, Sarah Joy? The day California seceded from the union was the day our lives completely changed. Of course, it was followed just a few days later by
Texexit, and then the New Federal Union closed the borders
to traffic and firewalled all internet relations with Texas and
California. Nothing was the same after that.

I can remember exactly what we were doing the day the news hit the web. There had been rumors swirling around for weeks, but nobody really believed that California would leave the United States of America. It was one of those moments that no one will ever forget. The whole world changed in the blink of an eye.

I have this distinct memory of Jack climbing to the top of this crumbling cement wall and laughing. This old broken down wall was jutting out in this field of mustard weeds and was covered in graffiti and was about seven feet high. It was pretty much all that was left of a tomato cannery that had been on the edge of town, where there had been a lot of big businesses and factories at one time before the real estate market collapsed and the City of Stockton was forced to declare bankruptcy. After that there were empty buildings everywhere, and some of them just burned down or fell apart like this one.

Jack was so strong and he climbed the wall easily. He just jumped and grabbed the lip of it and then he was up on top of it gleaming in the sunshine with his shaved head and his oxblood boots with the bright yellow laces.

"Watch this!" he yelled at to me. "Get a video! Get your phone out!" It was a hot spring day. How long had we been dating then? I can't remember. It must have been a couple of months. I wasn't too serious about Jack then.

This was just before I met your daddy, of course, I am getting to that, I promise.

Jack definitely wasn't part of my plan. I was almost done with school, I had great grades, and I was planning on heading off to a good Baha'i University to immerse myself in the study of my religion. I think Jack was still working at the Halal restaurant where all the black Muslims hung out all the time. He wasn't sure if he was going to graduate or not. He didn't seem too worried about it. I was sure we would break up at the end of the school year.

Anyway, I got my phone out and shot this great video. We used to watch it over and over again for years after that. I must have watched it about a hundred times. I wish I still had that phone so I could show it to you. There was Jack, way up high and all around him was just blue sky and white puffy clouds. In the video he does a little dance as he yells, "I want all you skinheads to get up on your feet! Put your braces together and your boots on your feet! And give me some of that old moonstomping!" And then he gets down in this crouch and starts swinging his arms back and forth back and forth and his eyes become little tiny slits, because he is concentrating so hard.

I remember, I was about to yell, "Don't do anything stupid!" but then he did. In the video he springs up and backwards with his arms swinging over his head, and then his feet swing up, and for a split second he is suspended above the dirt and the earth and the broken glass and the weeds and our stupid country and our stupid jobs and stupid Stockton and all the bullcrap! Then he completely rotates his whole body, and his big old boots fly over the top of his bald head, and BANG he lands on his feet laughing with dust flying everywhere and he is looking over at me with that big old grin of his to make sure that I had recorded the whole thing. He was the king of the backflip, Jack Martinez. Like a huge acrobatic skinhead monkey.

"You're crazy." I say just before I stop recording. I must have watched that video a hundred times back in the day. It's gone now.

I don't remember what happened right after that but he was probably running off to find something else to climb or some old windows to throw rocks at.

I was already pulling up my social media account to post the video, because that was something that everyone did back then. Everything we did, we recorded a video of and then posted it for the whole world to see. The internet was crazy like that and it was so addictive. You could just sit for hours on your phone watching your friends' videos or strangers' videos from the other side of the world. It's like the whole universe was just there in that little screen in the palm of your hand and a lot of people didn't even talk to each other face to face anymore because they didn't need to, and I don't really think I am doing a very good job of explaining it to you again right now but I will keep trying. I don't think I miss it, but at the same time... Yeah, I do.

Anyway, Jack from Spanish class and I had caught a bus way the heck out there to the middle of nowhere because some kid at my school had posted that there was supposed to be this store that didn't I.D. I think it was called Green Frog Liquors or maybe Lizard Liquors, but it doesn't really matter, and Jack was still only 18 but he wanted some beer.

When Jack stepped up to the counter, he was acting all blustery with his two twelve packs of PBR, ready to explain to the dude that he was 21, and in the military or whatever and that he had lost his ID. But the guy at the counter didn't even look at him. He just rang up the beer and took the money. His eyes were glued on the big flat screen TV on the wall behind the counter.

The news was on (the good news not the bad fake news) and the Governor of California was announcing that the California State Legislature had just voted to secede from the United States of America. It wasn't even a close vote. They called it a "bipartisan effort" because all the different political parties were agreeing that it was the best thing to do at that point because of all the crazy stuff the President was doing, and all the hardcore sanctions he had been putting on California, and how we had one of the biggest economies in the world even without the United States, and California was going to be strong together and stand up against nationalism, and racism, and misogyny, and in support of a healthy planetary environment.

There were a few other people there in Green Frog or Green Lizard or whatever, but no one was buying anything, everyone was just standing there watching the TV all slack jawed and everything. Half of them were wearing surgical masks. Some people were wearing them all the time in public because of the virus and everything. Jack and I didn't. Most young people didn't seem to care. We just watched quietly for a while because a lot of reporters were asking questions about what kind of money we would use, and would our jobs still exist, and what the heck would the crazy president do about it, and all that. But the governor didn't answer any of those questions too directly. He just kept saying that we needed to stick together. We would all be strong, together. He said California was going to come out on top and be a leader in the new world.

And then Jack and I slipped out of the store with our beer and my phone was just blowing up but I didn't want to answer it. Jack and I didn't even say anything to each other because we were both just kind of in shock and we didn't know how to deal with it all. We just held hands and walked back to the bus stop. We could always do that, Jack and I. Just be quiet together and think. He was a good friend and he did have a gentle side...

But that was before he ever went to jail. Jack was a heavy drinker, and drink is really what got him in trouble and that's why I knew I had to break things off with him. Sometimes he would just drink some beers and be silly and I loved that Jack. Other times, like that crazy night... Well, it got bad a couple of times, Baby. Jack would drink too much and become a completely different person. He could get really rough with other people, and once in a while he could get really rough with me...

So, that's how I met your daddy.

More Soon. Love you, Baby.

-Mommy

FOURTEEN

DAN'S PISTOL WAS STILL IN the cab of the truck. He stood shirtless in the dark kitchen, his hands still slick with Mary's blood, armed with nothing but his flashlight which he quickly switched off.

The beam from someone else's flashlight danced through the night at the back of the house. Dan watched as the light abruptly stopped, frozen when it landed on the dark face of one of the clones. Scar. Scar gazed back at the light with a determined silence written across a thick brow identical to Dan's.

Dan quickly rinsed his hands at the kitchen sink, where he was relieved to find the water running. Then he stretched his broad shoulders, threw his bare muscled chest out, and pushed the back door open noisily to make his large and intimidating presence known. Holding his large hands at the ready, he aimed his loud, deep baritone out toward the figure holding the light, "Something I can help you with?" There was more than a hint of a challenge in his tone.

"Easy, Man, easy. I'm not armed dude," came a response as the light splashed across the yard away from the truck and directly onto the tall well-muscled half naked Chicano. Dan held his left hand up to block his eyes from the light. He moved his right hand behind his back in a bluff that there might be a weapon there.

"Turn that shit off or I am going to shove it up your ass," Dan said firmly and slowly. The light switched off. Half-blinded, but not willing to show an ounce of weakness, Dan took four broad steps in the direction of where the light had been. This was all it took for him to be standing directly in front of the dark figure standing at the back of the truck. As Dan's eyes adjusted to the darkness again, he could make out a pale masculine face with a full beard. The top of the much shorter man's head was covered by a black knit beanie. He was a stocky man who obviously didn't scare easy; though he was much shorter than Dan he did not flinch or back away at the larger man's swift approach. Dan towered over his visitor by almost a foot, but the shorter man stood his ground and maintained a daring bearded smile, evident even in the darkness. Though he had to crane his neck, his eyes met Dan's confidently.

"Whoa, big man, whoa. Take it easy. I live next door," the bearded guest said softly as he held his hands up to show that they held nothing but the dark flashlight. "I'm not looking for trouble, just curious about the new neighbors."

"Who's with you?" Dan responded thickly.

"Nobody, Man. I am on my own. Right now, anyway. Hey look... These dudes in the back of the truck they all look like your twins, Man."

Dan did not move from his threatening position towering over the smaller man as his neck swiveled slightly to scan the darkness around them and peer into the recesses of the yard. He could find no sign that his guest was lying. He really did appear to be on his own.

Dan looked the smaller man over once more before moving to the back of the truck where he opened the tailgate and whispered firmly to the Five, "Out! Go to the bathroom!"

His five doppelgangers carefully clambered out into the dark weedy yard; their legs obviously stiff from having sat so long. The clones moved silently away from the truck, but not far. Each pulled down the cheap sack-cloth pants that hung loosely from their tall strong frames, and squatted to relieve themselves in the darkness. Dan noticed that Scar was the last to exit the truck bed, his black clone eyes still fixed on the stranger. When the Five had finished their business, they quietly and obediently returned to the truck stretching and scratching, their eyes watching Dan and waiting for direction.

"Dude! Who are these guys?"

Dan said nothing as he moved to the truck's cab to find his pistol and shove it into his waistband. He then unzipped a bag he had there and rustled around in it until he found a black t-shirt to put on. The barrel chested stranger watched him wordlessly still waiting for an answer as Dan fished two crude plastic bowls from the back of the truck. They were just empty plastic milk jugs that had been cut in half.

He twisted the handle of the water bib at the bottom of the large water container in the truck bed and held the bowls one at a time under the water keeping one eye on the stranger.

Dan took a long drink of water before passing on the dripping bowls. First, to Scar who drank deeply as the other clones patiently watched. When he was done, he passed the bowl on to his brothers.

Dan's visitor finally gave up waiting for an answer to his question. "Sorry, dude. I'm Trevor by the way. I'm the watcher on this block. You must be with the New Feds, right?"

Dan looked Trevor in the eyes thoughtfully as he carefully produced a red bandana and wiped out a third bowl to fill with water for Mary. "Why do you say that?"

"I mean if you are that's cool. If you're not that's cool too, Man." The thick brown beard parted to allow a quick chuckle. "I think this place used to be a safe house for New Union Feds, but no one has been here in a long time."

The clones shifted wearily on their feet. Scar was making a barely audible, "Ooh Ooh, Huff Huff" sound which he used to get his master's attention without annoying him. Dan knew they were hungry, but he needed to get back in to Mary and see to her wound.

Trevor held out a hand for Dan to shake. "I'm a councilmember on the board for the Reno Autonomous Collective. We're a co-op that maintains an independent self-governing hegemony here in Reno. We have no allegiance to the Feds or any other bureaucratic group outside of our own. We grow our own food, maintain our own justice and order, and promote the general welfare of all the members in the collective." Trevor's words sounded well-rehearsed.

Dan regarded the proffered hand for a moment. "Do you have any medical supplies?" he asked.

FIFTEEN

The following email Message appears to have been
sent by Dr. Abraha Tadese on May 13 ████, 12 days
after the incident at Adelphi. The message was sent
from an untraceable email account to Tricia Timm,
Wife of Dr. Derek Timm.

It is important to note:

- Dr. Abraha Tadese is alive.

- Whereabouts unknown.

- This email message was received by Tricia
  Timm. Operative Andrew Eldritch was
  immediately dispatched and Tricia Timm has
  been eliminated via drone strike.

Recommendation: ████████████████████████ —
Department Homeland Security NFUS

From: 389487476@anonomous.intel
Date: Tuesday, May 13 ▮▮ 1:30 a.m.
To: TriciaTimm@berkeley.edu
Subject: RE: Sofia and Marisa

Tricia,

Please forgive me for using your daughters' names in the subject line. I wanted to get your attention so you wouldn't think this message is junk. This is Abraha Tadese. It has been awhile, but I remember you and the girls very well. I ate dinner at your house many times and you were always a welcoming hostess.

I must be short. I am in danger and on the run. Please tell Derek that I am coming to California. I will contact him soon, but we must be very careful. Tell him to keep his eyes open in the next few weeks for a message or sign that I will relay to him in secret.

Tell him I said, "Where is Isaac Asimov when you need him?" He will know that it is me.

Thank you very much. God bless you.
-AT

SIXTEEN

Currently listening to: *Blister In The Sun*
by Violent Femmes

Dear Sarah Joy,   540 days

This song always reminds me of Jack. Sometimes I still
think about him even though all that is far behind me now. I
am going to write to you about the day that I decided to break
up with him. It was a strange day.

I can remember that it was scorching hot and we were waiting in a long line of cars to get gas at the Union 76. Tuesday
was my dad's scheduled day to pump his gas ration. Gasoline
was strictly regulated in California and everyone was assigned
certain gas stations to buy from on certain pump days. My dad
was working so he asked me to take his old Volkswagen for a
fill up that morning. Jack had offered to drive and wait with me.
We had heard some scary stories about things happening in gas
lines around Stockton.

The line stretched down the block and around the corner.
We were still about three blocks from getting gas and the line
was moving really, really, slowly. The VW did not have air conditioning and we had all the windows down. Just sitting there.
Sweating.

Jack said something like, "I don't know if it wastes more
gas to let the engine just idle, or to keep starting it and then
turning it off again every time we stop." My Dad had this med-
itation cassette tape in his radio, and Jack took it out and put in
The Old Firm Casuals. I think it was "Perry Boys" or maybe

that other song, "Strap in for a hell of a ride!" I knew all his music back then.

I had been reading from the Tabernacle of Unity a few days before and a line from Baha'u'llah had really jumped out at me like fireworks in my brain. "Noble have I created thee, yet thou hast abased thyself. Rise then unto that for which thou wast created."

I knew I was just abasing myself with Jack. He was just a fling. A good time. I had started dating him with my mind already made up that I would break up with him in a few weeks. The night before he had gotten drunk and, well... angry. That's when everything had changed.

You see, Sweetie, my faith in Baha'i has always been the most important thing in my life (almost as important as you!). Jack had no real interest in that. He drank too much and fought too much. I thought about how I would be graduating high school soon, and then I would move on to college... The last thing I needed was a crazy skinhead boyfriend.

Simple right?

Jack could be so sweet, he offered to jump out, run to the store, and buy me a Slurpee before the car in front of us moved again. But I didn't respond. My mind was flashing back to the night before. I had been trying to calm drunk Jack down, and he had knocked me over. He hadn't shoved me so much as just lurched against me, but the momentum from his big body had pushed me so hard I had fallen down in the street and scraped my shins bloody.

He was immediately sorry of course. All drunken apologies, but he had been so drunk, I knew he wouldn't even remember it the next day. He had stumbled on down the street and away all by himself. And sure enough, today he didn't even seem to know that it had happened. I was the one who had woken up achy, bruised, and hurt.

So, in my mind I had been getting my speech ready for him all morning; "I just graduated high school, you did not. You are supposed to be going to adult school to finish up a few units for your diploma, but you are not. I am planning on attending Delta College, and you are not..." Delta was our local community college. Sadly, going to school outside of the California Independent Republic was no longer an option. "I have a deep faith in Baha'i and you do not. You are a skinhead and I am not. You listen to this crazy music and I do not." Wait, I had to scratch that last one. Jack's taste in music was pretty good.

Anyway, I knew it was definitely time to say goodbye. I had planned ahead for that day. The gas line was the perfect place for a long reassuring talk if Jack should need it, but this was final. I would let him down firmly yet gently...

But... Jack's buddy, Cormac, had decided to tag along at the last minute. He caught me looking at him in the sun visor mirror and he winked at me. I just frowned over my shoulder at him. He was tall and thin and muscular. He had a toothy smile like a cartoon wolf. Cormac always thought of himself as a real ladies man. He was always flirting with me. All the girls thought he was so cute and it made him arrogant. He made some cheesy joke about Frappucinnos being cheaper than gasoline and said that we should pour those in the gas tank. Then he waited with this smirk on his face expecting peals of laughter. I didn't even smile.

I mean really, who tags along when you have to wait in line for three hours? Especially as a third wheel? Cormac apparently. So, I sat there in a pool of my own sweat, pondering whether or not it was kind and polite to dump Jack in front of his friend. It seemed like it would be pretty humiliating, for Jack anyway.

I could feel Cormac's eyes on my pale bare neck. I had just shaved a strip of short hair at my nape. I used to wear my hair up in a small ponytail above it. "Molly Ringwald Style," Jack called it. He told me it was sexy. Apparently, Cormac agreed. So, I couldn't say a word.

Jack was complaining about how much he missed soccer since the great firewall blocked all the gosh darn mother fricking Manchester City games and he had a hard time even getting the fricking scores (those aren't the words he used). I had to remind him to stop cursing so much.

I did not like being the harpy girlfriend! I added this to the list of reasons in my breakup speech. I didn't want to always be trying to change him. "Drink less! Fight less! Cuss less! Come to church with me!" It really wasn't working out.

"Jack..." I pushed his shoulder. Between the loud music and the fascinating conversation with Cormac, he wasn't hearing me.

I watched Cormac unbutton his sweat-soaked Ben Sherman in the vanity mirror. Underneath he wore only a wife-beater that was plastered to his pale muscular frame. He had a crucified skinhead tattooed between his pectoral muscles. He thought of himself as a real Martyr, Cormac. I hated him.

Then Cormac was complaining about the Defense Drill bombing sirens waking him up from his nap. And I was just getting more and more frustrated. I could feel the sweat trickling down my back and soaking into my shirt and I couldn't get a word in.

Then, Jack was telling us about the big riot at the Walmart on Hammer Lane the day before. It was over toilet paper. Toilet Paper! People went to the hospital over toilet paper. That's where we were at. Texas and California were both supposed to be having negotiations with the New Fed President to sort things out, but you didn't know if you could trust what you read anymore.

When the Honda Civic in front of us finally rolled forward one more car length, Jack started my Dad's old VW and rolled her forward slowly, two feet, six feet, ten feet closer to the gas station! It was still three blocks away.

We were going to run out of gas before we even got there.

Jack shut off the engine again and this time the music with it. He was keeping his eye on the guy in the Honda in front of us. The guy was shouting and making hand gestures at the car in front of him. Everything got real quiet.

I was just about to say, "Jack, I really need to talk to you," but the guy in the Honda was getting out of his car. He was a white guy with a tattooed neck, and he was dressed in baggy red shorts, a red shirt, and a crooked red hat. I couldn't make out what he was shouting.

Then the doors quickly swung open on the car in front of the red gangster guy in the Honda and two black guys popped out, both dressed in yellow and black. One was tall and skinny the other one was tall and fat. They were both shouting back at the white guy in red. I heard lots of angry cursing.

Cormac was halfway out the door. He wanted to go check it out.

I can remember Jack asking him, "You wanna get involved in that? Which side you gonna take?"

And Cormac said, "The white guy of course," without giving it a thought.

Jack and I looked at each other like, *what the heck?*

And Cormac was saying, "Come on, Man! You better have my back."

I grabbed Jack's arm and shook my head at him, but Cormac was out and his door slammed shut.

The guys in front of us had all left their cars and were continuing to shout and move toward each other. Jack started to open his door to go after Cormac, and that's when they started shooting at each other.

Oh! It was a scary day, Baby! Too much to write about in one sitting. I will write you down the rest tomorrow.

Love Mommy XXOOXX

SEVENTEEN

THE FIVE CLONES SAT AROUND a firepit at the Reno Autonomous Collective, each spooning up green mush from the wooden bowls they held in front of them and chewing hungrily.

Dan regarded his own bowl contemplatively, prying apart chunks of pink meat from the strangely textured green goo with a plastic spoon. They sat huddled on logs in the cool Reno night.

Trevor grinned, "They love it!" He reached out to pat Scar on the back, but the hulking clone flinched away from his hand, gave the short bearded man a disparaging growl, and then returned his attention to the strange smelling meal.

"It's my own recipe. I make the mush out of kale and wheat germ from the garden and then mix in a can of fried Spam chunks for texture. You get everything you need in a bowl of Trevor's Delight! Protein, vitamins, calories, fiber. That's really going to improve your bowel movement. Your next elimination is going to be an absolute pleasure."

The campfire was in what was effectively Trevor's backyard. His residence was a small craftsman house on the western edge of The Reno Autonomous Collective's block garden. Trevor still believed that Dan was working for the Feds and was happy to explain at length how the urban collective functioned. The group was an interesting one, consisting of a mashup of liberal Reno hippies and conservative desert survivalists. They had reclaimed several acres of land in a five-block area, pulling up the concrete and transforming it into gardens and towering wind turbines. The hippies in the group grew fruits, vegetables, and copious amounts of marijuana while the survivalists provided security in the form of regular armed patrols throughout the property.

"Our Council meets once a week to plan and make decisions on issues or problems. Larger issues are brought to the collective as a whole for a vote. At its heart, the collective is essentially a democratic venture." Trevor was happily explaining. "We tore down a bunch of houses and garages to increase our space for gardens. Most of the members of the collective live in the surrounding neighborhood."

Dan finally dug into his food, found it tasty, and nodded appreciatively toward his new friend. "Thank you for feeding us," he whispered huskily.

"Glad you like it," said Trevor with a smile. He then took a thick joint from his breast pocket, lit it, inhaled deeply, and blew a thick pungent cloud of sweet smoke out over the fire. He offered the joint to Dan who simply shook his head and kept eating.

Trevor continued to puff on the joint, often holding in the smoke as he spoke, "I'm actually surprised that you weren't spotted by a patrol when you came through, Dude. Probably because you tore ass straight to that Fed house. I don't think security even noticed you. I will have to bring that up with... Well, speak of the devil."

A tall figure strode into the circle of firelight and stood next to where Dan sat on the smooth white log with Trevor.

"This is our chief of security, Bill. Bill this is Dan."

Bill was a tall thin man in black fatigues who appeared to be of mixed Asian descent. He cradled a heavy assault rifle to his chest with an air of relaxation that displayed his comfort and experience with the weapon. He glanced back and forth from Dan to the five clones with a curiosity that Dan was becoming accustomed to. The clones had finished their meals and the Five were staring stupidly into the fire.

"Hey Dan. I'm Bill. Mind if I sit down, Trev?"

"Not at all. Care for something to eat?" Trevor asked with a smile.

Dan noticed that neither Trev nor Bill wore surgical masks, but they did keep a respectable social distance from each other, and from him. It had been a while since Dan had been around so many strangers. He was remembering the rules.

"No thanks." Bill tried to make himself comfortable on a short stump next to Dan. Dan noticed that he did not set the rifle down. He looked like he probably slept with the damn thing.

"Mind if I ask you a few questions, Dan?"

Dan shrugged and finished off the last few pinkish chunks of Trevor's Delight in his bowl.

"How'd you find us?"

Dan cleared his throat thickly, "Just come off the freeway and drove on down to find an empty house to put up in for the night."

"They came straight down Channel Street," Trevor chimed in as he moved to collect the empty wooden bowls from the Five, several of whom were starting to doze off in the warmth of the fire.

"And these guys are..." Bill indicated at Dan's tired quintuplets.

"They're my clones," Dan replied.

"I'm sorry, clones?"

Dan sighed and stretched his thick chest and arms in a yawn. He had explained the Five how many times now? How many more times would he before he reached Stockton? If he ever got there...

"They're harmless," Dan's thick voice rumbled out to his captivated audience around the fire as though he were telling a ghost story. "Few years ago, the New Federal Union ran an experimental program for citizens to clone themselves. After the Feds closed all the borders to immigrants, there was a real shortage of cheap labor. This was one of the President's ideas to make up for that." Bill and Trevor were listening attentively. "I signed on to have myself cloned six times. Lost one to influenza. Trained 'em as farm hands in Colorado." Dan spoke slowly with a heavy clarity.

Trevor and Bill both gazed over at the five clones and then back to Dan, with faces glazed in amazement. Bill produced a clear pint bottle half full of brown liquid from his pocket. He took a nip and passed it to Trevor who poured a bit in his coffee. When Trevor offered the bottle to Dan, the big man shook his head fiercely, almost angrily without looking at him. "I don't drink."

"So, what do they do?" Bill asked.

"They can't read or write or speak. Too stupid. Just capable of basic repetitive tasks with direction. Kind of like a smart dog. They're big and strong like me. Good farm hands until…" Dan's voice trailed off for a moment. He cleared his throat and spat into the fire before continuing, "Lost my farm a while back." He grew quiet again. "Gonna sell 'em in California."

The clones were stretched out by the fire leaning on each other. They had no idea they were being discussed at all. They sat slouched together against a log opposite from Dan and Trevor either with heavy eyes or snoring softly, except for Scar. Scar continued to stare vacantly into the flames of the campfire.

"I remember the television commercial. 'Clone yourself!' with the corny music. I didn't really think it was real," Trevor said with a yawn and a stretch handing the pint of whisky back to Bill.

"Interesting." Bill hugged his rifle tightly and downed the last two fingers of whisky. "I understand there is a 7th member of your party?"

Dan considered for a moment before answering. He had already bandaged Mary's wounds and left her sleeping comfortably in the safe house next door. "My woman. She's sleep."

"Are you armed?"

"I have a pistol."

"And how are you planning on getting into California?"

Dan paused again, "I was planning on just driving in... Repatriating. I was born there." Another pause, "New Fed soldier told me it's not possible."

Bill chuckled and shook his head, "It's possible, it's just not easy my friend."

Trevor joined in again. "The Republic of California will probably take you, Dude. They want solid citizens. It's getting out of Nevada that's difficult. The New Union isn't letting anyone out. They want to keep their citizens, and the border with California is completely shut down. I-80 and all other main routes are barricaded and no one is let through. There's no electronic communication with California, and there are no planes, cars, or trucks allowed to cross the border. The only real way into California is by boat from the Pacific Ocean to the west. The mountains here are patrolled by New Fed soldiers and heavily weaponized army drones."

Dan looked into his hands in silence. He had not considered this. He had been out of the loop too long and was unaware of heightened tensions between the California Independent Republic and the New Federal Union of States. "We will find a way through," he said to no one in particular.

"Huh. At least they haven't started building the wall on the border yet. Construction is supposed to start in a few months.

The New Federal Union loves their walls." Bill paused, his countenance thoughtful, "Trevor knows some homesteaders off the beaten track way high up in the Sierras, just past the Paiute reservation. Don't you Trev?" Trevor did not reply. "They live right on the border between the two states. Wild country though. A lot of Fundamentalist Mormons up there. Maybe they can help you get through." Bill stood to go offering an elbow for Dan to bump. Social distance. "I take it you will be leaving us in the morning?"

Dan bumped the offered elbow with his own. "Sure," he said.

"Good luck then." Bill and his rifle disappeared into the night.

Trevor sat staring into the flames as though he had not been listening at all. For the first time since Dan had met him, he was not smiling. After a few minutes he suddenly rose and disappeared with a quiet, "Goodnight" leaving Dan alone with the snoring Five.

Dan roused the Five and then made sure they were bedded down somewhat comfortably together in a nest of blankets and tarps in the bed of the truck before stopping in to check on his mysterious Mary. She had eaten the food Trevor had made and was sound asleep. The bleeding from her wound had stopped and Dan gently checked the dressing without waking her. Her lovely pale face glowed in the darkness of the empty abandoned house.

Dan knelt by her bed and offered ten Ave Marias before returning to the lonely campfire where he wrapped himself in an old Indian blanket. He was careful to avoid looking directly into the fire so he wouldn't be blind if he needed to look out into the darkness again.

Was Bill telling the truth? Was it going to be that hard to

get out of Nevada? He still had no idea who Mary was or what she was after. And who the hell had been shooting at them? Too much to think about.

Dan had just started to nod off when he was startled by a tall thick figure ambling into the orange glow of the fire. It was Scar. Dan rubbed his eyes in confused disbelief as Scar sat down next to him and picked up a stick.

He was Scar, and yet he was not. His eyes now shone with an intelligence that had never presented itself before. And then, when Scar spoke, it was with Dan's own voice, clear and deep and concise. It was something Dan had never heard before, his own voice not coming from his lips. The sound chilled him to his bones. None of his clones had ever uttered a word in their lives. They weren't capable of speech...

"Dan, it's time for me to tell you a story."

EIGHTEEN

SCAR POKED HIS STICK absentmindedly into the fire. Dan sat rigid; his face frozen in helpless astonishment. *This must be a dream,* Dan told himself. *You are just dreaming fool.* Dan relaxed a bit in the realization that this must be true. He leaned back into his blankets.

Scar began to speak:

Long ago near this very city there lived a mean old man. A man who had lived a dark life full of dark intentions and even darker deeds. He had made his living as a gunslinger. A warrior for hire. Well-practiced in the art of killing, his skills were for sale to the highest bidder.

Throughout his life he had killed many other men, and even a woman or two. Often, he killed for money. At times he killed drunkenly for no reason with complete abandon. Other times he killed because of pride. Now, in his older years, he often pondered upon the lives he had taken. He wondered if he should feel regret over the blood that he had spilt. He felt no such regret.

He had retired from violence a wealthy man. He was able to purchase a ranch here close to Reno. His bloodlust had been replaced by another form of lust. The lust for a woman, or rather for a girl. The ranch directly to the south of his was the home of a large family. A wealthy and well known farmer and his nine children lived there. The youngest of whom was the farmer's eleven-year-old daughter named Emma.

Emma was a bright-eyed and beautiful young girl. Once, in town, the gunslinger had heard her laugh loudly at something one of her brothers had said, and it was that laugh that first caught his attention. So confident. So pure. Young Emma had no inkling about regret or pain or murder. She was at the beginning of a journey that was sure to be much brighter than the one that was just ending for the gunslinger.

The gunslinger was covetous. He coveted the farmer's daughter. He knew though, that he was old and ugly both inside and out. Emma would not want him. Her father and her family would never think it proper for her to have any relationship whatsoever with an ugly old murderer like himself. Even back then, the desire to lay with one so young was considered anathema.

Once, the gunslinger would have taken the girl away from her family by force and done what he wanted with her. He had the skill. He had the power. He had the desire. Yet these times were very different from his younger years. The west had once been a lawless land where a man lived a violent life if he so chose.

But now, he was older. The gunslinger had the wisdom to foresee the consequences of such an action. The farmer had a large family including several strong sons and nephews. The sheriff in Reno was also a large and powerful man with many deputies.

Besides, the gunslinger was not desirous of merely a single night of pleasure with the little girl. He often watched her as she walked down a road near his small cabin on her way to town or to school. Sometimes she walked with her siblings, and sometimes she walked alone. Every time the old gunslinger caught a glimpse of her thin figure and fine auburn hair, his desire grew stronger. He was a lonely old man and he longed for the farmer's daughter to be his: a bright ornament that he alone owned and kept in his cabin to do his bidding. His cabin was dark and cold. Emma's bright light would shine even more brightly in his cabin. Emma's bright light would keep him warm.

So, the old warrior came up with another plan. And in his lonely dark little cabin he retrieved his guns from where they lay unused for years. He carefully oiled and loaded his guns as his tired old mind worked its way far back, digging deep through his disturbingly violent old memories to a story he had heard not once, but twice long ago.

Having heard the story more than once gave it validity, even if it sounded crazy. Once he had been told the story by a prostitute he had lain with in Winnemucca. He hadn't given it much credence then. However, he had been told the same story a second time by a man who was gut-shot in Sacramento. The gunslinger had listened to the dying man's story without any attempt to tend to his wounds or provide him with any comfort. He just watched as the gut-shot man lay bleeding his life out and into the dirt, mumbling to himself.

The dying man's tale was fantastic, as had been the whore from Winnemucca's. He told about an ancient shop that had been built a hundred years ago in an abandoned mining encampment deep in the Sierra Nevada mountains west of Reno. The shop was a mystical place that had somehow become blessed or cursed, neither the whore nor the dying man was sure which. In any event, any item that one purchased in the shop would remove years of age from the physical body of the buyer. If one bought a lamp that had been manufactured 20 years ago, 20 years would vanish from the buyer's age. If one bought a trinket that had been produced five years ago, the happy customer would instantly find himself five years younger.

The old gunslinger was thinking silently about all of this as he packed his leather satchel with supplies, strapped his guns around his waist and set off into the mountains in search of the shop. If he could remove 50 years from his ugly life, he was certain he could acquire the little girl who he wanted so very feverishly.

The mountains were full of snow at that time of year and the going was slow. Dan, I won't regale you with all the various perils and adventures that befell that ugly old man. One night in his sleep, he was attacked by a bear and despite being direly wounded, dispatched the beast with his knife in a bloody battle. Another day, crossing a stream, he slipped on an icy rock and plunged into the freezing water. If he hadn't found the strength to pull himself out and the wherewithal to get a fire started quickly, his dastardly existence would have been stopped cold there by hypothermia.

Suffice it to say that after two months of toiling through the mountains, the evil old gunslinger was near to shuffling off this mortal coil. He was frostbit, malnourished, and gravely wounded. He was out of food and the soles of his boots were worn through. He began to dream about just sitting at the base of a big tree and welcoming death to come take him. He did not want death sneaking up behind him, he wanted to see him coming just in case he found the energy to pick one more fight on this earthly plane.

Just as he was looking to pick out the perfect tree, he suddenly slipped and tumbled through the snow over a tall tree-lined ridge and into a small arroyo that shouldn't have been there. There had been no break in the foliage ahead of him, nor any dip in the terrain when he had looked down from the ridge above, but sure enough, when he had pulled himself up from the dusty ground he found that he had fallen into a small break in the rock that was devoid of any trees or vegetation. It was also almost completely dry, and upon stumbling into it, the old gunslinger felt an immediate warmth that chased the chill from his bones. Filtered light flowed through the rocks above in livered rays to reveal a short wooden boardwalk before him, ancient and splintered. The rotten and decaying planks led up the arroyo to a battered wooden shopfront. The word MER-CANTILE was barely visible in fading letters over a sagging door next to an ancient wooden cigar store Indian which had lost all of its paint decades ago.

The old gunslinger lurched forward and into the shop with his last shreds of energy. If he had believed in God, this surely would have been a moment for thanksgiving, but in all honesty the old warrior didn't believe in a damn thing and never had.

The interior of the shop was strangely well-lit by several hanging lanterns, although they gave off an acrid smoke that left a nagging need to hack and cough in the back of the old man's throat. Despite the lanterns being lit, there was no evidence that anyone had entered the crowded building in years. The walls were lined with shelves, packed full of items, covered in a thick layer of dust. The gunslinger left footprints in the dust on the floor as he walked to the small glass counter that was now so opaque with cobwebs that whatever might be inside was imperceptible.

Behind the counter, a strange thin mannequin was propped on a chair dressed in a crumbling fringed and beaded leather jacket and a moldy three pointed hat. Like everything else in the shop, the mannequin and its rustic garb were coated in a heavy layer of grime. The gunslinger nearly jumped out of his skin when the powdery layer encasing the countenance of the old mannequin cracked at the corners of its mouth and it spoke in a crackling monotone, *D'ye know the rules?*

The old gunslinger was more terrified than he had ever been in his life, but he had nothing to lose at this point. Without the energy to speak, he merely shook his head and continued to gaze about the shop.

Y'may pick one gewgaw, but only one. What ye pick ye must pay fer. How old yer gewgaw is shall be reflected in the price and the price twill be reflected in the years taken from yer carcass but not from yer soul, crackled the shopkeeper, for that is what he was.

The gunslinger's voice was barely a whisper as he found the strength to ask the one question that had hounded the back of his brain throughout his entire journey, "And if I pick an object that is older than I am?"

Ye shall cease t'exist! cried the dusty shopkeeper almost before the last word had left his tired customer's mouth. The shopkeeper seemed to almost rise up an inch or two in his insistence to answer the question, but he only settled down further into the dust and cobwebs that encased him.

As the shop's only patron stumbled deeper into its depths he was without hesitation. If he chose wrongly now it didn't matter. Death was at his elbow. His only recourse was to make a purchase.

The gunslinger considered a microscope for a moment, then a tattered flag bearing an insignia that he did not recognize. But a sharp icy wind filled his lungs as his gaze fell upon a small axe. It was a stout hand axe designed for chopping kindling and, out of jealousy, he had stolen a brand new one just like it from a boy who was much smaller than him when he was thirteen. The smaller boy had cried. The gunslinger, then but a lad himself, had pushed him face first down into the mud and walked away bearing his prize.

Thirteen. The axe had been brand new. Emma.

A gloating satisfaction filled the black heart of the evil warrior as he grasped the dusty old axe, brought it back to the counter, and placed it before the decrepit shopkeeper.

One final rule, croaked the dust covered corpse. *On the day ye lose yer purchase, sell it, or dispose of it, yer lost years shall be revisited upon yer head twofold.*

"Just tell me the cost," whispered the confident old gunslinger as he untied his heavy leather purse. He could feel death slinking away. Far away. If only for the time being...

Fifty dollars, replied the corpse of a shopkeeper.

The gunslinger smiled as he lay two heavy twenty-five dollar gold pieces upon the counter. And the decades fled from within him. The days and weeks spent alone in the dark, the drunken nights and saloon card games, the blind rages, the mornings he woke to find his hands covered in blood, the terror-filled dreams that haunted him at night. Fifty years of violence and hatred and despair effused from his corpulent existence and became trapped deep within the blade of the axe he had purchased.

And when the gunslinger went to reach for that axe, it was not with the hand of an old man, but that of a young boy. And when he used that young hand to wipe the grime away from a mirror hanging on the wall, the face of a handsome young lad of no more than 14 or 15 years of age smiled back at him and laughed out loud.

Axe in hand the young boy stretched his sinewy arms and shoulders, appreciating their power and flexibility as if for the first time. Then, he exited the shop ready to begin his arduous journey back through the mountains and to his ranch. His supplies had dwindled and his clothes were threadbare, but he already knew that he would need less and be able to travel much farther and much more quickly through the treacherous terrain with the renewed vigor of youth.

That first night he found a fallen tree with dry ground beneath. He built himself a fire to keep himself warm. With a solid THUNK he buried the blade of the axe into the old rotted stump left by the tree. However, as the dark of night settled around him, he heard a soft voice calling out pleading for mercy. The young boy looked all about, but quickly assured himself that he was quite alone in the mountains. Then he heard it again, still faint, but a bit louder than last time. This time he could make out the words.

Please don't kill me mister. I've got a family.

The warm blood pulsing within the young body suddenly chilled and froze the gunslinger's fresh muscles. He reached into his pack and drew out one of his pistols. The weapon was now large in his hands but the bone handle grips still felt as familiar as ever and he knew he held the gun with greater tenacity than ever before in his life.

He heard the pleading voice again even louder. *Please don't kill me mister. I've got a family.*

And his mind returned to a drunken night more than 20 years ago in Lovelock, Nevada when he had gunned down Joseph Poorgrass. Having taken two bullets already, Poorgrass had knelt in a mixture of his own blood and the mud before him in the street, begging those very same words. Then the gunslinger had shot him through the mouth blowing large chunks of brains and teeth out the back of his head and down the lane. Poorgrass never said another word ever again.

The young killer huddled by the fire wrapped in an old jacket much too big for him with his gun at the ready as Joseph Poorgrass's cry came again and again louder and louder still, *Please don't kill me mister. I've got a family.*

The wounded Poorgrass pleaded throughout the entire night until the words were ringing in the gunslinger's ears as though a banshee were screaming them directly into his skull. *PLEASE DON'T KILL ME, MISTER! I'VE GOT A FAMILY!*

PLEASE DON'T KILL ME, MISTER! I'VE GOT A FAMILY!
PLEASE DON'T KILL ME, MISTER! I'VE GOT A FAMILY!

And the gunslinger sat throughout the night clutching his pistol and listening without achieving a minute's rest.

As the sun began to rise, Joseph Poorgrass's cries finally began to subside. The gunslinger packed his axe and his last few provisions and started out into the snow again. All day he labored on his trek through the snowy mountains without stopping, dreading the moment that the sun would start to set in the west.

But set it did, and the young warrior was so exhausted that he had no choice but to again find a dry spot where he could lay out his meager bedroll and start the night's fire. This time he took the axe a hundred yards from his camp near a gently flowing stream. Here, he hacked at the frozen ground until he had created a deep hole. Therein he buried the axe, careful to place a pointed stone on top of it so that it could be found and brought forth again in the morning.

No sooner had he returned to camp however, when he heard a soft voice calling out to him. Again, the handsome young lad readied his pistol and he fixed his mind against the coming onslaught. He would ignore the voice tonight and think only of the sweet Emma and the delicious delight of her young, warm body in the darkness of his cold cabin.

But on this night, it was a different voice calling out begging, not that of Joseph Poorgrass. Try as he might to fixate on the bare, thin, hairless neck of young Emma, he couldn't help but hear the soft words echoing through the night, '*Go ahead and take the money, partner. Just don't…*' The final words of an unknown cowboy in Moapa, Nevada. The cowboy had been lucky enough to take the gunslinger's money in a poker game, but not lucky enough to keep his life.

Go ahead and take the money, partner. Just don't…
Go ahead and take the money, partner. Just don't…
GO AHEAD AND TAKE THE MONEY, PARTNER! JUST DON'T!

All throughout the night the bodiless cowboy screamed at the young lad hunched over his scanty fire. The killer only rocked back and forth. Back and forth. *It will all be worth it,* he thought to himself. *It will all be worth it when I have Emma.*

As the sun rose and the dead cowboy's cries dwindled, the young man went and unburied his axe. He was exhausted, but found strength in the sunny new day as the snow melted around him. He figured that he was a few days travel from his ranch and from sweet Emma. He set off again, strong enough during the day but always dreading the return of the night because…

The sun always sets. On the third night, the gunslinger had made up his mind to fight through his fatigue and continue moving down the mountain in the darkness. He could almost taste the salty sweat on Emma's sweet skin, he was that close.

However, as darkness fell and he shambled on through the snow, a new voice called out to him from the black night surrounding him. It was a voice he had long ago managed to forget. The voice of another very young girl begging for her life in three simple words. *I won't tell.*

The gunslinger slammed his fists against his ears over and over. He wrapped his scarf tightly around his head to block those three words, but nothing could keep them out. *I won't tell.*

And for the first time in his life the gunslinger felt a new emotion that smoldered in his chest like hot pitch. He remembered the little crippled girl from a neighboring farm on a summer's evening when he had been the same age he was now, fifty years ago. He had lured her into a barn and had his way with her. She had begged him to stop but he didn't. Then, she had begged him to let her go, but he didn't do that either. He had smothered her to death with an old horse blanket and left her body there in the barn for her father to find.

I won't tell, were the last words she had ever spoke. Tonight, the killer was hearing those last words over and over. *I won't tell. I won't tell. I won't tell.*

And as he continued to stumble throughout the interminably long blackness of the night, the words rang in his head over and over again until they were etched into his very soul. *I WON'T TELL.* And for the first time the gunslinger knew regret and he felt sorry. He was sorry for what he had done. He was sorry for the life he had led. He was sorry for the lives he had taken!

Just as he had shown no mercy to the many victims he had preyed upon throughout his life, there was no mercy for him on this dark, cold mountain night.

I WON'T TELL.
I WON'T TELL.
I WON'T TELL.

The gunslinger tore on through the night trying to outrun his past, stumbling and falling into the black snow over and over again. The words followed him through the black mountains and beyond.

But as the sun rose, he found himself nearing the end of his journey. Freezing, starving, and beyond exhausted, he was simply a few miles from the homestead of the rich farmer with the beautiful daughter. And, though his weariness hung upon him like a lead vest, he ran on. He could sense death very close behind him once again, yet he could also feel a new life waiting just a few miles ahead. On he ran.

However...

Despite the sunlight of the bright day, he found himself under siege from a myriad of voices from his past. The voices of so many he had wronged and hurt and killed.

GO AHEAD AND TAKE THE MONEY, PARTNER! JUST DON'T!

PLEASE DON'T KILL ME, MISTER! I'VE GOT A FAMILY!

DON'T SHOOT! I'M NOT ARMED!

PLEASE STOP! YOU'RE HURTING ME!

I WON'T TELL!

I WON'T TELL!

I WON'T TELL!

Running as fast as he could, the gunslinger could see the farmhouse just ahead of him. He could see one of Emma's sisters hanging clothes out on the line to dry. He could smell the warm welcoming smoke curling up from the chimney. He could reach the front door. With his last ounces of energy and sanity he leaned his thin frame on the door and pounded upon it with his fists.

And sweet young Emma bounded down the steps within the house and toward the loud banging with a curious look on her face. When she swung her front door open, it was just in time to see a very handsome young man on her porch who immediately proceeded to take a short stout hand axe in both hands and drive the blade directly into his forehead with all his might.

NINETEEN

Currently listening to: *Funky Kingston*
by Toots & The Maytals

Dear Sarah Joy,   541 days

So those were scary days! People were shooting at each other in line for gasoline!

I can remember the guy in red was holding a short black gun in his hand and aiming it sideways. The black guys were jumping back in their car. My ears were ringing and I could feel my heartbeat in my temples.

Jack grabbed the back of my neck (where I had just shaved it) and pushed my head down hard. He pulled his door closed. Cormac was back in and crouching in the back seat laughing, and shouting for Jack to get us out of there.

But when Jack turned the key... Nothing.

I could hear the POW! POW! POW! of more shots right next to the car but I couldn't see anything from below the dash where Jack had pushed me.

Jack was yelling at the car to start in his husky baritone. He tried the key again and this time the Volkswagen sputtered to life. Then Jack cranked the wheel and pulled us out of the line of cars and down Pacific Avenue. More shots were ringing out behind us.

Cormac was still laughing from his hunched position, "Fuckin' Stockton!" was all he said.

An hour later we had dropped Cormac off at his girlfriend's house, and we were miles away from the Union 76 gunfight, but my heart was still racing. Jack pulled Dad's VW into my driveway. The needle was still on empty.

He turned off the engine and smiled at me crookedly with his dark brown eyes sparkling.

And then I was crying and he was holding me close and kissing me softly over and over again. All over my neck and face. Everywhere but my mouth.

"Calm down Joc. Calm Down." He kept saying between kisses. "You're safe now. You're safe." And I did feel safe, for that moment, but it was all getting to me, Baby. Living in such a violent city where everyone was on edge not knowing what would happen next. We could have been attacked at any minute by our brothers and sisters in our old country. Or would they just blockade the borders and starve us out until we had to come begging back?

My emotions were out of control. Suddenly I was pushing Jack away and punching him. "I have been trying to talk to you all day!" I yelled at him.

Jack backed off a bit and held his hands out in front of him to keep me from hitting him. He was still smiling that sweet reassuring smile.

I looked up right into his eyes. He was so tall his shaved head was rubbing against the roof of the car, and I will never forget what he said.

"Listen, I would never let anything happen to you. Do you know that? Nothing. I will protect you no matter what. I know I drink too much sometimes, but the pressure of all of this is getting to all of us, right? You are the most important thing in my life. I love you, Joc."

Jack was usually so quiet, that was a really long speech for him. Sweet, too. To this day I remember every word.

And everything had been so tense lately. I mean, no one knew what was going to happen next with California. Jack was constantly worried about the future. Would the New Federal Union send in troops? Drones? Did we have a future in California? What would we do?

Everyone around us acted as if nothing had changed. People were still going about their daily lives, going to the same jobs, shopping at the same stores, but the tension was high. A manic high. Panic masquerading as normalcy. We all felt like it couldn't last.

Jack really internalized stuff like that and I knew he mostly worried about his mom and about me. Would he really be able to protect us? Could he keep that promise?

The timing for dumping Jack was perfect. Jack was low-hanging fruit to knock off the tree. But when Jack asked if I was OK...

I had forgotten my speech. The words were lost from my mind. I shook my head and looked away. "I'm fine," was all I could say.

"Hey, I was thinking about volunteering a couple of shifts downtown at the methadone clinic." Jack was trying to get my mind off of the gunfight by changing the subject. I knew him so well.

I was wiping at tears and looking away so he wouldn't see.

"What's *wrong*, Babe?" He was holding me again. "You just had a scare, that's all. Don't worry. I will always take care of you..."

And that's when I knew I wasn't going to break up with him. At least not on that day. I was angry at myself over it, for choosing a dumb boy over my faith.

"Calm down, Joc. Calm down." Jack was stroking my hair. For such a big tough guy he had the softest hands.

And I shook my head, pushed down my tears, and gave him a peck on the cheek. "Sorry. I'm fine. I'm fine," was all I said. Then I leaned back into the sticky hot vinyl-covered passenger seat and I didn't say another word. I didn't have the words to say.

Then, Jack got out of the car and jogged around the VW in the Stockton heat to open my door for me and let me out. And he was yelling, "Never Fear! Jack Daniel is here!"

So, Sarah Joy can you guess what happened next? I am sure you must have guessed the truth by now. Two weeks later, I was sitting in the bathroom at Jack's Mom's house with a pregnancy test. Jack was sitting on the porch with his pit bull, Goat, drinking a beer and he had this great Toots and the Maytals album spinning on his turntable with the speakers pointed outside the open windows so the whole neighborhood could appreciate a little 1960s ska music.

I had really come to appreciate that old record collection. When we first met, I thought it was cool and retro to collect vinyl, but not really very practical. Everyone was used to just streamed music on their devices from Spotify and Tidal. But of course, after Calexit, we didn't have that kind of cloud access anymore. The only way to listen to music was old school tapes, CDs, and records.

Jack had a nice record player and a great selection of old school Jamaican reggae, Northern Soul and punk. Plus, he kind of usurped his mom Rosa's record collection as well. Her records were my favorites, lots of 80s New Wave and ska and a lot of Morrissey! Can one ever listen to enough Morrissey?

Anyway, that was the day I figured out that I was pregnant with you. I could feel you inside me right away. I swear, when I was only a few weeks pregnant I knew you were coming. And,

I knew you would be bright and beautiful...

So, yes, Jack was your father. I know, I know what you are thinking: "That's not my Daddy!" But remember, Baby, there is a reason I am writing all this down for you. Anyone can father a baby, but it takes a special man to be a loving dad. Don't be mad. You need to read the whole story. Just keep reading.

Anyway, "Funky Kingston" was playing. That's a special song to me now. I know you know that one, Sweetheart. You've been singing along with it since you were a baby. "Hey Hey Hey!" I had just peed on the little plastic stick and I was sitting there on the toilet by myself watching it change color.

I was ready to cry. I was ready to scream and shout and throw things. College, the future, my deepening studies into the Baha'u'llah and my Baha'i faith...

But what I was most surprised to find out was that I wasn't sad, and I wasn't mad. I had this overwhelming sense of happiness. I was going to have a baby and nothing had ever made me happier.

And I knew that Jack wasn't the ideal father I might dream of, but that was OK. He was a good man and had a kind heart and if things didn't work out with him... well it would be me and you. We would make it on our own.

So then, I took that little piece of peed-onto plastic out on the porch, and I just showed it to him. The music was so loud that we didn't even say a word to each other. He just hollered a big ol' *Whoop!* into the air and threw his arms around me, and then we were out dancing on the dirt that used to be the front lawn and laughing and hugging each other while Toots was singing out to the whole neighborhood.

I was so happy that day, Baby! Even with everything going

on around us it was the best of times. Right when we didn't have any hope for the future, you came along and I knew I was going to find that hope in you. You were my future, whether I was ready for it or not! You still are. You are my light in the darkness.

More Soon. Love you, Baby.
-Mommy

TWENTY

The following is an encrypted message sent to
Operative Andrew Eldritch:

Intel reports state that CIRCA Operative Sister
Mary has been assigned to contact prime target Dr.
Abraha Tadese.

Target is reportedly traveling to California.

You have been assigned this mission due to your
prior experience with this CIRCA Operative. Sister
Mary's device has not been compromised at this time.

Directive: Respond immediately with confirmation on
the elimination of Tricia Timm.

Directive: Respond immediately with confirmation of
location of CIRCA Operative Sister Mary.

Directive: Shadow Operative Sister Mary to Dr.
Tadese and recoup prime target.

Directive: View enclosed report on Dr. Tadese.

All original orders stand.

                              —Department Homeland Security NFUS

Department of Defense
New Federal Union of States
Army Research Lab Nano Technology Division
(ARLNTD), Adelphi Maryland

AHRC-PDO-PA   **May 21, ▮**
Classified

MEMORANDUM FOR: Commander, Headquarters,
Agent In Field ▮▮▮▮▮▮▮▮▮▮▮▮▮▮▮▮▮▮▮▮▮▮▮

SUBJECT: Abraha Tadese, PhD Nanosciences and Nanoengineering ARTLNTD

1. The entire Adelphi Research Lab (ARLNTD) was destroyed June 1 by flood. The source of the water (more
than 60 million cubic meters) is unknown. Initial test-
ing of the water has shown that the water is absolutely
pure without a hint of salt or any other contaminant.
2. Water this pure does not exist naturally in such a
quantity anywhere on our planet.
3. The method for the transference of this much water
over a great distance is unknown at this time. Primary
theory: Project Adam's Ale (Classified).
4. Dr. Tadese, Dr. Frank Turner, and Dr. Shin Ha Kyo (N.
Korea) were initially presumed killed in the flood.
5. New intel illustrates that Dr. Tadese is alive and attempting to repatriate to California. He may be accompanied by Dr. Turner and Dr. Kyo.
6. Dr. Tadese is in possession of classified and highly
sensitive documents (Re: Project Adam's Ale) and has
the intent to disseminate said documentation in viola-
tion of the NFU Privacy Act.

7. It has become clear to this department that Dr. Tadese destroyed ARLNTD killing 567 souls in order to escape the NFU and repatriate to California.

8. It is the position of this department that locating Dr. Tadese and facilitating his continued work for the New Federal Union is of the highest emergency priority. Repeat. Priority One.

9. Immediate mission request.

The following communication was retrieved from the TEXTSECURE Ap on the mobile device of Dr. Frank Turner. Due to severe water damage it was only possible to partially unencrypt the following messages. Identity Tadpole431: Dr. Abraha Tadese. Identity Concentric23: Dr. Frank Turner.

5/24/█

Tadpole431: They've increased security on our wing ... does it seem ... not sure.

Concentric23: This is not a secure channel for discourse ... vis a vis required.

Tadpole431: ...germination.... attempt at 14:30 ... Shin's BOLT prototype will place nanoautomatons necessary for transference...

5/25/█

Tadpole431: Surely you realize the repercussions of our efforts here. Absolute ... autonomous memory. I believe that Adam's Ale is ready for ... the argument for weaponization ... control of ... Without your help...

Concentric23: This is not a secure channel for discourse! Please desist... consequences.

5/27/▮

Tadpole431: Burn after reading.

Concentric23: Your continued discourse is frustrating... change the way ... We can't possibly just ... removing myself from the ...

Tadpole431: ...responsibility is on our shoulders ... Calexit changed everything. If we allow the team to continue in this direction without ... got to give.

Tadpole431: Increased... new direction toward ... good conscience ... Adam's Ale.

Concentric23: Do you realize you could destroy the entire base? Why are we even discussing...

Tadpole431: ... not playing their game. I'm going home and I'm taking my ball with me. Consider ... choice do we have?

Concentric23: I want out. Your actions threaten...

Tadpole431: ...no longer have the option... Communicate with Shin regarding breathing apparatuses. ... June 1.

Addendum:

Mission request approved.

Initiate Operative In The Field: Andrew Eldritch

Reclaim target alive.

Agent Eldritch recorded response dated follows:

Confirmed kill- Tricia Timm. Her husband, Dr. Derek

Timm, should be unaware of her contact with Dr. Tadese. Encountered Opposing Operative (CIRCA) at contact point as expected. Good ol' Sister Mary. I know her well. CIRCA operative wounded in Reno. No sign of target, Tadese. Reconnaissance drone deployed and locked on Opposing Operative. Intel suggests she may attempt to enter California through the Paiute Reservation in the North. Operative currently housed in North Reno. She may need further prompting to move forward.

Will follow her to Tadese and retrieve Target.

Request: Immediate freezing and recall of all troops and drone activity in the area of the Paiute reservation so that OO may be allowed to proceed.

Request: Authorization for the continued independent use of Autonomous Hanwha Systems Unmanned Aerial Combat Vehicle MQ-9 Reaper with full armaments.

-Eldritch

Recorded response dated ███████ follows:

Eldritch,

Requests granted. Happy Hunting.

—Department Homeland Security NFUS

TWENTY ONE

ELDRITCH HAD NO PROBLEM evading the Reno Commune's security. He shifted the heavy automatic carbine with the large scope into a carrying position slung across his back. He then straightened his black cattleman's hat before he deftly and silently climbed a wooden fence. He rose up onto the roof of an empty greenhouse. This vantage point allowed him access to a view of the communal firepit, the adjoining garden, and collective areas as the very first dim light of dawn spread out over the mountains.

The neighborhood was silent. The Mexican that Sister Mary had hooked up with was sleeping with his back up against a log near the barely smoldering fire. The firepit was at the back of the house adjoining the one he believed Mary to be in. The Mexican's truck was behind that house.

Eldritch studied the sleeping Mexican. Who the hell was this guy? He had five brutish clones of himself who were all huddled together and sprawled haphazardly in the back of the truck. How easy it would be to slither over and silently slit his throat. So easy. But... that wasn't what the mission called for at this juncture.

He slunk down from his vantage point and padded silently back to the dirty white van he had left parked a few blocks away. Opening the rear of the van he reached inside to grasp two large black suitcases which he set down in the dust behind the van.

∅ ∅ ∅

Dan woke up stiff and uncomfortable under a musty blanket wet with dew by the fire. He stood to stretch and rub his eyes before thinking about the strange dream from the night before.

I won't tell, rang in his ears like a rusty bell. He looked over to where Scar and the other clones slept in the bed of the truck. He ran his fingers through his thick hair and wrinkled his brow. The rest of the dream was slowly coming back to him. He shook his head trying to wake up. *Scar can't speak,* he told himself with certainty. *Just a dream.* Then he moved toward the next house over to check on Mary.

Ø Ø Ø

Mary woke up slowly and cautiously, for a moment she didn't know where she was. On her first attempt to roll over a jolt of pain bounded through her side. Her leg was stiff. It felt six feet thick. She remembered. She was in the same small room where he had left her. There was a plastic bowl of water and a bottle of Tylenol on the small table next to her mattress. Morning sunlight was leaking in through a broken window blind. Everything was quiet.

Four Tylenol went down easily and Mary drained the water. She managed to swing her legs off the mattress and sit up when she noticed the cane leaning against a chair nearby. It was a nice thick cane that would make a good weapon. There was also a worn but clean pair of work pants and a light blue flannel shirt that smelled faintly of wood fire.

Before doing anything else, she dug through the stained and ripped rags that were her old pants and found her device in the pocket where she had left it. She powered it on briefly, concerned with battery life, just long enough to check for new orders. Then she quickly shut it down. Her holstered weapon hung on the back of the chair as did her leather jacket. Mary slowly and awkwardly got dressed into the oversized clothes and then sat down in the chair to rest her face in her hands.

There was a soft knock on the door. It was the big Mexican guy who had been helping her. His face was serious and his voice deep as a mineshaft when he asked, "You find the Tylenol?".

Mary just nodded. Her leg was still throbbing and she felt weak and a bit nauseous. "I've never been shot before," she admitted heavily to the floor. She wiped at a silent tear running down her cheek. She was having a hard time looking up.

Dan cleared his throat with a quick cough and then said, "You asked if you can trust me."

Mary nodded, wiped at her face with the flannel sleeve, and looked up into his eyes.

"I got the same question for you. Who was shooting at us?"

Mary took a deep breath and stared at the filtered beams of light that left white lines like bars across the floor. For a second, she thought she was going to stand up, but then she just sagged back into the chair. Dan leaned against the door frame and waited silently for an answer.

Mary thought for a minute before she finally started to speak. She knew she owed this guy an explanation, he had saved her life after all. But could she tell him everything?

"Look... Dan?"

Dan nodded.

"I don't know who shot me last night, I couldn't see. Don't you think it could have been random thieves trying to steal your truck?"

Dan paused and gazed off into the middle distance for a moment. Then he shook his head slowly and replied, his deep voice barely a whisper, "It's a coincidence I pick you up and an hour later I'm getting shot at?"

Mary said nothing.

"How'd you get stranded out in the desert?"

Mary examined the mote-filled beams of morning light searching for an answer. Then with a deep sigh she reconciled herself to telling her story to Dan. At least a part of it.

"OK. I'm going to be straight with you, big guy. OK? Because you saved my ass back there. I was out there in the Nevada desert with a group of..." Mary inhaled deeply again, "Friends. Some very, very close friends. Friends I had been working with for a long time." Her voice wavered a moment but then she continued on. "We were looking for another friend of ours. One who went missing a few months ago."

Dan nodded.

"We heard he was out there in the desert in Nevada. Near... have you ever heard of the Mustang Ranch?"

$$\varnothing \varnothing \varnothing$$

Dan regarded his former road companion warily. The illumination from the window shone through and around Mary's dark messy hair. Dan almost got lost in the thought that it looked like a crown of light.

But he was listening. Dan shook his head no.

"Well, Dan, it's a whorehouse just East of Reno. I've never been inside there myself, but behind it there is an unmarked hiking trail that leads out into the desert. About two miles out, there is a kind of hidden spot where mountain climbers and rappelers sometimes go called Diana's Throne Canyon. It's a slot canyon. Do you know what a slot canyon is?" Mary's eyes were dark and intense, her face pale and sad.

Dan shook his head again. In the back of his mind, a silent prayer formed and repeated itself over and over again without his consciously thinking about it.

"A slot canyon is basically a really deep, narrow, long hole in the ground. It's a canyon created by water long ago, but you can't just walk in or out. You have to rappel down into it by rope and then climb back out using rope again. Diana's Throne Canyon is, I guess I should say *was*, a very long and thin slot canyon. No one can get in or out without about 70 feet of rope. It's quite a long rappel."

Dan nodded again. *Ave Maria, maiden mild ... Thou canst hear amid the wild ... Tis thou, Tis thou canst save amid despair...*

"So, my friends and I got word from our... our other friend, that he was hiding out in this slot canyon a few miles behind the whorehouse. So, we went there to get him. All eight of us."

The prayer in Dan's head hushed. He focused on Mary's story.

"But he wasn't there." She said simply and quietly looking at the floor. "It was an ambush. Once we had repelled down into the canyon, we were attacked and... I guess it was like shooting fish in a barrel for... the asshole who attacked us. There was no easy way out once we were in. No place to hide... He slaughtered all my friends. Then he collapsed the canyon on top of us. Fucking asshole." Another silent tear rolled down Mary's cheek. She spoke softly and slowly like she was telling her story to a child. Dan wanted to reach out and touch her, but he resisted the temptation.

"I wasn't buried too bad. I dug myself out, but I couldn't find anybody else. There was dust and rocks everywhere. Then... I could hear muffled crying from David and Nia under the rocks," Mary paused. "I can still hear them. Calling my name. Calling for help. They were completely buried down deep under the rocks... I wanted to help... I wanted to dig them out... I... I... I just couldn't get to them. He had me pinned down. Every time I tried to move... Then, I waited for it to get dark. I thought I could get to them in the dark. I was yelling out to them, 'Hold on! I'm coming for you!'

Mary stopped herself for a moment. Her breathing was coming heavy. She rubbed her eyes, paused, and took a deep breath as if trying her best to compose herself before starting again.

"Their cries just got weaker and weaker. After a while they were just quiet. Just quiet. That was it... Then it started to finally get dark, and I snuck back to the rope, climbed up and then made it to the freeway through the sand storm." Mary's voice wavered for a moment but she pulled herself back together and continued, steely, with no more tears. "That's why I'm headed to California now. My friends are... gone, and we didn't find who we were looking for... But I think I can still find him. In California."

The room was silent again. No one spoke. The heavy slanted rays of morning light shown brighter than ever.

Questions swirled in Dan's head. The first two to come out were, "How did one person kill all your friends? The asshole. Who is this guy?"

Mary smiled grimly. "Eldritch? He uses drones." Mary's voice was flat without emotion. "Military attack drones. Several in the air at a time armed with missiles and light caliber guns. They are autonomous, they think for themselves. They kill on their own."

"Light caliber guns... How do you know all this?"

"Because he used to be my partner."

Dan's next question was cut short by a heavy knock at the back door. A brisk, masculine voice shouted, "Hello?! Come out! Unarmed please! Hands where we can see them!"

Mary slowly pulled her weapon from its holster.

Dan motioned for her to be silent with a finger over his lips. Then, he moved quickly and quietly to the backdoor of the house to see who was there.

TWENTY TWO

Currently listening to: *Red Lights Flash*
by Year of the Fist

Dear Sarah Joy,   674 days

In just a few months you will be two years old, Sweetheart!
Your daddy is already planning for your party. He is working
on something special for you. He loves you so much, Sweetie.

He's been running around the house hiding presents and
tying ribbons to everything to make you a big scavenger hunt.

You see, your daddy never knew his father too well. Your
"grandpa" was arrested for B&E when Daddy was just little and,
being an illegal, ICE deported him back to Mexico. Nobody
in the family ever saw him again. Daddy never talked about
him, except to complain about how much he hated the name
his dad gave him.

Why he thought it was a good idea to name his son after
his favorite drink... Well, I just don't know. Maybe he thought
it was funny.

But none of that is what I want to tell you about. I want to
tell you about the night Jack left me for good and your father
came into my life.

When I was six months pregnant with you, Jack and I drove
into Berkeley to see Year of the Fist, this awesome band front-
ed by two powerhouse females. I just put the record on and
it's bringing me back! They were opening for Swingin' Utters.
Or maybe Charger... Yeah, I think it was Charger because the

dude from Rancid was there just hanging out and he sings for Charger. But I don't know because we never got to see them.

Anyway, they were playing The Gilman Street Warehouse near UC Berkeley. That started out as such a such fun show! The place was packed with kids (of about every race you can imagine), and everyone was getting along great. Jack was drinking, but he wasn't dancing. I was pretty pregnant and he stayed in the back with his big arms wrapped around me the whole time and a big stupid grin on his face.

Then, when Year of the Fist finished with "Red Lights Flash!" Jack said, "Let's go up and meet the band!" But...

We could hear this chanting from outside. "SEND THEM BACK! SEND THEM BACK!" Jack looked at me confused and then one of his buddies grabbed him and motioned toward the door.

What we found outside was like nothing I had ever seen before. There were about 30 "Proud Boys" marching down the street in full force carrying burning torches and shouting their bigoted slogans. It was like a KKK rally, or something out of a movie. I couldn't believe it.

Ever since Calexit, there had been this big idea floating around to split the new California Republic up into three separate states. Stockton was considered Northern California, which was fine by us. LA and Southern California seemed like a different world. Very far away. But what always confused me and bothered the heck out of Jack was that the major supporters of Northern Statehood were motivated by race. You would expect something like that to happen in Texas or Alabama, right? Never in lovely liberal California! But racism was rearing its ugly head everywhere in those days.

The new NorCal movement was a very white movement, and the heart of the movement was being propelled by these

Proud Boys. Ug. I hated those stupid Alt-Right Frat Boys. The basis of their plan was to push all the Mexicans and the other immigrants back down south, and keep NorCal as Caucasian as one of the rallies for the NewFed President. Bullcrap.

And of course, what do these stupid Neo-Nazi Proud Boys want to dress like? Just to make my life difficult? Skinheads. Black Fred Perry shirts and Adidas Sambas on their feet. The only difference? These idiots don't shave their heads, they all have long beards and hipster haircuts. I couldn't stand them and neither could Jack.

I latched on to his arm right away. "Don't even think about it," I said. "Let the idiots march, Jack. Stay here with me."

But he just pounded his beer, smiled, and started taking off his shirt. "Sorry, Babe."

You see, Sweetheart, this is where Jack and I really always disagreed on the whole Anti-Racist Skinhead thing. I could understand his anger and his passion, I really could, but I could never convince him that violence wasn't any kind of solution.

Your father, Jack, just didn't see any peaceful resolution to the problem. If he saw a guy with an SS or a swastika tattoo, he was going to confront that guy. Immediately. "Hey, man, what's up with that tattoo? You a Nazi?" If the guy couldn't explain that it was a terrible mistake or that he was getting the tattoo covered up soon, he was getting punched. No if ands or buts. Whether it was at a show, in a supermarket, inside a church... none of that mattered. It was an issue of black and white (literally). Jack simply had zero tolerance for racists and bigots. It was the unflinching personal moral code that he lived by.

"Sweetie, you can't punch every single Nazi in the world," I pleaded with him.

Jack just looked at me with a condescending chuckle and

handed me his shirt. "Yes, I can, Baby. I'm going to kick all their asses." He was joking, but he was serious too, and of course more than a little drunk.

"SEND THEM BACK! SEND THEM BACK!"

The pack of Proud Boys with torches was just passing the venue marching down the street toward the university. The crowd fom the show was swarming out onto the sidewalk.

And then the bottles started to fly. Broken glass shattered inside and around the torch-carrying mob, and the Proud Boys stopped and turned their attention on us. It was a scary moment.

And that's when we saw him. He had grown a long beard but I could see those icy blue eyes flash, and the crucified skinhead peeking out of the top of his Fred Perry. Cormac was leading the Fascist march.

"Antifa!" he screamed pointing at us. And then he started a new chant: "YOU, WILL NOT, REPLACE US! YOU, WILL NOT, REPLACE US!"

The entire gang of radical hipsters took up the chant as they pounded the bottoms of their heavy long torches against the pavement.

"YOU, WILL NOT, REPLACE US! YOU, WILL NOT, REPLACE US!"

I could see Jack's eyes meeting his old friend Cormac's through the thickening crowd, and he threw out his chest and stretched out his thick shoulders before turning back to me briefly.

Jack was never one to be bossy with me, but that night, just before all hell broke loose, he gave me one quick bear hug, grabbed my shoulders and gazed into my eyes. "I love you, Joc. Now get the hell away from here as fast as you can." I just shook my head and tried to hold the tears in. I was beyond pleading with him. There was nothing I could do. I just started walking. I was six months pregnant with you and the last place I needed to be was in the middle of a race riot.

I was angry and scared and exasperated, and I did what he said. I walked away from the violence, and from Jack for the last time.

       - Love, Mommy

TWENTY THREE

MARY HEARD DAN OPEN the back door of the safe house and a muffled conversation. Then she heard the door shut and the house was quiet again. The cane that would make a good weapon was in easy reach and Mary used it to hoist herself up out of her chair before she strapped her weapon around her shoulders and threw her leather bomber jacket on over it.

In the backyard Dan was talking to a large man in black fatigues with a modified AR-15 strapped to his chest. Mary exited the house and moved unsteadily toward the truck where Dan had a garden hose in hand filling up his water tank. Another stocky man in a black beanie was loading some supplies into the back of the truck where the clones were seated waiting silently and patiently, watching.

As Mary moved closer to the truck, one of the clones suddenly jumped down in front of her, removed his large floppy brown penis from his pants, and urinated copiously into the dirt at her feet. He did not look up or acknowledge her presence in the slightest.

"Disgusting," Mary whispered with a shake of her head, and then she awkwardly maneuvered around the large idiot and over to the truck.

"Sorry," Dan said thickly. The clone was already bounding back up into the truck, leaving a steaming puddle behind.

"This must be 'your woman.'" The man in the black fatigues gave Mary a wide-eyed appraising look. "I'm Bill, head of security here at the Commune, and you are one lovely lady. How did you get hurt?"

Mary looked from the AR-15 up into Bill's smiling face

and then back over to the clones without saying a word. Dan hadn't responded either. The water tank had started to overflow and he removed the hose and began to coil it up as the guy in the beanie turned off the water.

"OK, OK, don't tell me." Bill was still smiling but an annoyed tone had crept into his voice. "But just remember, we didn't have to help you out with water and supplies here. We have been good to you guys."

"Nothing is free," Mary said as she handed him a short stack of green NFU bills.

Ø Ø Ø

Dan was looking through the supplies as Bill quietly pocketed the currency. Dan moved his gaze over to Mary and nodded. "How you feelin'?"

"Stiff, but OK." She turned to face Dan alone and spoke softly so the others wouldn't hear, "Listen, I'm not used to being taken care of. I usually take care of things myself."

Dan noticed Scar watching her from the truck. Was he listening? But when the brown clone turned his eyes to Dan, there was no hint of the intelligence that had been so obvious in his dream the night before, only the dull sheen of thoughtlessness.

"I just wanted to say..." She was having a hard time getting the word out, "Thanks."

"OK," Dan replied with a shrug.

Mary then turned back to the other two men, "We need to get into California as quickly as possible."

"Well, I know a route through the mountains that is generally safe. I'm Trevor by the way," the stocky man in the wool beanie extended a hand to Mary.

"Mary," she shook the hand. "Can you guide us through? I can pay you in cash."

"Dude... I would really have to think about it. I really didn't intend on heading that way anytime soon. I have a lot to do around here, and my..." Trevor trailed off and paused, as if searching for the right word, finally settling on "...friend up there may or may not be so happy to see me. What's the big rush?" Trevor placed a last rucksack into the truck.

A group of children ran through the conversation laughing, playing tag. One of them collided with Dan's knees and he bent to dust her off and help her up.

"I have an errand I need to attend to in California," Mary said.

"Errand huh? Sounds important. You guys are Union Feds, aren't you?"

The little girl looked up into Dan's face smiling. It was the same little blonde girl in the dirty white dress from the checkpoint! She had each of her index fingers shoved into empty brown beer bottles that she was tapping together, *clink, clink, clink...*

"Hey," Dan started...

Then, all hell broke loose as the house behind them exploded knocking all of them off of their feet. Smoke, dust and falling debris filled the air.

Dan was stunned. His ears were ringing. But he was unhurt and the first one up, brushing chunks of plaster and dust off of Mary and helping her to her feet. Commune members were running away from the burning house, shouting for everyone to take cover. Dan scanned the area for the little blonde girl but she had disappeared again. The empty beer bottles lay broken on the ground near him. Then an unfamiliar high-pitched humming echoed over the ringing in Dan's ears.

He could see Bill near one of the gardens perched on one knee looking through the scope of his rifle and scanning the skies above. "Drone attack!" Bill shouted, just before another explosion blew a hole in the earth right next to him sending him and several people near him sprawling. Through the dust and the smoke Dan lost sight of him. At least most of him. One jaggedly severed arm still holding the AR-15 landed near Mary's feet.

"Let's get the hell out of here," Dan whispered heavily. Mary tossed her cane into the bed of the truck and then threw herself over the side, landing on a grunting pile of clone flesh that broke her fall. She kept her weapon ready scanning the nearby rooflines but seeing nothing.

"Come on!" Dan yelled to Trevor and the two men ducked into the cab of the truck. They could hear more than one drone now, though they could see nothing in the skies above. A third explosion rocked the truck from a block away. Dan cranked the ignition and then the hit gas, sending dust flying as the truck broke through a decrepit old fence and bounded out onto the road and away from the commune.

Ø Ø Ø

Over a mile away, sitting in the back of a dirty white van, Eldritch recalled the drones with a tap of a button. He viewed the destruction firsthand on the screen in front of him via drone camera. The drones were completely autonomous and needed no immediate direction.

These things make the job too damn easy.

Having viewed the area ahead of time, he had simply set the coordinates, released the two drones, allowed them to scan the area, and then set them to "Havoc Mode." At that point each little killing machine, no larger than a child's tricycle, had unleashed 14-inch Red-Widow missiles on any viable targets nearby.

The drones were back a minute after he had recalled them: ugly, brutish little helicopters with four rotors each. Both still carried two more Red-Widows that they had not unloaded at the commune. Each missile was capable of completely destroying a 10-ton truck and raining shrapnel on everyone within a 25-foot radius.

Eldritch de-powered the two deadly little robots and started breaking them down and packing their parts back into the foam fittings inside their black suitcases. He took extra care and time as he detached the unspent Red-Widows and packed them into their own long case.

One of these has Mary's name on it, he thought to himself. *But today, it is in everyone's best interests if she gets away. She just needs to hurry the fuck up.*

He checked the black mirror of his device once again, viewing the feed from the third automated drone still monitoring Dan's truck and following from a safe and undetectable distance.

TWENTY FOUR

Currently listening to: *Heroes* **by David Bowie, but I am listening to the Hollywood Vampires version. That's Uncle Johnny's old band!**

Dear Sarah Joy,   677 days

Jack almost died that night. He ended up in the County Hospital with three broken ribs and 43 stitches in his face and arms. He was also under arrest. Handcuffed to the bed. At least, that's what I was told. I was not allowed to visit him in the hospital and I didn't want to anyway.

Cormac took the worst of it. Broken jaw and severe concussion. The last I heard of him he was still listed in critical condition. We never saw him again.

The California Republican Peacekeepers were not messing around. They charged Jack with aggravated assault and resisting arrest. He was sentenced to five months in the county lockup. I was due in three.

So, when you started coming early, it was really fantastic, but really scary, too. I was so excited to meet you, and I had already decided I could do it on my own, but once you wanted out early, I wasn't so sure.

My parents had had enough of California and had emigrated to Tucson where my mom had family. They were supporters of the President and the NFU, so we didn't talk too much after that. I was staying at Jack's mom's and looking for my own place, and his mom was really sweet, but... distant. I wasn't her daughter and she wasn't my mother.

It is hard giving birth without your own mother around. I hope when you have a baby someday, Sweetie I will be there for you!

Of course, my mom said she would have come if she could have, but the borders were already closed and no one was coming in or out of California from the East. My parents had been lucky to get out when they did. A lot of my friends had left Stockton at that point, either trying to get out of the California Independent Republic or just to a safer part of it. Stockton was getting pretty scary.

Jack's mother, Rosa, took good care of me but I still felt alone and that was pretty stressful. It didn't help that her house was in a really bad part of town. Maybe all the stress is why you started coming early.

The morning my water broke, I was walking to the corner store to get some milk for our coffee. It was only a block away. Rosa had a white iron fence around her front yard to keep Jack's pit bull, Goat, in and to keep the homeless people from sleeping in the front yard.

When I went to push open the gate that morning while Rosa held Goat back, I couldn't get it open because a crazy homeless guy had set up his tent (he was sleeping between two dirty shopping carts full of garbage with a ratty old blanket thrown over them) right up against the walkway.

The guy was so wasted he wouldn't wake up, even when Rosa threatened to turn Goat on him. It wouldn't have done any good anyway. That was the friendliest dog I ever met and he wouldn't have bitten a fly. So, both of us just had to push and push until we had forced his junk over just far enough that I could squeeze my pregnant belly through and get to the sidewalk which he had used as his bathroom before passing out.

So, I walked down the block and into the corner store,

almost eight months pregnant, holding onto you wiggling around in my big old belly. And I can remember, the prettiest and dirtiest little homeless girl playing out in front of the dingy liquor store. Just playing in the dirt. Writing words with a stick in the dust. She hardly even looked up when I walked by.

Rosa and I were in luck. There were a few slim cartons of milk that were not expired. I grabbed one, and I remember looking at the diapers on the shelf. They were size two diapers. I had been searching all over town for Newborn size, with no luck, so I was stockpiling whatever sizes I could find and afford. I grabbed a bag of those as well.

And that is why there were a few coins jangling in my pocket as I stepped out of the store and almost bumped right into the dirty little homeless girl. She must have been about six or seven years old. Just a skinny little thing with greasy blonde hair and wearing a dirty white dress.

She looked at me with her sad angel eyes and asked, "Spare any change, lady?"

And, of course, I reached into my pocket for that spare change, but I had to pause. Money was scarce and I wasn't sure that I wouldn't need every penny once you came. All the stress and the loneliness that I had been struggling with for weeks poured over me like a wave in one simple question: *Jocelyn, how can you bring a child into this world when you can't even spare a few coins for this poor little kid?*

And suddenly I was standing in a puddle of water, and I felt like someone had hit me in the solar plexus with a baseball bat. My water had broken and you were on the way! I looked around for the dirty little blonde girl but she was nowhere to be seen. I never saw her again.

I will write you the rest soon, Sweetheart!

Love, Mommy XXOOXX

TWENTY FIVE

DAN PUNCHED THE ACCELERATOR of the old Chevy, intent on guiding it back to the freeway. Trevor craned his neck out of the window of the truck, pistol at the ready, scanning intently for any vehicles following them. Mary and the clones were ducked down in the bed behind him. She kept her scarf tied tightly over her nose and mouth. Dan realized, with a mild tinge of embarrassment, that she was trying to combat the body odor of his clones, a smell which he rarely even noticed, perhaps because it was somehow his body odor as well. All five clones stared at Mary with childlike curiosity.

"Don't take the freeway, Dude!" Trevor called out over the roar of the road beneath them. "We won't get through that way. Turn left up here. We need to make our way North and then West. If we can get lost up into the mountains with a little luck we can sneak into California by some back trails. I can get us over to a little town called Graeagle off of the Paiute Reservation. I know people there."

"You point. I drive," Dan replied.

"Dude, that was fucked up." Trevor tried, and failed, to choke back a sob. "Did you see Bill go down? Goddam, he was a good guy. Who the hell was shooting missiles at us?"

Dan considered the question without responding. This was the second time he had been shot at since picking up Mary. The logical reaction was to pull over, throw her out and keep on trucking and minding his own business. But just the thought of her angelic face pulled prayers from his heart that his lips silently sent to heaven. *Ave Maria, Gratia Plena...* he mouthed the words without making a sound. Eyes intent on the road.

Trevor gritted his teeth in a wincing grin and looked back at the road behind them. "You talk to yourself often, Buddy? No sweat. No sweat. I can put up with a little crazy for a free ride to Graeagle. Looks like the Commune isn't such a safe place to be at this moment. I've been meaning to head to Graeagle for some time now anyway, got what you might call an old score to settle up there."

Dan was considering a response that wouldn't make him look crazy when Trevor barked an interruption. "Turn left here! We are going to head up to Cold Springs and see if we can get through there."

Suddenly Mary knocked heavily on the rear glass of the cab, shouting, "I need to know where we are headed gentlemen!"

Dan was still praying and before he could compose himself to respond, Trevor looked back at her and shouted, "I guess we are headed to California!" Dan looked into the back of the truck where the clone with the large scar was staring directly back into his eyes.

"I WON'T TELL…"

Ø Ø Ø

Almost a mile away and 200 feet above them a small black helicopter whirred away with a high-definition telescopic lens glued to their every turn. No one was directing the deadly little automaton which was laden with a payload of four Red-Widow missiles. All it needed was a remote command to destroy the target and it was easily capable of vaporizing Dan's truck and everyone in it.

Ø Ø Ø

The drive to Graeagle, California should have only taken a few hours from Reno, but Trevor was hyper-paranoid, and with good reason.

He had them stop often, just to sit parked in silence and listen for any sign of patrols, drones, or other vehicles. They often started up dirt roads for a few hundred feet before Trevor ordered Dan to turn around backtrack the way they had come and then take another route.

At their first stop under the shadow of a collapsed railroad bridge Dan got out to water the clones. There were no fires out in the wooded mountains where Trevor had led them. No traffic either. High walls of granite and beautiful redwoods were all that surrounded them. Trevor couldn't help but cling to the idea that they were getting away too easily. Maybe it was just good luck that there was no sign of either army or of drones. He pushed his gnawing suspicions down and kept his eyes and ears open.

Dan was also glancing about suspiciously, seemingly ready for another attack at any moment. He had taken his pistol from under the seat and kept it tucked into his belt.

Mary hobbled up to the passenger window, "What is our plan here, gentlemen?"

Trevor lit a joint and inhaled deeply, holding the smoke in as he spoke. "Well guys, I don't know who is trying to blow you up, but I am doing my best to get us all into California, and far away from the Commune. My..." he paused to exhale, "my friend has a ranch just on the other side of the border. We can probably hide out there for a night or two and get some gas. After that you two are on your own." He offered the smoldering joint to Dan and then Mary. They both declined. "Suit yourselves." Trevor took another hit.

No one said a word for a few moments as Dan's clones stood and stretched, scratching at themselves amiably.

"Why do you need to get to Berkeley?" Dan asked nodding at Mary. "Someone sure wants you dead, and he's got some fancy toys." His thick voice was little more than a deep whisper.

Mary mulled over her response before speaking. "Look, the less you guys know the better."

"You're with CIRCA aren't you?" Trevor asked.

Mary did not respond. She only looked away.

"Chriiiiiist! I knew it!" Trevor took another massive hit on his joint and held the smoke deeply in his lungs managing to squeak out. "I first thought the New Feds, but I shoulda' known better. Damn, who's chasing you lady?"

Dan shot glances from Mary to Trevor and back again, confused, "Wait a minute, what's CIRCA?" he whispered.

Trevor exhaled, "Fuckin California Independent Republic Counterterrorism Agency. She's a fuckin spook, Dude. Black ops shit. Real badasses."

"That means what? The NFU is trying to keep you out of California? The guy who is trying to blow us up works for the New Feds?"

Again, Mary affirmed Trevor's speculations with her silence.

"So how are the hell we going to get you into the middle of California, with all these flying toys trying to kill you?" whispered Dan.

"Whoa! No 'we', Dude. You're leaving me in Graeagle." Trevor tugged lightly on what was quickly becoming a small roach pinched between thumb and forefinger.

"Where are you going?" Mary pointed a finger up at Dan.

"Stockton." Dan's baritone was little more than a rustle.

Trevor produced a well-weathered map from his pocket.

"I was going to give this to you for the trip." He pointed out Graeagle, California. Mary placed a finger on the black dot representing the small mountain town and then traced a line to Berkeley. Stockton was not too far out of the way.

"What do you think about Berkeley, big guy? You've brought me this far. You know who I work for and you know who's after me."

Dan was quiet for a moment gazing into her eyes with an odd reverence before nodding. "I got you, Sister."

Mary turned to Trevor, "Can you blow that smoke in another direction please?"

"Sorry," he replied with a cough and flicked the roach past her out the window

She pulled the door open, pushed him over on the bench seat hauling her body into the truck with one leg and her arms.

Now it was Trevor's turn to be confused. "Hey, wait a minute, what about this errand you were talking about?" Dan had already restarted the truck and they were making tracks down another dusty mountain road. Mary didn't say another word.

∅ ∅ ∅

Two hours later, after repeated redundant backtracking and several false starts checking different roads, a route to Graeagle became clear in Trevor's mind. His paranoia was finally subsiding. It was replaced with a nagging question that had been hanging over him for almost two years now. What the hell was he going to do when he got to his father's ranch in Graeagle?

Trevor hadn't spoken to his father in almost three years. Now he was preparing to challenge him.

TWENTY SIX

The following is a non-electronic paper letter
intercepted on ███████████ The letter was sent via
private courier from Dr. Derek Timm in California
to a ████████████████████ Be advised this is a
copy. Delivery of the letter to ██████████████ was
permitted.

It would appear that Dr. Derek Timm has no
contact with Target Dr. Abraha Tadese at this time.

Recommendation: No action at this time

                    —Department Homeland Security NFUS

Dear ████████
  It has been far too long my friend. Welcome to the
future where all of our technological advances have
brought us back to the ancient practice of writing letters on paper and then putting them in an envelope and
mailing them. This courier service has served me well
in the past, and I hope this letter reaches you.
  So much has changed in our lives since Calexit. The
Great Fire Wall keeps us from any direct contact with
people outside of the state. I am not sure how much
news you receive from California, but any news we receive from the New Federal Union is heavily filtered and

one-sided. I imagine your experience to be the same. Which is why I am writing you with the heaviest of hearts to inform you that my dear wife Tricia died twelve days ago. The girls and I are fine. We are dealing with the loss the best we can. I am encouraging the girls not to let this tragedy take any time away from their education. They are here at home with me now, but will both be returning to school in the next few days.

I am sure you heard about the earthquake that rocked San Francisco in April. The California Independent Republic has certainly had a rocky start as a new nation. The earthquake, the wildfires, the slow start for the new economy, and not to mention the lack of communication with friends and family in the NFU. At this point, in my view, things have to get better. They certainly couldn't get any worse.

In any event, the earthquake was absolutely devastating. There are still teams excavating collapsed buildings and searching for remains after all these months. The list of missing and dead is over 4,000 names now. Almost a quarter of the population is homeless due to collapsed buildings, or structures being so severely damaged they are no longer safe for habitation. One out of every four buildings is no longer habitable.

They say the aftermath of an event like this is often worse than the event itself, and that is definitely the case with the quake. With the collapse of both the Bay Bridge and the Golden Gate Bridge, San Francisco practically became an island. These were the main thoroughfares for citizens to enter and leave the city as well as the main supply lines for food and water. With these routes gone, supplies and relief must come up the peninsula from the South where the freeways were also severely damaged, by boat, or by helicopter.

Across the bay here in Berkeley, the damage from the quake was far less significant, but watching the smoke rise and boatload after boatload of refugees arrive dirty and starving was difficult for us. Especially for Tricia.

I know how close you two were. You know better than anyone how much Tricia loved San Francisco. You two grew up together there. You also know what a kind and loving soul Tricia was. ██████████████████████
████. She joined the relief effort right away.

Her main concern was for those who refused to leave the city. You know how proud San Franciscans can be. Tens of thousands pledged to stay and rebuild. With the lack of running water, the collapse of the electrical grid, and the short supply of food, there have been outbreaks of cholera, corona, and viral hepatitis.

Tricia dove right into the relief effort, organizing boats to ferry supplies of food, water, and temporary shelters across the bay. On the day she died, she was leading a team of volunteer physicians into the Marina district, which was especially hard hit, to set up a temporary health clinic at the old Bus Stop bar on Union Street. I am sure you remember that spot well.

Shortly after she arrived at the Bus Stop on ████████ there must have been a seismic shift or aftershock that directly struck that block of Union Street. This caused the building to collapse burying Tricia and three of the doctors that were with her. I am told that she was instantly killed and did not suffer. Her body has yet to be recovered, but an effort is underway.

Grief pours over me like bay fog in October. I am having a hard time functioning. I have been working on this letter paragraph by paragraph for three days now. I need to walk away from it again now...

You were one of the first people I thought to contact. Tricia loved you very much. I wanted you to know that Tricia died helping others. She made the ultimate sacrifice for her hometown and for the people of San Francisco. I hope you will light a candle for her and remember her fondly.

It is my unfortunate task to write several of these letters to our friends in the NFU. Tricia loved and was loved by so many people.

I am adding an addendum to each letter asking for a favor. My good friend Dr. Abraha Tadese has gone missing in Maryland. Reports of flooding and a possible radiation leak in the area have reached us, but I am asking all of our friends to please keep an eye out for his name in local news and to please contact me if you hear anything of him or his whereabouts.

██████████ I don't know if our paths will ever cross again. I hope that someday we will be able to sit down and remember Tricia together. I hope ██████████ are well and these troubled times are treating you with more kindness than many of us here in California.

██████████████████████
██████████████████████

Your Friend,

Derek Timm

TWENTY SEVEN

DAN PULLED THE TRUCK OVER underneath a large thatch of enormous redwoods near a cold clear waterfall along the dusty mountain road about a mile from the gated entrance to the Graeagle ranch. Trevor's paranoia was working overtime again, with good reason. He repeatedly shushed the group to listen for the hum of drones and often jumped out of the truck to check the road for booby traps.

"So, maybe it's time you told us about your friend with the ranch?" Mary asked Trevor as he ground the last millimeter of a charred roach into the gravel at his feet.

"Yeah, Walter..." Trevor paused. "He's my dad. He has a compound about a mile from here. It should be pretty well fortified and even booby trapped."

"Your dad?" Dan was unloading the Five who immediately began to stretch and relieve themselves. He turned to Trevor. "I'm thinking about taking these guys for a run. I need to keep them in shape if I'm going to make any money off them." Dan smiled sheepishly. "It's easy, all I gotta do is start running and they follow."

Trevor nodded; he was in no hurry to confront his dad. He wandered over to a boulder near the rumbling white waterfall and sat down. "Yeah, you guys want to hear a story first?" Mary ambled to the back of the truck and dug around in the C-rations until she found two black packages. She threw one to Trevor and then limped over to a rock near him and sat down.

"Growing up Mormon wasn't easy, especially not in a sin filled city like Reno," Trevor started.

Mary chuckled, "You're Mormon?" She tore open her

package to reveal pink spongy meat. "Gross. You want this Dan?" She showed him the contents. Dan peered at the pink meat food product and nodded, eyes intense with hunger.

"You want to hear this story or not?"

"Sorry Trev. Go right ahead. I need to think about something else besides getting blown up anyway." Mary handed Dan the black packet without getting up. Dan snapped out a thin shiny blade and started to eat with a grin. The clones were looking over his shoulder to see what he was eating, dull eyes flashing a mild curiosity. Trevor lit another joint.

∅ ∅ ∅

"Growing up Mormon wasn't easy. Church was three hours every Sunday in a starched white shirt and tie. Seminary was an hour every morning at 6:00 A.M. before high school classes.

"Then, Dude, after all of that, my mother expected me to serve a two-year mission for the church as soon as I turned 18. College was a peripheral priority after service to the church. Can you imagine that? Two years. Maybe I would get sent somewhere interesting like Spain, but more likely someplace miserable like Tijuana or Bakersfield.

"When I was younger though, I never questioned my faith. I would never even consider disobeying my parents. I walked the straight and narrow path! I held fast to the iron rod of righteousness all throughout my teenage years."

Trevor paused to regard the smoldering joint in his hand. He inhaled until his lungs began to protest and held the smoke in as he continued his tale. "I never broke the Word of Wisdom. It says thou shalt not partake in the drinking of beer nor wine nor liquor nor coffee nor tea nor the smoking of tobacco. It leaves out cannabis, but Mormon's read that in-between the lines... Most of my friends didn't give a damn about the Word of Wisdom, but I was a good kid. A believer.

"But, when the United States began to fall apart, and Texas and California started talking about seceding from the Union to create their own sister nations, my faith became an immediate luxury. My family's survival became the priority at that point. The hotels and casinos in Reno began to close one by one leaving thousands of people without work. When the border to California closed and the influx of fresh vegetables and meat from the West ceased overnight, Reno transformed from a fun vacation destination to a dead-end hole on the edge of nowhere.

"My dad, Walter Menasco, is a big strong guy. Bigger than you maybe Dan. He had run a successful collision repair shop for years, but after Calexit, there was very little traffic passing through Reno. After a while there were just no more customers. Menasco Body Repair closed the same summer that the wildfires in the East began to burn unchecked. After that the Nevada skies had a constant unhealthy red stain. Every time we went outside, we had to cover our mouths and noses with wet bandanas just to breathe."

Trevor flicked his small roach into the waterfall that poured out its own story next to him. Dan had finished his meal, and the Five had followed him back to the truck looking for more, without making a sound.

"Then, my mom was diagnosed with cancer." Dan and the clones stopped what they were doing and looked up at the short husky stoner as one.

"Since Reno General Hospital was closed, the nearest treatment for my mom was in Phoenix, Arizona, but there was no money for traveling, and no healthcare or money to help pay for her treatment. It didn't really matter anyway because

Mom accepted her illness as the Will Of God. She decided she would rather meet her maker than struggle to eke out a few more months of misery in a dying town on the edge of a crumbling country. She just wanted to spend a little more time with me and my dad in her own home."

Trevor stopped to wipe at his eyes. As he blinked away the sweat and dirt and tears, he watched the five clones staring intently at Dan, who held a finger to his lips as he continued rummaging for packets of pink sponge meat.

"I did the best I could to make her comfortable. My eighteenth birthday was coming up and, get this, I had actually started looking forward to serving a mission. Serving the Lord in a distant land far away from Reno was sounding great to me. But, it wasn't meant to be, you know? My mother needed me, and so did my dad.

"See, my father had been a devout Mormon since he met my mom and converted, but his faith wavered and faltered. He got really bitter about the unhappy path his life had taken. My mom was so healthy one minute and then the next... he was scrounging back alleys for pain meds for her. Black market opioids. She was in a lot of pain. I don't know when he started taking them too, but after I turned eighteen... he just wasn't around much. He was either out scrounging or he was nodding off in his Lazy Boy. I ended up taking care of Mom 24-7.

"There is no mention of prescription drugs in the Word of Wisdom. A lot of Mormons take pills without an ounce of guilt. I finally figured out that Dad's addiction had taken over his life. On top of being stoned all the time, he was losing a ton of weight, really unhealthy. But you know what I think? It wasn't the actual drug addiction that was killing him. It was the guilt in his heart because he was using the pain meds that should have been helping my mom... ya know? There was never enough for the both of them.

"He'd quit for a few days and just be sick as a dog, throwing up stomach bile. Not able to hold anything down. Then I would be out scrounging around for pills to keep Mom from screaming in pain. But sure enough, when I got back, half the pills would disappear, and Dad would be snoozing in the Lazy Boy again.

"What a mess. He couldn't stand to see my mom like that, so he took her pills. Then he felt incredible guilt at having taken her pills, so he took more. He stopped eating, wasting away to nothing, just like my Mom. And it changed him. He wasn't the same dad that I had as a kid.

"On good days, Dad worked odd jobs, sometimes he could get mechanic work, but the lion's share of his earnings went to get those damn little white pills that fed his addiction and fought Mom's pain. Meanwhile, Mom was slowly deteriorating at home unable to get the chemotherapy that would have only given her a slim chance of survival anyway."

The waterfall rumbled on. Dan and the clones were eating from black packages of rations. Dan's eyes were on Trevor, even the clones seemed to pay him rapt attention.

"Sorry to be long-winded you guys. I want you to get a sense of why my dad is the way he is now. I guess I am still trying to wrap my own mind around it...

"Mom's final days were brutal, just brutal. Her pain was agonizing. There was no food in the house. There was no electricity. Water was strictly rationed and only available for certain hours on certain days. The Church provided some food and supplies for the family, but it was never enough.

"That's when my strung out, addicted, guilt-ridden dad became really embittered toward the Church. He didn't think our fellow Mormons were doing enough for us. I mean, I understood, we were far from the only needy Mormon family in Reno. Mormons are famous for taking care of their own, but the church's resources were just spread too thin. There wasn't enough to go around. I don't hold anything against them. I still respect the church very much. My dad on the other hand..."

Trevor's voice cracked a bit and he coughed, releasing some of the anguish that congested him. Mary reached out and patted his knee in support.

"When Mom finally passed, Walt would not let the Sisters in to dress her in her garments for her burial. He would not allow the Elders to come and pray over her. He cursed all of them from the front porch. He brushed the dirt off of his shoes at them!"

Dan and Mary shared a confused glance.

Trevor was incredulous, "Dudes! That is an ancient curse from the Old Testament! Mormon's believe it's the gravest spiritual action, like invoking the wrath of God on a person! It just isn't done." Trevor thought about this for a moment and shook his head at the ground. "Anyway, Dad wouldn't allow a Mormon service for his beloved Shenandoah, even though that's what she had wanted more than anything. More guilt for him, and I was the only one there to watch my dad crumble and fall apart.

"I ended up being the one to dig a shallow grave for my mom in the backyard. I was the one who carried her stiff frame out of the house for the final time. She weighed almost nothing. Just bones. The cancer had taken everything from her.

"Dad didn't help. There was no more medication to be had. He was too sick to go out and try to work or steal to get more. He stopped noticing me, or anything else in the world for that matter. I just sat back and waited for my dad to die too."

TWENTY EIGHT

Currently listening to: *Tenderness* **by General Public**

Dear Sarah Joy,   679 days

Hi, Sweetheart! Where was I... Oh yes, you being born! So, from the dingy corner store, I managed to waddle back down the block, over the homeless guy and back into Rosa's kitchen crying. My contractions were starting. Rosa got me into her car and rushed me to the hospital.

I was lucky. They put me into a room and I got to see Dr. Singh right away. There had been talk of a doctor shortage since California left the Union. You never knew what to expect. The wait time at the emergency room was being measured in days not hours.

Luckily, Rosa had retired from St. Joseph's, the nearby Catholic hospital and I think she still knew people there, so we were treated just fine.

I remember Dr. Singh well. He was a Sikh. A very kind gentleman. He wore a baby blue turban and a neatly trimmed beard that left the slightest dandruff on his dark blue shirt. His message to me was a scary one though, "You're not dilating, Jocelyn," he told me in his soft sing-song Indian accent. "The baby wants to come, but your body does not want to open up. I think we should be considering..."

My anxiety rose and I interrupted him quickly before another contraction could hit me. "Doctor, I am Baha'i. We do not believe in using drugs or alcohol because we know they cause serious health problems. I absolutely will have a natural birth without any drugs or surgery. My mind is made up." I would have gone to a doula if I could have found one, but like I said it was a difficult time and we were lucky to get a doctor.

I was very blessed to have a wise and willing doctor who said, "OK then let's wait and see." And that was the start of a very long and exhausting day for me. I was in labor with you for 24 hours and I was alone for most of it. Rosa and the Doctor were in and out, but that day is all a blur of pain and crying and loneliness to me. In the end, everything I went through didn't matter. My cervix never dilated.

During that time, they kept offering me painkillers and I kept saying, *no.* When the doctor would check on me, I would ask him to wait a little bit longer. I was sure you were coming naturally. Women have been giving birth to babies for thousands of years, there was no reason why I shouldn't be able to do it.

And the contractions, came and went, came and went. All day and all night long. I ended up completely exhausted and feeling so alone. I missed Jack terribly! I didn't realize how much until then. I started crying loudly and getting loopy but I couldn't sleep because I was still having contractions.

And then, right at about the 24 hour mark, Doctor Singh came in one more time, and said the words I had been dreading to hear. "It's time for an emergency C-Section, Jocelyn. We are going to sedate you now." He had decided to cut me open and take you out. I got very upset. I didn't want that at all. I started screaming and crying really loud and I can remember Rosa trying to calm me down, and I can remember the doctor telling her, "If we don't operate soon, she could die..."

And, I felt completely alone in the universe. Like there was no one who understood what I wanted, and I had no control over what was going to happen to me, or what was going to happen to you.

So that's when they filled me up with drugs and rolled me onto the operating table. It was the about worst-case scenario I could have dreamed of, except for one thing.

While all the fuss and the arguing and the contractions and the pain was going on, Jack was being granted early release from the County. With Calexit happening, most state agencies were slashing budgets and they released all of the inmates in for less than five years. A sheriff even gave Jack a ride to the hospital once they understood that I was in labor at the very same minute. California seemed to be falling apart all around us, but there were still kind people. And the system kept on working, someway, somehow.

So, I didn't even know it, but right after I passed out, Jack was there just a minute or two later. He was just in time to be holding my hand while they operated on me. He was there in the room when they took you out. He was one of the first people to hold you. And, he was there in the room, with you in his big strong arms when I woke up.

God is good. Despite the fact that nothing went the way I wanted; it was the best day of my life. I take a life lesson from that, and I hope you do too. The whole world seemed stacked against me until you were in my arms and Jack was by my side. I had learned that I was a strong enough and brave enough woman to be on my own, but that life was easier with a little help and with a little love.

And in the next few days, our lives just revolved around you. Getting a car seat strapped into your father's truck just right, making sure your crib was safe, learning how to feed you and change diapers. Those were wonderful days. We took you home to Rosa's house and Jack chased the homeless people away, but still, whatever was happening outside her door didn't matter a bit because we had you.

And you weren't my only miracle, Baby. In those days I realized that Jack was a different person. Jail had been tough on him. He never talked about it, but I understood. I think. There were no Mexican Skinheads in County. No one he could align with. There were the gangsters and Cholos on one side and the white power dudes on the other. He didn't fit in with anyone so he had to be on his own. I think he fought his way through the entire three months he was there.

Still, I explained to him that I was ready to go it alone. To get my own place and raise you by myself. "It's time for you to choose, Jack. If you want to be with me and Sarah Joy, it's time to give up the drinking and the fighting. It's up to you."

I only had to say it once. He knew I was right. He knew.

And so that was the day the daddy you know now really came into our lives. Jack hasn't had a drink or been in a fight since; the angry skinhead side was pushed away.

We were both so happy that you were with us. You looked just like your daddy and you still do. You are the best of both of us and nothing will ever matter to me more than you. I love you, Sarah Joy!

The big problem we then had to face was the hard reality outside of Rosa's front door. Politically, economically, socially, nothing was going our way at that time in California, let alone poor bankrupt Stockton.

But God is good. It was the time of miracles, and the third miracle arrived in Rosa's mailbox the next day in the form of a letter from my Uncle Russell.

Can you guess what he wanted, Sweetheart? He wanted us to move out here to the farm and help him. Leave all the political BS and the trouble with the police behind in California and come to Colorado. He told me about how beautiful it was out here. Nothing to worry about except taking care of the animals and the crops.

Growing cannabis was a bit of a controversial idea for me at first. In The Most Holy Book, the Baha'u'llah wrote that we should avoid all intoxicating substances. They make us stupid and they inflict harm upon the body. I don't smoke, and I hope that you never do either. But... I knew that God had given us this opportunity for a reason and I had to reconcile myself with it. I am glad I did.

When I showed the letter to your daddy, he was nowhere near as excited as me. Change was hard for him to accept and there was a lot of change going on in his life right then. "Let's go to Colorado! It will be a new start for you! We can raise the baby in the country, on a farm!"

He just looked at me sadly with his big dark eyes and said, "Stockton, California is my home, Babe. All my friends are here. My life is here."

And you know I am the farthest thing from a bossy person, Sarah, but I told him, "Jack, if you want to be with Sarah Joy and me, you need to make a change now. If you are serious about giving up drinking, the best way to prove it to me is with a fresh start. A new life. We can always come back to Stockton, someday." It was time for me to take charge.

-Love, Mommy

TWENTY NINE

ONE OF THE CLONES FARTED loudly and scratched his back by rubbing it against a huge granite boulder. Dan reached out to slap his shoulder. The hulking brute recoiled and bowed his head silently in groveling supplication.

"So, your father didn't help you bury your mother?" Mary looked at Trevor, horrified.

"Like I said, my dad had been a large powerful man. A six-foot five-inch body builder of 325 pounds. His addiction and his sorrow had eaten him down to nothing. He was chasing after death just like he had chased after black market Oxycontin on the Reno streets the months before. I could've picked him up and carried him at that point, just like I had Mom.

"But he didn't die. Now, he tells the children in his new family that God had other plans for him because... It was at this time, in the depths of Dad's despair that the Fundamentalist Mormons knocked on the Menasco family's door.

"Fundamentalist Mormons are an illegitimate branch of the original Latter Day Saint Religion. They still practice polygamy and live an old-fashioned way of life. Very cultish and closed off. I hadn't realized that there were so many Fundamentalists in the mountains above Reno, but I guess there were, or are.

"They were also worried about survival. While financially they were faring better than the more conventional Mormons in the area, they needed people, or I guess I should say men. They would call them Patriarchs.

"They were seeking out disenchanted Saints to join their ranks and help provide for their community. The offer they pitched to both Dad and I was a generous one. 'Come and work with us and be a part of our community in the mountains. You will be rewarded with fertile land and several young wives. You shall want for nothing more.'

"While I was sitting there thinking, 'No thank you!', Dad was feeling reborn. What they were selling is exactly what he was looking to buy.

"And that was about the same time that I discovered the Reno Autonomous Collective. I won't regale you with that story, but let's just suffice it to say I met a cute little hippy girl in the neighborhood who introduced me to the tender mercy of the organic marijuana that she grew there and I... Well I found a second home. A new home really. So, while Walt was getting clean and being rebaptized as a Fundamentalist Latter Day Saint, I became a member of the collective, and moved in with them.

"Through the Collective I learned about Fog Catchers, which were doing wonders in places like Morocco, turning deserts into farmland. You guys must have seen them back in Reno, the large mesh nets that we position to capture droplets of water from the fog that rolls down from the mountains? That fog can be condensed into pure water for drinking and irrigation."

There was a noticeable gleam in Trevor's eyes as he spoke of horticulture. Obviously, this was his true passion. Mary was surprised when Dan spoke up, hoarse and husky, "That's brilliant. You gotta tell me some more about that sometime."

"Sure, Man. We became very successful at it, and at reclaiming city land for the growing of food and powerful strains of weed."

Dan nodded. Trevor patted the breast pocket of his flannel shirt, found it empty, frowned, and continued on.

"And my dad did overcome his addiction. He regained his strength and moved up into the mountains with the other Fundamentalists. Right between the CIR and the NFU. Here in Graeagle the old man started a small cattle ranch far away from the rest of what was left of society, and he has been very successful.

"He asked me to come with him... but there's no weed in Graeagle, California. It is a purely Fundamentalist Mormon survivalist community. Outsiders and nonbelievers are not welcome. They don't barter with anyone else; they don't communicate with anyone else. They are a completely closed-off community of their own."

"I stayed in Reno. I felt needed by the commune. I had purpose there. And for heaven's sake, I had had enough of religion."

With the help of her cane Mary stood on her one good leg to stretch. The clones were now napping piled on top of each other in a spot of filtered sunshine under an enormous redwood. Dan was looking drowsy himself leaning against his boulder.

Trevor's story, while moving, begged an important question, and Mary was not afraid to ask it. "So, you haven't seen him since? I guess I am not seeing the point of your story here Trev. Are we going to be welcome in Graeagle or not?"

Trevor studied his hands for a moment. "Well that's where it gets interesting. I was able to visit my father, but just once. It was about a year ago. It's hard sneaking into California, but up here in the mountains it can be done if you are careful. I did it on horseback the first time, at Dad's request. 'Come see how we live, Lil' Trev. You will love it here.'

"So, I went, but I was..." Trevor looked from his hands up into the thick green pine trees surrounding them, "I was..."

Trevor, who could obviously spin a good yarn, was struggling for the right words. "I was... well... Dude, I was disgusted by what I found at Walt's ranch. My dad's an old man now, but he's still strong as an ox. He had taken on three young wives, Judy, Elizabeth, and Emily, but he treats them like... like slaves. He may have more wives now. I'm not sure.

"Those teenage spouses serve Walt hand and foot. They are only allowed to dress in long old-fashioned gingham dresses. They cook and clean for him, and take on most of the grunt work on the ranch. They have their own bedroom they share, but... Walt sleeps with each of them in his room in turn. He treats it like a reward. Whoever is working hard and pleasing him most can spend the next few nights in his bed. While I assume he enjoys having sex with different young girls each night, his main goal is to impregnate them, over and over. More children means more ranch hands.

"The sons will work and grow the ranch. The daughters will be traded off at an ungodly young age to other Fundamentalists to become young wives to other old Patriarchs in exchange for expensive dowries. It's quite a racket."

"At the time of my last visit, I already had a one-year-old half-brother, a two-year-old half-sister, and another half sibling on the way, all with different mothers. I guess you could call them my step moms."

"Wow." Dan's voice was quiet. "That's some way to live."

"And his wives are... happy?" Mary asked, her voice ringing with feminist indignation.

"I think two of Dad's wives are happy with their lot. They contentedly toil for Walt's pleasure because it is God's will. I mean it could also be worse, they could be starving in the streets of Reno. But... Walt's youngest bride, Judy, the one who was pregnant at that time was different. She kept pushing against the Fundamentalist programming. She often disobeyed my dad. She had tried to run away twice. He told me this himself. He thought it was funny.

"In fact, Walt was laughing as he told me the story. Here is the poor girl serving us at the dinner table, the dinner she had made, even though she must have been eight months pregnant. Walt just sat there waiting to be served, and laughing and telling me in his great booming voice, 'The second time she tried to run away she had almost made it to Sacramento. I tracked her down though, with the help of some of the Brother Patriarchs. I brought her back to the ranch. I said, how can I make sure she understands not to do something this stupid again? So, as a punishment I used hot branding irons on her feet. Made her sister-wives hold her down while I did it too. She couldn't walk for weeks afterward. She won't try running away again. I promise you that.' His laugh was as loud as thunder.

"And while Walt is telling the story, Judy is bringing in the bread, and then going back to the kitchen for the corn, and her head is just bowed, her eyes focused on her feet. But I could see that she was gritting her teeth, and I could feel her raw desire to stab her husband in the neck with his own steak knife. At least I think I could."

$$\varnothing \, \varnothing \, \varnothing$$

Squirrels chirped and chased each other in the trees overhead. There was the slight whisper of a breeze in the trees. Other than the rush of the waterfall the forest was silent. Trevor collected himself and finished his story, but why he chose to go into such detail for two people he had just met and five brutish, non-comprehending clones, he could not say.

"She was beautiful and sad. And you know what, I kinda

decided that I hate my father. I hate what Walt has become. He didn't used to be like that. He would have never treated my mom like that. All those pills he took, all that sickness, and my mom's death, it changed something inside of him.

"I felt like I should do something, or say something. But I didn't. I went back to Reno the next day and left him there with those poor girls."

Trevor remembered, but did not tell Dan and Mary what he had been thinking from the back of that horse the entire way home. *If you were a brave man, Menasco, you would have done something. You would have rescued her. You should have rescued all of them.*

"I always figured I would go back someday. I just didn't plan on these circumstances. To be honest, it's all stressing me out a bit. Dude, I hope there's some more weed in my jacket."

Dan and Mary had listened quietly without a word. They looked at each other as Trevor made his way back to the truck in search of another joint. Dan's clones had roused themselves from their nap and were milling around the rocky pool under the waterfall lapping at the icy water they scooped up with their hands. They made soft "ooh" noises as they pointed at the silver fish that swam there.

"Shiest!" Trevor shouted from the truck. "I am out of weed. Well, I guess that does it. Time to go see Daddy! I will walk in from here and make sure that we are all welcome. I'll come back for you guys in a few hours."

"What if we aren't welcome?" Dan's voice was a hoarse whisper.

Trevor shrugged. "Should be, but if you haven't heard from me by nightfall then you are on your own. Good luck. Maybe someone can sell you some fuel in Graeagle."

Mary glanced over at Dan, trying to gauge his reaction as she shambled over to lean against the truck's rear bumper near him. But Dan's solemn face expressed nothing. He just nodded at Trevor and told him, "Good luck," and the shorter stocky man turned and started down the dusty road.

"Later, Dan! Later, Mary!" he called over his shoulder.

As he walked away, Trevor heard Dan say to Mary, "I should change your bandage." The heavy Mexican's voice was somewhere between a purr and a growl. "Take off your pants."

THIRTY

Currently Listening to: *Please, Please, Please Let Me Get What I Want* **by The Smiths- (My record on your daddy's old turntable)**

Dear Sarah Joy,   680 days since you were born!

We got big news today! Very exciting. But I will get to that in a minute. First let me see, what was I writing about last time...

Oh yes, that's when we left to come here to Colorado, Baby. You are getting so big now, and I am writing this journal for you because… I don't know… to keep some sort of family history alive? I want you to know about how your daddy and I met, and about Jack, even though we left him behind in California. Our lives have changed so much since we came here and moved in with your Uncle Russell and met your Uncle Johnny.

The big earthquake hit San Francisco just after we left. We were lucky to miss it physically, but it still hit us just as hard. Luckily, Grandma Rosa's house in Stockton survived, but we had lots of friends in California who were not so lucky, especially in San Francisco.

With the Bay Bridge completely collapsed, relief teams had a hard time getting food and water to all the people trapped and stranded in San Francisco. There were wildfires burning out of control in SoCal. The New Feds had blockaded the borders and created a total embargo on all sales and trade. It was dark times in California. Really dark times. We were lucky to get out when we did.

But these days, it's hard to know what is going on back

home. When we left California, we left the CalWeb behind us. And there is still no signal out here in the country. Probably half of the New Union is still without internet and the other half, on the coasts and in the big cities, have their content heavily regulated and censored by the NFU. The government blocks all contact with Texas and California now and they only allow pro-government subject matter to be promoted online here in Colorado on the NFUNet, so what's the point of going online anyway, right? I missed my phone for the first year. Now, I can't remember why I needed it so much. All I need is right here in front of me in real life, not on a little screen.

I am so glad we moved. When your daddy gave up drinking and fighting, he became a new person. He left Jack behind and he just goes by his middle name now. Even I don't call him Jack anymore, which was hard at first. But, he's just Dan now. Moving to Colorado was like a rebirth for him. I would say he quit being a skinhead, too, but down deep he really still loves it. He never hung up his boots.

Your grandma Rosa's goodbye present to your Dad was a new truck. We packed all his records, and everything else we could fit in the back, bundled you up and headed out of Stockton, through ugly Nevada and Utah and then into Colorado. We brought your daddy's record player, of course. I am listening to it right now.

Uncle Russell and your daddy worked together to get the family a work visa (which is a nice way of saying they bribed some people in high places), and after a few months of wading through red tape, our application to become citizens of the New Federal Union was granted. It took a long while because we got held up getting over the border into Nevada for two days, but in the end somehow it all worked out.

We crossed Nevada and Utah pretty much non-stop as fast

as we could. Your daddy wanted to leave California far behind. You slept a lot on that trip, but I remember how pretty it got when we first entered Colorado and then I will never forget the first time we drove into Loveland, it was just lovely.

We passed Deer Mountain, then we followed the Big Thompson River down the mountain, into the rolling green foothills, and then all the way down into the valley, to Uncle Russell's farm. This is as close to paradise as I can imagine. If I look up, I can see Deer Mountain looming to the West like something out of *The Lord Of The Rings*. The Big Thompson River passes just to the south of our land so water is never a problem, and we can eat fresh fish whenever we want.

I hope you remember these days when you are older Sarah Joy! Feeding the goats and pigs and old Jezebel the cow. Weeding the garden and picking the fresh peppers and kale while you run around between the rows and rows of vegetable plants. These have been the happiest times of my life.

Your daddy turned out to be a natural born farmer, too. He and Russell spend most of their time in the greenhouses tending to their cannabis plants. There are five different greenhouses all at different stages of grow right now. The first house is full of brand-new baby clones just a few inches high, and the fifth house is in a state of harvest. We are always busy cutting down the plants, trimming up the buds, hanging them to dry in the barn, and then shipping them off for sale in Denver. That's why Dan decided he could use some help.

And that is our big news today! Your daddy is applying to the New Federal Cloning program to have himself cloned! Imagine if we had five or 10 more men just like your Daddy! We could expand the farm and build another ranch house. I'm not too sure how the whole thing works just yet, but we should hear back in a week or two.

He applied to the program up at Johnny's house on his old computer. I guess I should write to you a bit about your Uncle Johnny. He is the thin old man that owns all the vineyards up the hill to the west of our land. He always wears funny hats, rides horses everywhere, and has little braids at the sides of his white hair. He looks like he is a million years old but he is still so handsome. He reminds me of what it meant to be cool.

You won't appreciate this until you are much older, but he was once one of the most famous movie stars in the world. We have a bunch of his old DVDs. Movies he made years ago, but you are still too young to watch most of them. *Pirates of the Caribbean* is my favorite. If anyone had told me when I was young that I would end up living next door to Johnny Depp someday, I never would have believed it!

Guess who is knocking on the door right now? Uncle Johnny is here to take you for a horseback ride. Love you, Sweetie!

-Love, Mommy

THIRTY ONE

TREVOR WALKED THE ROAD alone flexing his heavy muscles and thinking. He was still a bit stoned but hyper-aware of his surroundings. He was pondering the ancient Chinese proverb that said, *The fish cannot sense the water*, but he was not sure why.

Walt's ranch was set in the heart of the Sierra Nevada mountains, and the rocky road Trevor walked cut through large granite outcroppings and grove after grove of towering redwoods that swayed and rustled in the breeze. The road took an unexpected turn up into a steep ravine. There were no body bags this time. Walt had a habit of bagging up any looters or trespassers that he shot, covering them in lime and then leaving the bags for months at a time here at the mouth of the ravine. It was his father's way of warning unwelcome guests that they were walking down the wrong road.

Must not have had any trespassers recently. Trevor turned up the sharply vertical road, and climbed over a locked cattle gate that barred the way into the compound. Instinct told him to place both hands on his head as he walked. His pistol stayed tucked in his belt at the small of his back. Bright fingers of sunlight poked themselves through gaps in the trees overhead shining into his eyes as he walked. Trevor kept a mindful observation of his surroundings and moved with great care, watching for the tripwires that he knew his father liked to lay out around the ranch. "If my booby traps don't catch an interloper, they might catch dinner!" Walt had bragged to him.

As he rounded a granite boulder the size of a small apartment, Trevor came upon four young girls in long-sleeved gingham dresses that hung down to their ankles. Though Trevor had been very careful, they had already sensed his presence, standing in the middle of the road, staring at him as he rounded the huge rock. Two of the smaller girls held empty five-gallon water jugs. The tallest girl in the center of the group stood heavily with both legs set firmly into the dirt balancing her body into an A-frame. She held a large, deadly looking revolver up in front of her with both hands. The hammer was already cocked back, and the barrel was trained at Trevor's head.

Trevor stopped in the road before them, his hands still on his head. No one said a word for a few minutes. The tall girl shifted her sweaty hands on the bone grips of the revolver, betraying her discomfort with the substantial weapon. Trevor locked eyes with her. She was pale and pretty, 18 or 19 years old, with her long blonde hair pinned up in the same messy old-fashioned bun that her sister-wives wore.

She also appeared to be eight or nine months pregnant.

Trevor tried to smile through his pounding heart and firing nerves as he gave a short wave.

"Hi, Judy."

Ø Ø Ø

With a fresh bandage wrapped not too tightly around her thigh, Mary sat on a large boulder dangling her pale feet in the crisp cold pool at the bottom of the waterfall.

The five big clones splashed and made soft noises at each other glad to be out of the back of the truck. They were trying to catch fish with their hands.

Dan returned to the pool from the truck with another bundle of old United States Army C-Rations. He placed the bundle on a rock near Mary and opened packets of salted crackers and orange jelly one at a time. "Maybe you will like these better than the meat. Used to be my favorite."

There, deep in the wooded mountains, Dan and Mary munched quietly on crackers and jelly. The Five played and splashed with the mindless abandon of toddlers in the loud musical lullaby of the waterfall that washed over them.

Dan glanced at Mary from time to time but made sure he did not stare. She sat half in the shade and half in the dappled sunlight which recreated the halo around her thick dark hair. Dan said a silent prayer. Though they had only known each other a short time, theirs was the growing bond between a caregiver and an independent soul not used to being in need.

Mary looked up at Dan and caught his glance before he could look away to where one of the clones had actually caught a small silver fish and was vocalizing an excited, "Ooh Ooh, Huff Huff" noise. The other four scrambled through the water to see it.

Mary broke the silence, "Are you really gonna sell these guys in Stockton?"

Dan flinched, startled by her clear voice ringing out into the quiet of the forest, but he did not look up at her. He kept watching the Five, and finished the twenty Hail Marys he was saying in his head.

"I mean, you seem pretty attached to them. They kinda seem like your family."

Dan flinched again, but answered, his voice flat and low. "I ain't got no family." He looked down into the dirt. "Lost my farm. Don't need these guys anymore. Need money for a new start."

"Who are you going to sell them to?"

Dan examined the dirt at his feet for the 20 heartbeats that fell in time with his final prayer before answering. "San Joaquin Valley's still fertile and being farmed. Heard farmers there pay good money for trained laborers."

"And what if you can't find a buyer?"

Dan's voice was almost a whisper. "Then I sell them on the cheap to the protein factory. Make food out of 'em.'"

Dan could see the wariness and mild disappointment in Mary's eyes.

"What about you? Gonna tell me about this errand you have in Berkeley?"

Mary nodded, took a quick breath, then began to speak, slowly at first.

"I'm on a mission to save a man's life, and if I save his life, I can save California, maybe the whole world." She glanced at Dan. "I am aware of how insane that sounds. The man is a scientist from the NFU who has made an amazing discovery. They call it Project Adam's Ale. It's something that everyone wants." She paused, "you can go ahead and laugh, Dan."

But Dan did not think that anything she said was particularly funny, or impossible; he had five clones of himself that he was trying to sell.

"His name is Doctor Abraha Tadese, and he has discovered a way to digitize water."

$$\varnothing \, \varnothing \, \varnothing$$

Two thousand feet above a silent black helicopter no bigger than a lawn mower trained both an HD telescopic lens and a long-range parabolic microphone on Dan and Mary, recording every word. Even if they had looked directly in the drone's direction, they would neither have seen nor heard it. It was too far away for them to even see the long black missiles mounted at the ready beneath its four whirring rotors.

Ø Ø Ø

Mary sat alone by the waterfall while Dan took the Five on a short run down the gravel road a ways and then back. She was still thinking about Dr. Tadese when they returned.

"There are a lot of people after him. Some want to kill him. Some want to weaponize his invention and use it against their enemies."

"And this guy who's trying to kill you?" Dan asked.

"My old partner. Andrew Eldritch. He's a trained assassin working for the NFU. He taught me everything I know. Now he's trying to grab Tadese and bring him back to stay in the New Federal Union."

The clones were splashing each other again in the cold shallow water. Were they smiling? Kind of. Mary spent a heartbeat wondering what went on in their simple minds.

"My Chief says that it may be the single greatest discovery of our time. Imagine the fires raging out of control here in the West, and then imagine the flooding happening out East. If we could, I know this sounds crazy, but if we could email tons of water, digitally send it from one place to another in the blink of an eye, millions and millions of gallons of pure H2O…"

"There would be no more floods or fires," Dan finished for her. "Nobody would be thirsty. Everyone would have water."

Mary nodded, "You get it."

"I get it," Dan replied, his voice funeral-grim. "I lost my entire farm to a flood in Colorado. It destroyed… everything."

Mary looked deeply into the big man's eyes, but he was only looking at the rocky ground. He seemed overcome with emotion, unable to speak. Mary placed one hand on his bulky shoulder, and they sat together in silence for a while.

Mary knew next to nothing about the hulking Indian except that he had, at some point, decided to clone himself five times. He had seen her in various states of undress in the past 48 hours, but she always sensed a deep blush under his dark skin and he always averted his eyes from her thin pale legs and belly.

She was glad she had trusted him. She missed her team. Soon it would be time for revenge and she would need his help.

THIRTY TWO

The following document is a copy of a personal letter from Dr. Abraha Tadese's Classified Dossier regarding: Project Adam's Ale. This information is considered extremely sensitive and requires Level Four Security Clearance for viewing.

Directive: Delete and purge after reading.

—Department Homeland Security NFUS

Let me do my best to explain the project I am working on. It is quite unlike anything else I have worked on before! Sometimes I feel like I am in the middle of a Science Fiction novel. It would not be bragging to say that my associates and I here in Maryland are *altering the very fabric of reality.* We are making the impossible possible. I hope you can approach this letter with an open mind, otherwise you may not believe the sheer magnitude of the technology we are working on.

I am sure you are familiar with my previous work in the field of nanorobotics and their use in medicine. You know we are talking about machines that are built on the scale of the nanometer and they have many practical uses. We are trying to reimagine new uses for these machines that we never thought possible before.

Remember, if you cut one hair from your head, the surface of that one cut would be 80,000 nanometers. One nanometer is one billionth of a meter. We could place 80,000 microscopic machines on the surface of that one cut hair. Nanoautomatons are so small, a teaspoon could hold three billion of them.

Previously, these nanoautomatons have been used on a molecular level to repair faulty heart valves, cauterize brain hemorrhages, the medical applications are innumerable. We inject them into the body directly through the blood stream and program them to do all kinds of amazing life-saving jobs.

But now, we are beyond even this amazing technology my friend! Now, we have found an amazing new use for the nanoautomaton. Each one of these microscopic machines are autonomous much like your Tesla which is capable of driving itself. Nanoautomatons are capable of steering themselves, thinking for themselves and working on projects without direct instruction from a human. They are completely powered by externally generated magnetic fields.

Here is the leap of faith. Imagine each of these billions of nanoautomatons consuming one atom of matter, let's say an oxygen atom. The nanoautomaton is able to eat the oxygen atom and then excrete pure energy in the exact signature of that type of atom. That energy can then be digitized into information. This process is called nanoinformatification.

Now comes the really exciting part. The informatificated oxygen atom can be stored digitally on a computer or sent in something as simple as a text message via a WIFI network. At the other end of this transaction, a similar nanoautomaton can consume that piece of information and then excrete it once again as an oxygen atom. Nothing is destroyed or created, but the molecule has been transmuted into information and then back into a physical atom again.

Now, keep in mind old Star Trek episodes where Scottie beamed Captain Kirk down to a planet. The atoms that make up Captain Kirk's physical body were transferred into energy (or information) and then reconstituted back into atoms of matter at a different location. Of course, the human body is far too complicated for our technology to even attempt such a feat at this time, but the nanoinformatification of single atoms is within our reach. So why not nanoinformatificate simple molecules as well?

This is my immediate goal, and we are on the brink of making it all a reality.

So, to finally get to the point! Let's examine a single molecule of water. H2O. A large grouping of Nanoautomatons could break each water molecule down to its base, two Hydrogen atoms and one Oxygen atom. Then another group of our friendly little Nanoautomatons consume those atoms, informatificate them, and excrete them as energy which is digitized and sent to another location. At their new home they are transmuted back to atoms and then reconstituted as water molecules again by another teaspoon of billions of nanoautomatons.

By this method, billions of simple water molecules could be sent in an email or a text message and then be reconstituted by another grouping of nanoautomatons somewhere else. In simple terms, this is the digitization of water.

On a large scale (which is ironically actually quite small when considered through nanometrics) we could digitally move billions of gallons of water from the center of the Atlantic Ocean to the middle of Death Valley in the blink of the eye, leaving all the salt and any other contaminates behind. The process only informatificates the prescribed atoms, so the water that comes out the other end would be absolutely pure.

Imagine the possible applications for this process. We are talking about the end of drought on a worldwide scale. The absolute extinction of wildfires or floods. No one on earth would ever be thirsty again. Every desert could be transformed into forests to cool and oxygenate the climate, or into fertile soil ready to be farmed. Colonizing the moon or Mars would be no problem. Desalinization of the oceans? No problem. The possibilities are endless.

The technical █████████████████████████
██
█
███
████████████████████████████████████
We are on the brink of ████████████████████
██
██████████████████

However, the NFU

I dream of the day when this discovery can be put into use to save our dying planet and revitalize humankind. I believe that day is very close.

████████████████████Please let me know what ███

Your friend,

Dr. Abraha Tadese

THIRTY THREE

THE OLD FORD DIESEL WAS powerful and towered high off the ground, as did its owner. Though Big Walt was in his early sixties, he was still every bit as formidable and intimidating as the orange diesel truck that he had been driving for as long as Trevor could remember.

Trevor recalled Walt's drug-addled days when his mom was still sick. Once a man had shown up at the house looking for money that Walt owed him on a drug deal. The man had started kicking Walt's big orange Ford truck, angry that he wasn't getting his cash. Walt had picked up a large rock from the yard and smashed it into the man's face, knocking out several teeth and fracturing his jaw. Walt almost beat the man to death that day in his own front yard while Trevor sat and watched from the porch. When he was done, he handed the bloody rock to Trevor and said, "That guy was really asking for a rock massage."

Now father and son sat together in the cab of the same orange behemoth as Walt navigated it down a canyon so narrow that redwood branches brushed against the roof. Trevor sat in the middle of the bench seat between his father and his very young and very pregnant "stepmother" Judy. They passed granite boulders that missed knocking the lateral mirrors off by inches. Obviously, Walt had driven up and down this road many times.

"Family is one thing, but strangers are never welcome on my ranch, right, Jude?" Walt said staunchly. "You of all people should know that, Trev."

"They're not strangers, Pop. They're friends."

Judy remained silent.

His father's short beard had more white in it than Trevor remembered, but his full head of hair was still predominantly a light brown making Walt appear much younger than he was. His muscled frame had never turned soft and fat with age. Trevor had been pleasantly surprised that his father was happy to see him. There had been no hugs or handshakes, but Walt's face had lit up in a big smile when his wives walked Trevor up to the ranch house. As soon as Judy had recognized him for who he was, she had tucked away her heavy revolver and the sister-wives had escorted him home, where Walt was cleaning freshly caught trout in the shade of an oak tree.

However, Walt's demeanor had quickly changed when Trevor told him that he had several friends waiting for him down the mountain a bit.

Despite his obvious reservations, he had offered to drive Trevor down to meet the interlopers, although what was going to happen when they got there was going to be entirely up to Walt, and his moods were ever changing like the winds through the redwoods.

"And how many of these *friends* did you bring with you, Lil' Trev?"

"Just two…" Trevor remarked, his mind elsewhere as the truck skidded to a dusty stop in front of the cattle gate and Walt bounded down with an agility that belied his age and girth. Before he swung the gate wide open, he busied himself with a set of loose dusty wires that wound into the mesquite bushes at the side of the road. "Glad I didn't set off whatever that was," Trevor told his father as he bounded back up into the cab that sat a good five feet above the ground.

Walt looked at his prodigal first born gravely. "Yes, you are," he growled as he turned the orange machine down and into the main road. "And why do I get the feeling there's more than two?" Trevor took note of the two natural bone handles protruding from below the truck's dash where a large revolver and long, hand-forged knife were mounted on either side of the steering wheel. Walt also had a gun rack in the back window of the truck that held a black 12-gauge riot gun and a modified AR-15.

"Well, two humans... The guy I am traveling with, Dan, he has a group of clones of himself..."

"Clones? Fuck. Sounds like a lot of mouths to feed, Trev. You know, I already have five wives and eleven kids to watch out for. Two of the girls are pregnant, too! You and I are blood, Trev, I always have a place for you, but I don't know about this shit where you show up with a bunch of fucking people I've never even seen before. What in the fucking world made you think that would be OK?"

"Shush, Papa. Don't talk so." The quiet young pregnant woman broke her silence.

"Woman, I only brought you along because you asked so nicely. Don't try my patience."

"But I say unto you, that whosoever is angry with his brother without a cause shall be in danger of judgment: and whosoever shall say to his brother, Raca, shall be in danger of the council: but whosoever shall say, Thou fool, shall be in danger of hell fire." Judy spoke without blinking an eye.

"Aw hell, Woman, don't recite scripture at me." Walt replied. Trevor moved his hand to his mouth, hiding a slight smile. For Walt, the hardest part about being religious was all the religion.

"You sure aren't *sounding* very Mormon these days, Pop."

"Aw, shut the fuck up and answer the question. Why are you trying to bring strangers into my home?" Walt slowed the truck over a particularly rough spot in the road.

Trevor chose not to point out that it would be impossible to do both. "They're on the run, working for California and the New Feds have someone chasing them. They're headed to Berkeley. I know how you feel about the New Feds. I thought you wouldn't mind lending a hand. This is the only way I know to get into California without hassling with checkpoints and soldiers. Besides, I wanted to see you."

Walt balked at this with a sarcastic snort. But, when he glanced over at Trevor again, his eyes betrayed his pleasure at his oldest son's answer.

Judy gazed on quietly at the road ahead. Trevor could feel her left thigh rubbing gently against him as the truck bounced on.

∅ ∅ ∅

When Walt stopped short at the waterfall, he parked nose-to-nose with Dan's truck, which immediately looked tiny in comparison to his own. Walt grabbed the riot gun from behind him and dropped down into the gravel.

Dan brushed the cracker crumbs from his black T-shirt and stood up from his seat in the rocks to meet Trevor's dad.

"Shit, you didn't tell me they was Mexican." Walt leveled his shotgun at Dan's belly and looked past Dan at the Five. "Aren't there enough Beaners in this country already? Why the hell would we need to clone some more?"

He pumped the shotgun chambering a buckshot shell and raised the gun to his shoulder with a bead on Dan's face.

Cradling her swollen belly in both hands, Judy stepped away from the truck and in between her angry husband and Dan. "Stop, Papa. Peace."

"Woman, I already told you not to preach to me. Get out

of the damn way!"

"Dad, put it down!" Trevor shouted. An automatic pistol appeared in his hand as if from nowhere. He held it steadily trained on the big old man.

Walt did not lower the loaded weapon despite his pregnant wife standing directly in front of the short ugly barrel and his firstborn son standing next to him with a weapon of his own at the ready.

Dan stood frozen in place directly behind Judy watching the entire tableau as an eerie, unsettling calm descended upon them all.

∅ ∅ ∅

Mary had gone a little way down a game trail to relieve herself. When the gunfire exploded, reverberating through the quiet of the mountains around her, she buckled up and hobbled back to the waterfall painfully, but as quickly and quietly as she could. The rapid succession of shots were still echoing through the forest when she arrived upon the bloody scene.

THIRTY FOUR

Currently listening to: *Clones (We're All)*
by Alice Cooper

Dear Sarah Joy,   730 days since you were born!

Happy birthday, Sweetheart! My sweet two-year-old girl. We love you so much! It's hard to believe we have been here in lovely Colorado for more than two years now. I hardly keep track of the date anymore. You are my calendar, Sweetheart! My whole world revolves around you.

I just spent the nicest day with you and your Uncle Johnny out in the garden and in the stables.

I wish I had a camera to take a picture of you and Uncle Johnny feeding the chickens (your daddy never did find me that Polaroid). These days Johnny rides down to see us at least once or twice a week. He always says he likes my coffee, but I think he really comes to see you, and help you with the chores. His eyes light up like stars whenever he sees you. I think he is a very lonely man, and a little sad because his own family never comes to visit him.

The other day we were sitting on the porch having coffee and I asked him, "Johnny, why are you here in Colorado?"

He told me, "I came here to escape California, just like you!" He was wearing a silver or gold ring on every single finger and had little beads in his white hair. He still dresses like a pirate even if he is not in the movies anymore.

"Well, maybe not just like us. We left because we were too poor, but I think you left because you were too rich!"

He told me, "I left 'cause I wanted to get lost. Here in the mountains, this is the perfect place to get lost. When I look up at that blue sky, and listen to that river pouring by, there is no place I would rather be. I hope nobody ever finds me." He is the nicest old man and he is still really cute, too.

After we fed the chickens, we checked on the goats and old Jezebel the cow, but it's not our job to scoop their poop, because your daddy has his clones do that every day now. Then we went out and watched the clones pull weeds in the garden. I am still getting used to having five more of your daddy around, but it's really not so strange once you get used to it. They really are a lot like him, just stupider. They work hard and eat a lot.

Johnny was out there with you in the garden, picking cucumbers and one of the big idiots almost stepped on you so I guess Johnny smacked him a good one and he ran off blubbering. It was pretty funny because those clones are the same size as your daddy, like a foot taller than Johnny. I think that clone could have crushed him if it had a mind to. But, you know, they say Uncle Johnny used to be quite a fighter back in the day. He must still hit hard, even though I can't really imagine him hurting anyone any more. Kinda like your daddy, huh?

So, after that, your Uncle Johnny said, "Listen, Joc, do you really trust these big oafs? I don't think they are safe to have around Sarah Joy. Why don't you guys get rid of them and get some normal human laborers in here to work?" He is super protective of you and doesn't think we should let the clones around you at all. But you know, sometimes old men worry too much. I don't think any of the Five (that's what your daddy calls them) would ever hurt you, at least not on purpose.

Besides, now we've realized just how much we need them. Johnny really knows that too. Since we got them, the work around the farm is so much easier.

And that's what I want to write to you about today while you take your birthday nap. You should really hear the story about how we got the Five since you are growing up with six daddies, five dumb ones and one smart one. So, here is your birthday story, Sweetheart:

Uncle Russell invited us to come and live with him out here in Colorado to help with his cannabis farm, and it is a lot of work. Cannabis is still in big demand in the NFU, especially the organic stuff from Colorado which has earned quite a reputation over the years.

Your daddy loved all the hard work, of course, and he dove right in. He had never experienced anything like farm work growing up in the city, but he was seriously working 12 to 14 hour days seven days a week. I think he really felt the need to prove himself to Uncle Russell since Russell was basically supporting us when we first moved here. It was really important to Dan that Russell see him as an asset. Your daddy does not want to be anyone's burden.

One strange thing we learned about your Uncle Russel is that he disappears for a week every other month. He always lets us know ahead of time and he tells us he is going on another "business trip," but we never know where he goes or what he gets done. Now Uncle Russel is my mommy's brother, but he is not Baha'i. He was raised in the church but doesn't practice. He doesn't have a wife, and he doesn't drink, so I think he goes off on a bender and just cuts loose somewhere in the city on these trips. He works so hard when he is here, he just deserves it, so we never say anything.

Anyway, your Daddy has to work twice as hard when Russel goes on a "business trip." So, it was after one of these trips that Dan came back from town one day with this brochure that he had picked off of the bulletin board at the Farm N Feed. At first, he was just joking about it.

"Do you believe this?" he said when he first showed it to me. "Human cloning is a real thing now. You can have 10 husbands exactly alike Jocelyn. Twenty if you want!" He made a couple of sexy jokes about that, but I don't think I will write those down here.

But, it turns out that pamphlet was pretty persuasive and it started to make a lot of sense to your daddy. The most persuasive part was the part about free labor, and it turned out to be true. There was no cost at all to us, it was a new experimental program. So, all your daddy had to do was provide his DNA, and the New Federal Cloning Program would pick up the cost and print up to 10 exact replicas of your daddy the same size as him, the same age everything.

The Mexican border has been completely walled off and closed for two years now. The NFU forcibly deports every illegal they find (or anyone who is brown and can't prove their citizenship for that matter) or sticks them in the ICE concentration camps. I don't even want to think about those places. We are so blessed to be where we are and have what we have.

But now farm workers and laborers are really hard to find. Maybe that genius of a president of ours saw cloning as a way to build the manual labor force back up. Anyway, the NFU was all about the cloning program for a minute. All of that ended up changing pretty quickly though.

-Love, Mommy

THIRTY FIVE

AS THE TALL THIN DARK-SKINNED MAN moved through the parking lot, heat waves shimmered across row after row of dusty cars, trucks, and vans. There was not a cloud to be seen above. The July Indianapolis sky was the color of turquoise.

The tall man moved from car to car head bowed, hands in pockets except when he reached out to try a sizzling door handle. The commuter parking lot at the train station was crowded with vehicles, many of which looked as though they had been in the same spot for a long time. The busy morning rush was over and there didn't appear to be a guard on duty.

Running a hand over his head to wipe the sweat from his short curly hair, he tried a dusty Toyota. Locked. A large white van. Locked. A newer model Honda Civic. Locked. An old Mercedes diesel station wagon. The handle clicked and the door popped open. And then Dr. Abraha Tadese was seated in the sweltering leather driver's seat of the vehicle with the door shut firmly behind him. He had been looking for an open vehicle for hours doing his best not to appear suspicious.

"Don't get too excited," he spoke out loud to himself. "You still have to figure out how to get this thing started." Tadese caught a glimpse of his face in the rear-view mirror. His greying hair had just started to recede giving him a hawkish widows peak. His bespectacled face at first glance appeared African American in origin, but on closer inspection one might determine that he might be of Middle Eastern decent. He had been called "ethnically ambiguous" in the past.

Abraha checked both sun visors. No key. Then he sent a silent prayer up through the Mercedes's torn and tattered roof and into the dry Indiana firmament before snapping open the center console between the two front seats where a ring of keys awaited him.

"Thank you, Lord!" he breathed out loud as he fit the key with the Mercedes symbol into the ignition and turned the car over. She came to life immediately blowing a thick cloud of smoke out of her rear end. The gas tank showed full. God was good.

The station wagon was indeed old and worn, but she ran strong and steered easily through and out of the parking lot. Ab steered her around the corner and behind a crumbling drug store where a short, black haired figure leaned in the shade of the building near a dumpster.

Abraha nodded to the short Korean man. He pulled up to the dumpster as Dr. Shin Ha Kyo pried his sweaty body from his shady spot to access the passenger side of the dusty vehicle. His short sleeve collared shirt was tucked into a pocket and he wore only a sweat-stained white under shirt and thin grey slacks.

Shin spoke with a heavy Korean accent, but his English was still concise and clear. "Air conditioning?" He turned on the fan and even hotter air blew out over the two men as Abraha steered the stolen vehicle out of town and toward the highway.

Abraha's own voice was deep and only tainted by what people in Maryland had called a California accent, "Man, we got lucky, Shin. This is the car for us. I don't care if the AC works or not, this is the one. She's going to get us to California; I know it. I had a car just like this in high school. These diesels run forever."

The vents continued to blow hot air as the two men drove on in silence with Abraha checking his rearview mirror regularly for police lights.

Two of the greatest scientific minds on the North American continent cruised out of Indianapolis on the 36 toward Illinois in their stolen station wagon.

Abraha Tadese's North Korean passenger drifted in and out of an uneasy but much needed sleep next to him. In his relative solitude Abraha began, as he often did, a silent one-sided dialogue with God. Though he often waited patiently for a response from the Almighty, the Lord had yet to respond to Abraha's prayers. *Someday*, he told himself, *someday*.

Dear God, thank you for this Mercedes station wagon, and please forgive me for the crime of stealing from my fellow man and bless the poor soul I stole it from. May he get home safely by some other means.

This seemed like a good start to his first prayer in days. Shin was finally snoring softly beside him, which was good. Abraha felt as though he had a lot to say to his maker today.

Lord, if you allow me to get to California...

He started again and stopped. Abraha wiped the sweat from his eyes and kneaded his temples.

Lord, I need your help...

He stopped again and shook his head. He glanced over at the snoozing scientist next to him then back to the clear road ahead. The sun was setting. He was driving with a precision born of necessity, keeping the stolen car at two or three miles per hour under the speed limit. There were very few other cars on the road anyway. Almost dinner time. He jumped right to the heart of the matter.

Lord, the guilt. Please Lord, give me some relief from the guilt. I killed hundreds of people, many of them were good people with children and families who were just doing their jobs.

I didn't mean to kill them, Lord, but I was aware that it might happen. I vastly overestimated how much water it would take to create a large enough distraction for us to escape. I didn't want to kill anyone.

Tears streamed down Abraha's face and he wiped furiously at his eyes to keep the road clear in front of him. It had been difficult, even for a mind like Abraha's, to calculate how many cubic meters of water would transfer once the nanoinformatification transference began. He had opened the process window for three minutes, expecting the ADELPHI Lab to flood heavily. He had not expected the entire valley to flood with billions of gallons, covering the roofs of every building with 60 to 70 feet of pure blue water.

He had swum up toward sunlight, scuba diving gear on, past lifeless body after body floating steadily on their own. He had seen Frank Turner. He had tried to pull Frank up with him, but had lost his friend in a sudden vortex created by too much matter moving too suddenly...

Forgive me, Lord. All I wanted was to make sure that no one used my work as a weapon! In my efforts to do so, I have become the first person to weaponize my own discovery. I am my own worst nightmare. Dr. Tadese drove on into the setting sun racked with guilt, blinking back tears, and begging forgiveness from his maker.

THIRTY SIX

BLOOD SPLATTER MISTED over Judy's face as she stared in shock. Dan stood frozen in place behind her. He hadn't even had the presence of mind to pull out his own weapon. It had all happened too quickly.

Walter staggered forward ever so slightly before turning his heavy frame away from Judy and Dan to face Trevor who stood on his right. Trevor, whom Dan now knew to be the now dying man's firstborn son, had just unloaded his 9mm pistol at the big man, hitting him at least seven or eight times until the gun clicked repeatedly, empty.

Mary was already crouched behind a rock with her weapon sighted on Trevor, her training lending her the speed and presence of mind that Dan lacked. He looked back to Trevor's father, amazed that the old man was still standing and holding the riot gun. Blood was soaking into his shirt from the many holes that had punched through his flesh in the hail of bullets. Still, he managed a shambling step toward his son and killer, as fear washed over Trevor's face.

Blood gurgled from Walt's mouth as his lungs tried to suck air making a whistling sound where his ribs had been torn and smashed. "Lil' Trev… My boy..." he managed to say.

Judy screamed.

Then Big Walt dropped the riot gun, pitched forward onto his knees, and onto his face in the dirt at Trevor's feet. Trevor, Dan, Judy and Mary all watched in silent horror as the old man writhed there in the thick mud made of his own blood for almost a full minute before the holes in his lungs finally ceased whistling and he expired and lay still.

Mary stood at an awkward angle, favoring her good leg still holding her weapon though it was at her side and no longer aimed at Trevor. "What the actual fuck?" was all she could say.

Judy was kneeling in the dirt next to her dead husband, one hand still cradled her unborn child, the other lay gently on the dead man's shoulder.

Mary looked from the young pregnant woman to Trevor who was sobbing softly to himself as he stood over the body of his dead father. "That was your dad?" she asked incredulously. She received her answer as Trevor collapsed to his knees next to Judy with tears streaming down his face.

Dan had not moved. His ears still rang from the shots. When he finally was able to tear his eyes away from Walt's bloody carcass, he saw that all five clones had stampeded off into the woods in fear. He moved to go after them, but had a second thought and walked over to where Trevor stood shaking and staring at his dead father. Dan took the empty gun from Trevor's hand, then scooped up Walt's heavy riot gun and walked over to place them both on the rock beside Mary. Then he slipped off to find the Five. He knew they wouldn't be far.

∅ ∅ ∅

A few hours later, after Dan had rounded up the Five, calmed them down, and gotten them into the back of the truck, he and Trevor got to work building a stone cairn over Walt's shallow grave.

Trevor still had not said a word and Dan was silent as well. He could see that Trevor was struggling with what he had done. Dan was used to working with quiet patience. He figured Trevor would say something when and if he was ready.

Judy sat in the truck.

They had buried Walt's body in the small quiet meadow next to the pool at the bottom of the waterfall. When the two men had piled enough rocks over the dead man to bring the cairn close to the level of Trevor's waist, he knelt before the pile in silent and earnest prayer.

Dan respected this and stood by, revisiting his own Hail Marys and Our Fathers for several minutes until Trevor suddenly spoke out loud, "We didn't prepare the body properly, but he wasn't an earnest Saint anyway."

These were the first words any of the party had uttered for hours. Mary limped over, relying heavily on her cane. Judy bowed her head and pressed her palms together in supplication.

Trevor continued speaking from where he knelt in the tall grass, "Lord, please accept my father's soul into your kingdom and forgive me for what I have done."

Dan, with Mary at his side, waited for him to continue in patient silence.

"My father was not a good man. He was a racist. He was abusive. He was a misogynist who mistreated his teenage wives as if they were his slaves. Those girls are widows now. Please bless and protect them all."

Mary and Dan exchanged a quiet glance but kept their heads bowed as Trevor continued.

"Walter did love my mother. That was a long time ago, but I remember his capacity for love. I have buried both my parents now with my own hands..."

Trevor's voice trailed off and he sobbed quietly for a few moments before continuing his prayer.

"He claimed to love you, God... He also said he loved me... I guess none of us knows what is truly in a man's heart except for you, Lord.

"I came here knowing clearly that it might come to this. I alone am responsible for my actions. Whether it was the right thing to do or not... I will have to live with that question until it is time for my own judgement at your feet Lord. God, please rest his soul, forgive my sin, and ease my tortured mind. In Christ's name I pray. Amen."

Trevor slowly stood and turned to face his companions.

"What are you gonna do now?" Dan finally asked.

"Who? Yeah... What now?"

Judy left the safety of the truck and hobbled over to Trevor to put an arm around his shoulders supportively.

"I'm gonna go back to his ranch and tell those little girls that they are free. I am going to tell them that Walt died... in a rock slide. Terrible accident... Not sure if they will buy that or not..."

He looked to Judy who nodded her assent.

"Then I am going to start working his ranch. Seems terrible and strange to say that out loud but... I'm not going to let everything he built go to waste. All those children up there on the ranch need to be provided for. I took away their provider, so I will have to make sure they are taken care of... If they will let me."

"Don't stand too close to me," Dan whispered in Mary's direction. "People keep getting blown up or shot when they stand too close to me."

⊘ ⊘ ⊘

Trevor drove the big orange truck back up the mountain with Judy at his side and Dan, Mary, and the Five following close behind in Dan's truck.

Walt's four young wives watched as they pulled up, all holding babies in their arms and surrounded by a small flock of toddlers of varying ages. The oldest was a stocky boy, dressed in a western shirt and worn but clean blue overalls. He was the spitting image of a six-year-old Trevor.

None of the girls were armed this time. They stood on the porch of the small well-kept ranch house at the top of the arroyo that enclosed the ranch. The children stopped their play and ran to hide in their mother's long skirts as Trevor jumped down from the truck alone and then moved to help Judy down.

One of the young sister-wives stepped forward into the sunlight, plucky and a few months pregnant, asking loudly, "Where's Papa Walt?"

Dan's old diesel coughed itself into silence as he and Mary stepped out of their truck behind Trevor and Judy. Then, there was no other sound except for the soft wind blowing through the giant redwoods all around them.

Walt's family waited for one heartbeat. Two. Three… Then Trevor broke the silence. There was a new authority in his voice that Dan had not heard before.

"Walt's not coming back. He met with an accident down the road…" He was unable to finish, but Judy again moved to put an arm around his shoulders, her long blonde hair falling out of her messy updo as she did so. She then threw both her arms around Trevor and starting sobbing into his shoulder.

The other four girls stayed on the porch but began wailing and screaming in anguish as they held onto their children. One fell to her knees as she did so. This started all of the babies and children crying and screaming.

Dan gritted his teeth against the cacophony of emotion, his own eyes welling with tears at the regurgitated memory of his own loss. Mary kept her sidearm in hand but pointed at the ground, ready in case one of the young mothers decided to act out in vengeance.

Trevor closed his eyes and returned Judy's embrace, with a look of joyful release on his face that Dan had seen in the mirror the day his daughter was born.

THIRTY SEVEN

Currently listening to: *Save It For Later*
by The English Beat

Dear Sarah Joy,   731 days since you were born!

Anyway, this last Spring, your daddy ended up applying for the Federal Cloning Program. He went up to Johnny's ranch to do it. Johnny still has hardwired access to the NFUNET which is the New Federal Union's version of what we used to call the World Wide Web. It's heavily monitored and censored by the New Feds, but your daddy was accessing one of their websites, so it was no big deal. Bioserv.nfus.gov

Here is your daddy to tell the story. He's going to talk nice and slow, and I'm going to try and write it all down for you as fast as I can:

"I guess not a lot of people had applied for the program. My application was approved within just a couple of days. Then they invited me out to Denver. That's where the Cloning Program was based. It was a short drive. Bioserv ran some different tests on me. Took blood. Had me run on a treadmill. Read my vitals. That sort of stuff.

"Then, I filled out a bunch of paperwork on what I wanted the clones to be like. They asked me, what 'developmental stage' I wanted them produced at. I told them I wanted them just like me. There was a question of their intelligence level... I got the feeling that the doctors weren't really sure about how smart they would turn out. It was all a big experiment.

"Anyway, Dr. Tsai, the project director told me they did not create what he called 'sentient product.' I think he just meant smart clones. They claimed it was because of the limits on the technology. But you know what? I think something else was going on. Maybe they just really didn't know what the heck they were doing. Maybe they were worried that if they made the clones too smart there would be a clone rebellion."

Your daddy's imagination runs away with itself sometimes.

"So anyway, the Bioserv people told me that my clones would have about the intelligence of an average Labrador Retriever. They would be able to learn around 20 words or commands. They wouldn't be able to talk. Easy to control, they said. Docile, they said.

"Other than that, the clones were s'posed to be patterned exactly like me. Same age, same height, same musculature. My exact sextuplets.

"Then I got to visit the laboratory. I got a tour of the tanks they would use to grow my clones in. Crazy tech. Like out of a movie. Then they took another blood sample so they could replicate my DNA and grow the embryos. I'm 22 years old so... somehow, they were able to develop and grow the cloned embryos in their tanks to my exact same age. To the day. Can you imagine that? They explained it to me too, but to be honest, I really didn't get it.

"Then I drove home. And, even after all that, I think I was only semi-serious about the whole thing. I mean, did I really expect what happened next to really happen? A month later the Bioserv van pulled up to the ranch and unloaded the six clones they'd produced for me. That was before Six died. End of story."

Thanks, Daddy.

Sarah Joy, when those six clones first arrived here at the ranch, I have to admit it was really strange, Baby. They just

kind of loped around looking at everything with their big ignorant amazed eyes. They reminded me of huge toddlers. They
got spooked and cried really easily. Bioserv gave your daddy
instructions on a whole system for training them. Lots of pos-
itive reinforcement.

They liked granola bars a lot, so that's what we always
used for rewarding their good behavior. They learned really
fast. The most important thing to those clones was pleasing
your daddy. They loved him like a dog loves its master and
they were always trying to snuggle with him and be right next
to him. It was really awkward! Just the slightest attention from
him would make them so happy they would fall all over themselves.

All we really had to worry about was feeding them, making
sure they stayed pretty clean, keeping them in simple warm
clothes, and giving them a comfy place to sleep.

We were given a tablet that was in direct contact with the
laboratory, and we were supposed to record everything about
them. Take their temperature (anally yuck!) every morning and
every evening, monitor their blood sugar, record what they ate
and how their bowel movements looked. It was a lot of work
those first few weeks.

But then, out of nowhere, the Bioserv laboratory was
bombed! Completely destroyed! Whoever did it killed three
doctors (including Dr. Tsai) and destroyed the embryonic tanks.
That brought a quick halt to the whole program.

Your daddy says, "The New American Christian Terrorists
saw cloning as an abomination in the eyes of God, like abor-
tion. They had no problem breaking a few commandments
(like Thou shalt not kill) in order to stop it."

New American Christian Terrorists. Huh. How is that a
thing? What are their meetings like? Anyway, they took credit

for the bombing. Then there was supposed to be an investigation. Then it was just never in the news again. Swept under the rug by the NewFeds as if Bioserv never even existed.

The Senate introduced legislation to ban human cloning in the New Federal Union of States right after that, and they never reopened the lab. No more emails, no more reports, no more Bioserv Inc. We expected somebody to show up and take the clones away at some point, but no one ever did. They were just ours.

Turns out there were only about five other citizens in the whole NFU who tried the program and received viable clones. Some others tried and failed because the system didn't work for everybody. Your daddy was lucky.

He is saying, "We should track down the other successful clone recipients and have a big family reunion." Good one Daddy. We don't know who or where they are though. The whole program is dead. A failed experiment.

We did lose one of the boys (he didn't have a name before he died, but now we call him Six) to the flu in the first month, but the other Five have always been healthy, hard-working, and even... kind?

So, it's like I told Uncle Johnny a few weeks ago when he asked, he doesn't have anything to worry about. You play with the Five all the time. I would never leave you alone with them of course because they are huge, and stupid, and strong, but as long as someone is watching them and telling them what to do, we have never had a problem. They never disobey us. Besides, they're just part of the family now.

So, I got that story down. I hope it will be important to you someday. Now it's time to wake you up for your birthday party! Uncle Johnny brought a big box down from his ranch for you! It's all wrapped in pink! So exciting. I love you so much my two-year-old girl! May God watch over you and may we always be this happy.

Love and kisses!
-Mommy

THIRTY EIGHT

The following was transcribed directly from digital audio recordings of an interview with the former Hollywood actor Johnny Depp. The interview was recorded on ███████ by Dr. Nathan Jensen in anticipation of writing a biography on Mr. Depp. Dr. Jensen completed his book but publication was blocked due to ████████████████████████████ ██████████████

The interview has been included here for the purpose of ████████████████████████████████ ██████████████

Mr. Depp is considered to be ████████████████ ████████████████████████████████

██

—Department Homeland Security NFUS

Is that thing recording?

Yeah, man, I don't really do interviews. Well, I haven't done one for years anyway.

Well, I don't give a shit.

No. That simply doesn't matter to me. You do what you want.

Life here in Colorado? Sure. Where do I begin?

My neighbors? Yeah, that's an interesting story.

So, Sarah Joy turned two last week, and I guess that means that it has been about two years since Dan and Jocelyn moved out here to Colorado with that little baby girl.

When I first met Dan? Let me tell you, I was just stopping by Russel's farm to pick up some weed. We have been neighbors and friends for years and I often stop in on my way back from town. He had decided it would be a funny joke to tell me Dan liked to be called by his full name, "Jack Daniel." I really shouldn't listen to Russel. He's a son of a bitch.

It was a lovely spring day and Dan was walking me through the farm and telling me all about the harvest that was underway. I already knew most of what he was saying, but I listened politely. I can do that sometimes.

I remember watching him, oh so carefully pulling small green caterpillars off the huge pot plants to show me. He held a little devil wriggling between his thumb and forefinger for a second before he crushed it.

"See here, Mr. Depp, how the bud is brown at the tip?" I took a closer look at the thick green bud and it was just covered in little red hairs and white crystals. It made my mouth water. On closer inspection, I could see that there was indeed a brown rotten spot on one of the large lower buds, so I nodded my affirmation.

"That's worm sign. There is no reason for a healthy plant to get brown spots like that unless there is a worm somewhere inside there, eating away. The longer you leave them uncaught, the bigger they get, and the more they eat."

We were standing in an enormous field filled with row after row of pot plants. Dan was moving slowly from one plant to the next running his hands over the large coned colas the plants produced. Sometimes he would pull a small pair of scissors from his belt to trim a wayward branch or a yellow leaf. Then he would just let the cuttings fall to the ground.

Russel and Dan's pot farm is less than a half mile from my ranch where we are now. We're just outside Loveland, Colorado. I got lost here years ago and then I never left. Yeah, lost is the right word for it alright. People used to come looking for me, but I never wanted to be found. Now, since the whole country has been going to hell and falling apart all over the place, everyone seems to have forgotten about me. That's just the way I like it.

A nice little house, a couple acres of wine grapes, a half-dozen horses, three ranch hands. What else do I need? Yachts? French Villas? Those days are gone. I left that all behind decades ago. Traded it all in for the mists of Blue Mountain and the roar of Big Thompson River.

Anyway, yeah, I remember Dan cursing whenever he found another dead spot on a plant. He pinched at the dead place, pulling away small chunks of dead, brown flower and examining the plant closely until he made a satisfied grunting noise and held up another small wriggling worm for me to see.

"The netting is supposed to keep the butterflies out," He motioned to the light green nets that stretched out overhead throughout most of the field, "but the little buggers get in once in a while anyway and then they multiply." His voice was deep and rough, barely louder than a whisper, much like the slight Colorado breeze that wandered through the plants and rustled the heavy buds ever so slightly.

"It's always the worst just before harvest time. Of course, the easy thing to do would be to spray poison to keep the bugs off, but we can't do that right?"

He was still a little starstruck that day. I could tell. People generally react one of two ways when they meet someone famous, or someone who had been famous previously, years ago, I guess I should say. They either clam up and can't find a word to say, or they treat me like a best friend they have known for years and talk my ear off. Dan had started out the first way, but he was now working his way into the second.

"Why don't you just spray non-toxic insecticide Jack Daniel?" I already knew the answer, but he was enjoying himself so much, I was just taking pleasure in the sound of his voice. He was such a solemn, quiet guy, listening to him open up about a topic he was so passionate about gave me great gratification. Besides, who didn't want to spend a sunny morning walking through a large field of thousands of luxuriously fragrant marijuana plants so near to harvest?

Dan glanced at me from the corners of his eyes as he pinched the little green monster until green juice squirted out between his fingers. He then dropped it into a glass bottle half full of rubbing alcohol that was strapped to his belt.

"Come on, Mr. Depp, do you really think I am gonna spray anything even close to insecticide on all this lovely Colorado Organic OG Kush? It wouldn't be worth a dime if I did." He walked on to inspect the next plant. I followed a few steps behind him sipping on a mug of coffee and reminded him, "I thought I told you to call me Johnny."

Russell had always grown good weed, but now that Jack Daniel was helping out, they absolutely grew some of the dankest pot I had ever experienced, and trust me I was used to having really good shit.

I once had a personal joint roller on staff. Tony was on the payroll for several years, if I remember correctly. I used to call him my weed butler. I had paid him a healthy salary to find the very best weed, grind it up and roll it into fresh joints for me every single day. That had been back in my Hollywood days. I have no idea where Tony ended up, or if he was even alive, but he would have shit a brick if he were standing in this field with me now.

Back then, the news media had all said I was spending more than two million dollars a month. They said I was being sued by my ex-wives, my ex-lawyers, not to mention two or three guys that I had purportedly punched "for no good reason." Trust me though, I have punched a few guys in my time. It was never without good reason.

The fake news media had also said that despite being one of the highest paid actors of all times, I was broke. All these mean articles came out about how I couldn't afford my lifestyle. Personal chefs, personal assistants, personal joint rollers, IRS problems, unpaid loans, 70 guitars, Basquiats, Warhols, a $30,000 a month wine tab (that one was laughable- it was actually much more).

Anyway, I stopped following the news media. No need for all that fake news in my own little private Colorado paradise.

Can you turn the recorder off now, please? I have to go to the bathroom.

THIRTY NINE

DAN WATCHED AS Trevor gingerly lowered himself into what had obviously been his father's favorite chair, an overstuffed leather armchair ensconced between the fireplace and a large bookshelf crammed full of novels and religious doctrine. The significance of Trevor's actions was not lost on Dan.

Judy handed Dan a hot roasted grain beverage that she called "Postum." There was no coffee or tea in a Fundamentalist Mormon household. He sipped on the thick bitter liquid as Trevor rose from his chair and began to build a fire in the fireplace.

Judy brought Trevor a steaming mug with a smile and a swish of her long dress. "Thank you, Judy," he told her as he watched her pregnant but still slight figure slip back out of the room. Dan looked away, uncomfortable, and scratched the back of his head. *He looks like the man of the house alright.*

Eight or nine children were gathered around the kitchen table passing plates of biscuits and fried trout that their now-deceased father had caught that morning. They ate with an introverted shyness, glancing up at Dan and Trevor from time to time with questions in their eyes.

Mary limped into the living room with her own steaming mug and took a place on the sofa next to Dan.

"We need to get moving. I have to get to my errand."

Trevor was the first to respond. "Berkeley should be a straight shot from here. Four or five hours at the most. It's dark now, and it has been quite a day. Why don't you guys crash here tonight? I can re-provision you with gas and food for the clones. Send you on your way first thing in the morning."

Dan looked to Mary, who only nodded with a profound weariness as she stared into the flames forming in the fireplace. The children were finishing their food and taking their plates to the counter for their mothers to wash.

Dan stared for a moment as one little girl walked past him toward Trevor. She wore a long white dress creased with dust. Had Dan seen her somewhere before?

"My Papa's not coming back?" she asked Trevor.

Trevor held the little girl's chin in his big hand, "I'm sorry, Sweetheart," he said. "But I'm here to take care of you now."

Dan started to stand, but when the little girl turned her face to his, he realized that she was not the same little blonde girl he had been looking for. Her eyes were darker and her lips thinner. Then she was gone, running up the stairs with her brothers and sisters. Dan shook his head to clear it and leaned back into the couch.

Somewhere else in the house a door slammed. Two of Walt's wives were upset about the day's turn of events. They were making a loud fuss about packing up their clothes and their children's clothes to leave the ranch the next day.

"And what about you Trev?" Mary asked softly. "You're going to stay here and… take your dad's place?"

Trevor looked at the floor and nodded.

"Most of these kids are probably too young to remember their… your… real dad," she added. "You're planning to… raise your half brothers and sisters in your dad's place? Like they are your own kids?"

Trevor did not look up. He just nodded again. Judy had slipped into the room to stand next to him and place a hand on his shoulder. Trevor looked up at her and smiled placing a hand on her hand.

"I'm going to go back to church. Back to the real Mormon

church. The true church, not this Fundamentalist madness. I need to give up the smoking and atone for my mistakes. I need to find a way to be good again."

Judy returned his smile.

Then Trevor turned to face Mary and Dan, "Clones comfortable out in the barn Dan?"

Dan sensed Trevor's eagerness to change the topic and nodded as he lay back into the couch, sleepy in the glow of the growing fire.

"And what about this errand of yours, Sister? You are on a mission for California? Are you out to save the world?" Trevor's grin betrayed that he was only half serious, but there was nothing but cold hard reality in Mary's reply.

"Yes, I am." She glanced over at Dan as she sipped her Postum and grimaced at its bitterness. "We are."

Over the crackle of the fire, Dan could barely hear a baby crying softly from the second floor. Judy patted Trevor's shoulder as she withdrew her hand from his and moved away toward the stairs.

"What's your scientist's name again?" Dan asked in his gruff whisper. "And how are we s'posed to find him?"

"Dr. Abraha Tadese." Mary replied pulling her small black tablet from a pocket in her jacket. "I'm not directly in contact with him, but I am in touch with a man named Derek Timm in Berkeley. He has been communicating with the doctor and we will be setting up a meeting place in the next few days."

"And are we still being followed?" Dan's voice was barely a gruff murmur.

"No way." Trevor replied, his voice shot through with confidence. "You may have picked up a tail on the way to the Reno Commune, but I was extra careful getting us here. No one knows where you guys are. I can guarantee it."

Dan's eyes were drooping with exhaustion, but he was still looking at Mary. His mind was on autopilot and praying on autopilot, *Ave Maria, Gratia Plena*... It was time for bed.

Ø Ø Ø

Dan awoke with a start. He was cold and alone on a cot in a small room off of the kitchen. The house was dark and quiet, but something had roused him.

From the crack under the door he could see the reflection of bright orange fire flickering across the black tile floor. Someone had gotten up to stoke the fire. It should have burned down to embers by now.

Dan's skin prickled with goose bumps as he lowered his feet to the floor and moved to open the door that led out of the room, careful not to make any noise. Even before he opened the door, Dan knew what he would see.

He peered through the dark kitchen and into the living room, where Scar sat in Trevor's leather armchair nudging absently at the fire with a heavy iron poker. Everyone else was sound asleep elsewhere in the house.

Scar looked up at Dan and nodded. He was waiting for him. The gleam of reason sparkled in his eye.

Dan's mouth fell agape. He could not understand how Scar had gotten into the house. He wanted to yell or run out into the night, but he was frozen, immobile. Trapped in what could only be a dream.

"Sit down, Dan." Scar's voice was strangely his own but somehow wrong, like hearing a recording of his own voice.

"I have another story to tell you."

FORTY

THE DUSTY MERCEDES STATION WAGON pulled over to the side of the dark empty road.

"There, Shin. The mailbox on the corner. Get out, grab the package, and get back in. Hurry!" Abraha Tadese directed the short Korean man beside him.

Dr. Shin Ha Kyo fumbled with his door handle and then stiffly spilled out of the car onto the gravel pathway beside the car. He had been sitting for a long time. They had been driving for almost 20 hours straight, stopping only once for gas, urinating in empty bottles and then pouring the thick hot piss out of the windows. They were getting better at not getting it all over their hands, but the exterior of the station wagon was not smelling so good.

There was no moon and the countryside around them was a deep, funeral black, save for their headlights. Cicadas sang in the trees. There was no other sound.

The doctors had stopped in front of what appeared to be a deserted warehouse somewhere in Nebraska. In front of the warehouse there stood a tattered grey mailbox. Inside the mailbox someone had left them a package, as Abraha had expected. Shin Ha Kyo grabbed the package and then he was back in the car nervously saying, "Go, go, go," in his thick North Korean accent.

Abraha wasted no time in gunning the car, sending gravel and dust flying off into the night behind them. He aimed the old diesel machine back toward the freeway that the two had left behind them 20 minutes ago.

Shin tore open the brown paper package to reveal a short

black mirrored device.

"Power it up, please," Ab said glancing back and forth from the road to Shin as he drove.

With the tap of a button the black mirror lit to bright white in Shin's hands. They waited a few moments as the screen read:

Primary Encryption status... verified
...
...
Secondary Encryption status ... verified
...
...
Tertiary Encryption status ... verified
...
...
Incoming call ...

"Should I answer it?" Shin's voice was barely a whisper over the thick hum of the diesel engine.

Abraha thought for a moment, eyes intent on the dark road before them. They were passing the orange glow of a fire. These fires had been visible from the road with more and more frequency in the last few hours. "Yes. Let's do it." His voice betrayed the lack of confidence he felt in the depths of his stomach.

Shin's finger shook as he tapped the screen which was instantly filled with a kind intelligent face that Abraha knew well.

"Derek Timm!" Dr. Tadese called out in elation. The car swerved a bit and he overcorrected but managed to guide them back onto a straight path. Shin held the small tablet so the camera would register Abraha driving.

"Abraha! You're alive! I can't believe it. I have been waiting two days for you to activate that device. I was starting to think you weren't going to make it."

"Did Tricia get my email?"

Derek glanced away from his camera for a moment. He was a handsome man in his late fifties with a pronounced widows peak of sandy blonde hair fading to white. The creases at the corners of his eyes furrowed as he looked back at his friend Abraha gripping the steering wheel, surrounded by darkness.

"Tricia died three weeks ago, Ab," Derek stated gravely. "She was caught under a building collapse in San Francisco."

The station wagon nearly swerved off the road again, but Ab continued staring straight ahead for a moment. When he glanced back at the device Shin was holding, there were tears forming in his eyes.

"My God, Derek, I am so sorry. I didn't think they would be monitoring her email as well." He brushed at his eyes with the sleeve of his shirt. "I never thought I would be responsible for so much… death."

"Wait," Derek's face was suddenly pale on the screen. "You can't think that…" The car continued on in silence for several heartbeats before Derek continued, his voice so soft Abraha had to strain to hear it over the engine. "It was an aftershock… From the earthquake…"

"God, I hope so," Abraha said stifling a sob at the back of his throat. "God, I hope so." Then he turned back to the glowing screen, "Derek you have to know you're in danger. You have to get somewhere safe."

"I'm safe, Ab. I'm in the middle of California for heaven's sake. There were just two CIRCA agents here an hour ago checking in to see if I had heard from you. They said they would swing back through this evening. They left a car watching out front."

Abraha thought about this.

"What the heck happened at Adelphi, Ab? I have had conflicting reports. The New Feds say it was a radiation leak, but rumors were circulating online that there was some sort of flash flood?"

"I did it. I flooded the place. I killed them all. I didn't mean to. You have to believe me. There was a slight miscalculation on my part."

"But how is that possible?" Derek was incredulous.

"I used my friend Shin's robot."

Dr. Shin Ha Kyo turned the device's camera on his own face for a moment giving Derek a respectful bow of his head before turning it back to Abraha's fatigued form.

"Dr. Kyo had a Broad Operational Language Translation prototype robot. He used it as an assistant, and it was allowed off base to go shopping at the Korean market for him. I sent it to the Potomac river with several ounces of liquid packed full of trillions of nanoautomatons. He poured them right in. We used them to nanoinformatificate water molecules from the river and then transmuted them back into water molecules at the base. We only opened the window for three minutes. I didn't realize the sheer proportions of matter we were dealing with. I thought I would flood the base with 10 or 12 feet of water..." His voice trailed off and he wiped at his eyes again his gentle sobs mixing with the hum of the tires over the road.

Sensing that he was done, Shin turned the device back to his own face.

"Dr. Timm, I have been trying to convince my friend Dr. Tadese that it is not his fault the entire base was destroyed." He spoke with a rapid precision, his Korean accent betraying no emotion. "There was a grave miscalculation and we flooded the entire valley that held the ADELPHI base under... I would guess 50 or 60 feet of water. Abraha, Dr. Frank Turner, and I were prepared with oxygen tanks and breathing gear since we did intend to swim our way out. Abraha and I were barely able to reach the surface. Dr. Turner was caught in a vortex and did not survive. I am guessing that there were hundreds of other casualties as well, but again I do not believe that Abraha is to blame. We were being held against our will."

Derek was stunned into silence. "I... I... I don't know what to say. Are you telling me you can transport water electronically?"

"Yes, sir. Digital water. Your friend Dr. Tadese has made this possible."

"Listen, Derek. We should sign off now just in case we are being monitored and the New Feds triangulate our location." Abraha had regained some of his composure. He was exhausted, but felt a steely conviction nonetheless. "None of this will matter if they get ahold of the nanoinformatic technology. I am convinced they only want to use it as a weapon. I have faith that California will see the moral value of my discovery and put it to use for the good of the world, not for violent purposes. At least, I hope they will."

"And where is the technology, Ab?" Derek asked from the screen.

"I destroyed all evidence of my work from the lab before the flood," Ab responded. "The nanoautomatons in the Potomac are in hibernation mode, but I can re-establish contact with them any time. I am the only person in the universe who can do that. They are impossible to locate for anyone else.

"Other than their existence, all the code, all the schematics for producing more technology exists only... here." Dr. Tadese took his hand from the steering wheel long enough to tap his brown bespectacled head. "And here," he reached into his pocket and revealed a small glass vial full of clear fluid to the camera.

"One billion nanoautomatons right here." He returned the sealed test tube to his jeans pocket.

"Christ almighty, be careful with that," Derek spoke from the tablet.

"It's unbreakable, and they are harmless unless activated by my privately coded network," Ab replied continuing to drive.

"Well, take careful care of that head of yours as well, Ab. I'd like to think it's unbreakable too. I assume you're headed west?"

"I am on the way to you, sir. Thank your friends at CIRCA for putting this device in our hands. It is good to be back in touch with a sympathetic soul."

"Travel safely, Ab. I will have CIRCA contact you and guide you into the state when you are close. I will keep my end of the line open 24-7. Contact me when you need me."

"Will do old friend."

"And, Ab," Derek spoke in a broken staccato, as if grasping for the right words to say. "Tricia… The base at ADELPHI… None of it is your fault… You're a good man. If everything you have told me is true… The ends will justify the means."

"The ends will justify the means." Abraha repeated in a whisper wiping again at his eyes with his sleeve. "I will be in touch, Derek. I will see you in California."

Shin closed the connection as the device again scanned for possible indication of eavesdropping and, finding none, shut itself down.

The dirty old Mercedes sped on into the West through the smoky night.

FORTY ONE

The following is an encrypted message sent to Operative Andrew Eldritch:

Be advised: Dr. Abraha Tadese's direct contact person within the CA Republic is Dr. Derek Timm. Dr. Tadese has gained access to an encrypted fire wall jumping device. Sister Mary deemed nonessential. She is out of the loop.

Troops and reinforcement agents are available at your request.

Directive: Enter California and apprehend Dr. Derek Timm as well as his encrypted device. Timm can be leveraged to gain access to primary target, Dr. Tadese.

Directive: Apprehend and return Dr. Tadese to the New Federal Union immediately. Dr. Timm will be considered nonessential after Dr. Tadese's apprehension.

—Department Homeland Security NFUS

FORTY TWO

The continued transcript of Dr. Nathan Jensen's
final interview with Johnny Depp in Colorado
follows. These recordings were obtained from Dr.
Jensen's hard drive without his permission. It is
pertinent at this time to note that Dr. Jensen ▮▮▮
▮▮▮▮▮▮▮▮▮▮▮▮▮▮▮▮▮▮▮▮▮▮▮▮▮▮▮

-Department Homeland Security NFUS

Alright, alright, alright, Nate!

Well, turn the damn thing on then. What was I talking about?

I was walking through the cannabis field with Dan...

I could see five figures following Dan and I through the fragrant field. They were emulating Jack Daniel's actions pretty much exactly. They follow him everywhere he goes and they do exactly what he does. They can't talk, but they seem to understand everything he says to them. It's just a little surreal.

I remember when I paused to set my coffee on the ground so I could light a joint, and one of the clones moved over to inspect the plant right next to me. That was the first time I had ever stood close to one of them. He was a hulking brute, the same height as Dan. Hell, he had the same face, the same dark brown skin, the same broad shoulders. But still, I would never have mistaken him for Dan, even in a dark alley. I still struggle for the right words to describe Daniel's relationship with his clones. Is he their father? Their brother? Their owner? Their master? Anyway, I noticed right away that there was something missing from that clone's eyes, some register of intellect that Dan had but his five clones all lacked.

The clone made an excited huffing noise whenever he pulled a worm from a plant and squished it. He was hoping to get noticed. They live to get a little praise or a treat from Dan, just like the family terrier who catches a rat and brings it to his master for approval.

"Did you find a big one there, buddy? Good worm?" I asked him, but the words didn't register. He glanced at me, but I didn't register either. It is like he saw me, but he was just looking through me at the same time. Only his master mattered. Yeah, master. I think at this point, master might really be the right word. So, the clone, he went back to work examining plants for dead spots without so much as a nod in my direction.

Maybe I should get myself cloned, huh Nate? I could just imagine what fun the news media would have with that information. Headline: Recluse Johnny Depp Clones Self Out Of Pure Loneliness. Ha ha.

They love me. They hate me. They want to see me fail. They are rooting for me to succeed. Hell, they just want to sell more magazines, or web memberships, or blog subscriptions, or whatever. I am just a money sign to those vultures. Everyone loves to read about the golden boy taking a shit and throwing it all away. Man, I hate people.

That's why I gave it all up. I walked away. Hollywood? London? St. Tropez? Left it all behind for a little ranch in Colorado. No threat of viruses out here. We are too far away from the city and all that madness. I haven't visited any of my properties in decades. I said, 'if the kids want to see me, they can come here to Colorado.' But they don't come. Lily-Rose came for a Christmas a few years ago with her kids. It didn't go well.

I haven't heard from her since. My lawyer keeps me updated a bit once in a while. Says she's doing fine...

I think, that for the most part, the world has forgotten about me. It was bound to happen eventually. In any event, I forgot about the world. I just settled into my little compound here and focused on raising horses and growing wine grapes. I drive into Loveland once or twice a month just to get a good coffee. I don't even get recognized any more. The world's obsession with my life and career faded like a pre-teen's love for a boy band. Replaced by rappers with tattooed faces and the newest American Idol contestant. Or whatever is important to people these days.

It took me a few years to really let it all go. I had to fortify the ranch to keep out photographers and pilgrims. I almost had to give up the internet entirely. I haven't had a smartphone or a tablet for more than ten years now. Just an old desktop computer I boot up once in a while, as seldom as possible.

After all, I do still need to communicate with my financial team. Lawyers and CPAs. Shiest, I hate those guys the most. A necessary evil. There are still decisions to be made for the family's sake. I leave most of the day-to-day operations up to my sister. Even though I haven't appeared in public for so long, the money keeps rolling in. Captain Jack Sparrow for Christ's Sake.

But, out there in that huge pot field, on such a beautiful morning with the sun rising up over the mountains, none of that really mattered. A hot cup of good coffee, a nice joint to puff on, that's all that mattered. I picked up my coffee, and plodded on through the field. I couldn't help but reach out and caress a thick sticky bud on a nearby plant. The residue stuck to my fingers like invisible fragrant glue. I held them to my nose to inhale the fresh aroma.

"Hey, Jack Daniel, how long until harvest?"

He was a few plants ahead of me, but he turned to regard me stone-faced. "Nobody calls me that," he said. I could sense his solemnity. His mood had flipped on a dime from cheerful to deadly serious.

"Um… Sorry, I thought Russell always…"

"Russell only calls me that when he wants to piss me off. It's just Dan now. It used to be Jack… but nobody calls me Jack Daniel. That was my old man's favorite drink. A couple pints of that and then he would start knocking me and my mom around." His eyes were smoldering. Russel had told me he had a violent past and a quick temper. I did not want to piss him off. Fucking Russel.

"Shit, sorry Dan. I thought… I didn't realize…" Damn that Russel and his practical jokes.

"I'm sober now. I don't need to be reminded of that shit." That big man was about to square off with me in the middle of his pot field.

"Won't happen again, Dan. And I am Johnny. Don't forget."

Then, Jocelyn swished out of the house and into the field in her long colorful hippy skirt. Music was pouring out of the windows. What was that old song she was playing? It seemed so apt at that moment. The one that goes, "You lost a lot when you lost me…"

Joc was bringing the baby out to her daddy, and I was glad for the interruption. And Dan cast off the shadow that had hung over him for a moment and he walked over to her his face alight with love at the sight of his family.

I was impressed by Dan's beautiful wife and even more impressed by his beautiful daughter, Sarah Joy.

"Morning, Johnny," Jocelyn had a pot of coffee in one hand and the baby in the other. She passed the baby to Dan and filled my mug with steaming dark brew.

"There's my girl! My girl! My girl!" Dan held the little bundle close to his heart. She was barely two months old then. A marvelous little treasure. He was no longer angry with me, thank God.

"I think we will cut down next week. Are you going to come help us trim? There will always be a lot of scissor work to do this time of year...Johnny."

"Sure, Dan. Wouldn't miss it."

Interesting guy Dan; he carried the swaddled baby out into the field with him, a tiny bundle in his huge brown hands. The clones were still going plant by plant picking worms. I had caught a flash of the skinhead Jack that Russell had told me about. I wouldn't want to get into a fistfight with that guy, especially with his five devoted disciples to back him up.

Fuckin' Russell, Jocelyn's Uncle... he still always says with a laugh, "When you're ready for your comeback, Johnny, I will be your manager. The Ed Wood to your Bela Lugosi."

But there won't be no comeback. I can't imagine returning to Hollywood now. I'm too old. No longer the handsome devil I was in my prime. Besides, California has become her own nation now. I keep my head out of the politics these days the same way I keep my head out of the entertainment game. No need for any of that anymore. Everything I need is right here.

Did I mention that my neighbor grows weed? Yeah, I guess I've been talking about that, but I mean what could be more perfect right? I grow grapes for my own wine, and my neighbor has this huge cannabis farm.

And on that day, when I stubbed out my joint and held my hand out to brush another plant as I moved on, Dan was just ahead of me, Dan was next to me, and Dan was behind me.

Federally subsidized clone workers. I never would have believed it if I didn't see it with me own eyes! They come help me with my harvest season now, too. Crazy.

Hey you want a drink, Nate?

Come on man. Don't give me that.

Do you know how many assholes out there would give their left testicle to be sitting here interviewing Johnny Depp for an authorized biography? If we hadn't been friends for so long, I would have told you to go fuck yourself.

Come have a glass of wine with me.

FORTY THREE

Scar relaxed back into Trevor's overstuffed leather chair and continued to poke into the fire with his heavy tool. Dan sat on the edge of the couch, his movements robotic, as if his body was following pre-programmed commands. Dan couldn't bring himself to call out or to walk away, but he didn't really want to do either. Dream or not, he needed to hear Scar's story.

Scar stared deeply into the fire as he began his tale.

A long time ago in a city far away from here called Osaka, there travelled two brothers. The two brothers were very handsome, and shared the same intelligent countenance, but despite the good looks they had in common, they were two very different people.

The brothers were both salesmen. They travelled together from city to city peddling their wares.

The older brother was short and stout. His name was Gunzo and he sold the knives that his father had forged back in the small village where the boys had been raised.

The younger brother was tall and thin. His name was Akari and he sold silk ribbons that his mother had dyed deeply in bright colors back in the village.

Both brothers had black, deep set eyes and high, sharp cheekbones. That they were related was always immediately obvious to others.

The two boys also had very different methods of selling their goods. Gunzo had a high, sharp voice and as they entered each town or village, he would walk the streets calling loudly, *Knives for sale! Knives for sale!* Potential customers might come out to see him if they were interested in making a purchase.

Akari, on the other hand, had a melodious baritone and as he walked the streets he sang a lovely tune, *Ribbons for all the pretty misses, so their boys will give them many tender kisses!* This brought him many customers, especially amongst the pretty young rich girls of the city.

One night the two brothers were camping on a lonely embankment, in the moonlight outside the city of Osaka. After working hard all day to sell their merchandise, they sat upon their bedrolls around the campfire counting the coins they had earned. On this day, as had happened upon many others, Akari had once again sold many more ribbons than his brother had sold knives. Akari's leather purse was full to overflowing while Gunzo's was still very nearly empty.

Tomorrow I will return to our village, Gunzo, to share my earnings with Mother and Father. Good night. And with that, Akari rolled over and went to sleep.

But Gunzo could not sleep. He stayed awake for several hours staring into the fire. He had seen the same firelight glinting over his younger brother's pile of coins. Now he could think of little else as his eyes drifted again and again to where Akari's purse lay just jutting out from under his pillow.

Is it my fault that I have not a beautiful voice? Gunzo thought to himself.

Mother and father will truly be so proud of you, Akari. Gunzo imagined the party his parents would throw for his brother, and the fine silk robes they would buy for him.

It's not fair. He thought. *It should have been me.*

And it was on this night, with a bright crescent moon shining down, that Gunzo rose up from the fire. Mad with jealousy over his brother's successes, Gunzo took his sharpest knife, slunk to where his brother was bedded, and firmly seized a handful of his brother's thick black hair.

Akari's eyes popped open in time to see the glint of the knife and the spite in Gunzo's eyes, but not in time to save his poor life as his brother was already sawing briskly at his throat. And through the spraying blood, the flailing limbs, and the final gurgled screams, Gunzo did not stop his sawing until he had completely severed Akari's head from his lifeless body.

The sun rose the next day to shine upon a desolate and sleepless Gunzo covered in his brother's blood still grasping the severed head in one hand and the gory knife in the other. His eyes grew wide with amazement gazing upon what he had done. It was only when the sun was high in the morning sky that Gunzo finally roused himself enough to wipe the carnage from his hands. Then, his first act in the new day was to empty his brother's purse into his own.

Gunzo buried his brother's body, head, and empty purse in a shallow grave below the embankment where they had slept by a thin river underneath a Mimosa tree. He washed himself in the river, packed his things, and thought to himself, *I can never return to our village now. Oh, brother, they will surely know what I have done. I will make a new life for myself in Osaka.*

And this is what Gunzo did. He went to Osaka and, with the coins from his brother's heavy purse, he purchased a pawn shop in a wealthy neighborhood. There he did brisk business for years and years becoming a very rich and successful merchant.

Gunzo never saw his birth village nor his parents ever again. He married, had children, and grew old enjoying his wealth and all the pleasures that vast sums of money can bring.

Still, somehow it was never enough. Gunzo was always jealous of those who had more than he. There was always someone richer, someone with a robe of finer silk or with a better pattern than his own. And Gunzo was often cruel to his wife, his children, and to others in the town. He was a spiteful man who only thought of himself.

He never thought of his dead brother. Ever.

Until one day, a very old woman entered Gunzo's shop. She was dirty and her robes were tattered. Gunzo was motioning for his oldest son to eject the peasant woman from his fine store until she placed a very intricately engraved and heavy wooden box upon the counter before him.

Her face was a mask of wrinkles caked in a fine white powder that gathered thickly at the corners of her eyes. *Shopkeeper, what'll ye give me for this fine treasure?* She asked as she opened the large box. She reached inside with both hands and produced a human skull of perfect translucent ivory which she carefully set down before Gunzo.

How morbid, said Gunzo. *What should I want with this disturbing object?*

The smooth bone of the skull glowed in a dull iridescence shining from a brow that was vaguely familiar, but…

Without answering, the old woman suddenly cried, *Sing Skull sing!*

And Gunzo's eyes grew large with great shock as the skull opened its ancient mandible to produce word for word the lovely song the short stout brother remembered well from his past: *Ribbons for all the pretty misses, so their boys will give them many tender kisses!*

Though Akari's skull no longer had a face or throat, his beautiful baritone voice was unchanged. When his song was done, the old woman firmly grasped the skull and placed it back in the box.

Gunzo was beside himself. He could not believe what he

had just witnessed. He glanced about the shop and was relieved to find it empty save for his son who was busy with inventory.

What'll ye give? the wrinkled old woman demanded again.

Without a word Gunzo placed 25 pieces of silver on the counter. The old woman shook her head, and he added five more silver pieces to the pile. With a smile the dirty old woman swept the coins into a pocket concealed in the sleeve of her threadbare robe and was gone without a word, never to be seen again.

A horrified Gunzo took the heavy wooden box and placed it on a dusty shelf in a corner of the back storeroom. There it sat for many years until Gunzo again had another opportunity to trade upon his brother's talents for his own benefit.

In his later years Gunzo had taken to gambling. He loved the excitement of it, and of course there was never enough money in the world to satisfy his lust. He often won and was considered to be very lucky by those with whom he played. His favorite opponent was Ichika Yui, the wealthy samurai who ruled over the entire province.

Ichika Yui had often lost bets to Gunzo and in the many hours the two had spent rolling dice or turning tiles he had looked deeply into his opponent's eyes. Ichika Yui saw Gunzo for what he was, a bitter, greedy and spiteful man. For this reason, the samurai had decided to no longer play games of chance with the wealthy shop owner.

However, Gunzo had other plans. In the same hours spent rolling dice and turning tiles with his opponent he had grown jealous of the samurai, and covetous of his kingdom.

Is it my fault that I was not born into a wealthy samurai family? He often asked himself. *It's not fair. It should have been me.*

And these were the very thoughts on his mind on the morning that Gunzo's fine carriage pulled up at the gates of

Ichika Yui's palace. Gunzo withdrew from the carriage and up the steps to his adversary's door carrying the finely engraved heavy wood box.

The short stout merchant found the samurai breakfasting within the palace on a sunny veranda. He placed the box before him, removed the skull, and placed it on a heavy mat upon the floor.

I have one final bet for you my dear Ichika Yui. I know you will not deny me this. I will bet you that I can make these dead bones come to life and sing for you.

Skeptically the samurai poked at the grinning alabaster cranium. But his curiosity was peaked. *What's the bet shopkeeper?*

If I can make the skull sing then you must gift your kingdom and all it contains to me.

The samurai was annoyed and distrustful of the merchant but he was also intrigued. He considered Gunzo's offer for several minutes before stating, *I shall take your bet. However, if your skull does not sing, I shall take your life.* He then placed a hand upon the razor sharp katana tucked into the silk sash at his waist.

It is a bet! cried Gunzo already savoring the vast wealth and power that was just within his reach.

Sing Skull sing! shrieked the greedy merchant, but his words were carried away by the wind and met with only silence. The skull did not make a sound.

Ichika Yui did not waste a moment. With one fluid motion visible only to the quickest eye, he drew his flashing sword and severed Gunzo's head from his thick frame.

And it was at the very moment that the merchant's head struck the floor sending a cascade of blood spraying out into the rays of the morning sun that the skull sang loudly in a beautiful baritone, *Ribbons for all the pretty misses, so their boys will give them many tender kisses!*

FORTY FOUR

NATIONAL ALERT OF IMMEDIATE IMPORTANCE TO ALL OPERATIVES

The following emails were intercepted in conjunction with operation ███████████ Operative Eldritch ███████████ several enemy states. ███████████

—Department Homeland Security NFUS

From: Eldritch666@glorious.intel
Date: Monday, July 15 ███ 3:12 p.m.
To: AGolosenko@svr.gov.ru
Subject: The time we spoke of has come (encrypted)

Alexei,

Your comrades in Russian Intelligence should have no problem unencrypting this message immediately, though with a little luck it will take our own agents here at the New Federal Union a good week should they intercept it. That leaves you and me one week to come to an agreement.

I will have possession of Dr. Abraha Tadese in the next few days.

Dr. Tadese is the genius behind Project Adam's Ale. Dr. Tadese is responsible for destroying and completely submerging the entire Adelphi Research Lab (ARLNTD) in Maryland in a matter of minutes. I am confident that you have an intelligence briefing on this extraordinary event. This man controls the secret of DIGITAL WATER.

As we discussed, I have grown tired of the petty arguments between Texas, California and the New Federal Union. I no longer have any alliances here. I have come to the realization that Dr. Tadese, along with all of his knowledge and skills, would be put to better use by a foreign power that would be more hospitable and generous to myself and the good doctor.

Of course, I thought of you immediately.

The two of us could be available for extradition along the California coast within the week.

Please contact me here using the same encryption with a proposal from the SVR. Time is of the essence.

-Eldritch

From: Eldritch666@glorious.intel
Date: Monday, July 15 ▮ 3:13 p.m.
To: FMChan@mss.gov.rs

Subject: The time we spoke of has come (encrypted)

Feng Mian Chan,

Your brothers with Chinese Intelligence should have no problem unencrypting this message immediately, though with a little luck it will take our own agents here at the New Federal Union a good week should they intercept it. That leaves you and me one week to come to an agreement.

I will have possession of Dr. Abraha Tadese in the next few days.

Dr. Tadese is the genius behind Project Adam's Ale. Dr. Tadese is responsible for destroying and completely submerging The entire Adelphi Research Lab (ARLNTD) in Maryland in a matter of minutes. I am confident that you have an intelligence briefing on this extraordinary event. This man controls the secret of DIGITAL WATER.

As we discussed, I have grown tired of the petty arguments between Texas, California and the New Federal Union. I no longer have any alliances here. I have come to the realization that Dr. Tadese, along with all of his knowledge and skills, would be put to better use by a foreign power that would be more hospitable and generous to myself and the good doctor.

Of course, I thought of you immediately.

The two of us could be available for extradition along the California coast within the week.

Please contact me here using the same encryption with a proposal from the MSS. Time is of the essence.

-Eldritch

From: Eldritch666@glorious.intel
Date: Monday, July 15 ▮ 3:14 p.m.
To: MAHAlavi@ministry.intelligence.iran.gov
Subject: The time we spoke of has come (encrypted)

Mahmoud Alavi,

Your brothers with Iranian Intelligence should have no problem unencrypting this message immediately, though with a little luck it will take our own agents here at the New Federal Union a good week should they intercept it. That leaves you and me one week to come to an agreement...

Operative Andrew Eldritch has gone rogue. Eldritch has stolen weaponry and technology from the New Federal Union and has threatened to sell state secrets abroad. He is considered a traitor and an enemy of the Union.

Directive: All agents be on the lookout for Eldritch. Subject is armed and dangerous. Shoot on sight. His termination is New Federal Union priority number one.

—Department Homeland Security NFUS

FORTY FIVE

The continued transcript of Johnny Depp's final
interview with Dr. Nathan Jensen's in Colorado
follows. Note Mr. Depp's interactions with Jack
Daniel Mero's clones. In retrospect further
surveillance would have been prudent. There is
no further evidence of Mr. Depp's whereabouts
subsequent to the conclusion of this interview. Mr.
Depp is believed deceased.

–Department Homeland Security NFUS

Yeah, the wine helps huh?

No, I'm not drunk, asshole.

Yes, there is a point to my story, I was just getting to that.
Like I said, the wine helps.

Dan and Jocelyn were my neighbors in Colorado for almost a year before I really felt like I got to know them. People
are always a bit standoffish with me. The old movie star who
gave up all the fame and money to become a hermit in Colorado... Does that sound like someone you'd want to be friends
with? Maybe. Maybe not.

It's mostly my fault though. I keep people at arm's length
because hey, people always want something from me. It's been
that way my whole life. People I have considered friends, family,
they always act like they love me, like they have my best interests at heart. But they don't, do they? Everyone is just looking
out for themselves. Everyone around me is thinking, "If I am

hanging with Johnny Depp good things are gonna come my way! I will be on TV! In a movie! His fame will rub off on me!" Everyone is just looking out for number one.

Dan and Jocelyn were different though. They didn't come here for me. Hell, I don't think Dan has even seen any of my movies. They just moved out to Colorado to get away from tough times in California. They just wanted to grow some really good weed on this beautiful little ranch, and when they met the old guy next door, it just so happened to turn out that he was famous a few years ago.

The most they want from me is a little help at harvest, some conversation, and to swap weed for wine, which is OK by me. They're not trying to get one over. They're my friends. Maybe the first real friends I have had since... I dunno, since my career started maybe.

When their daughter, little Sarah Joy, learned to walk last summer she started following me around. She calls me, "Uncle Johnny" which is pretty damn cute. My own kids and grandkids have pretty well given up on me. They have their own lives and their own problems. I only hear from them when they need something.

Little Sarah Joy is something else. All that curly brown hair, and dark eyes that are too big to be believed. Like a little pink Muppet, but too cute for TV. And what a personality. You would love her, Nate. Next time you visit, if the weather is better, I will walk you down to their ranch. She's really going to be something when she gets older, that little girl.

Dan and his clones are so very protective of her, which is understandable. But man, those five clones really confuse me. I still don't understand how those things work, or what the hell they think. I do know now that they love Sarah Joy. I wouldn't have thought they were capable of love, but I saw it with my own eyes. I almost died finding that out.

Last fall we had a mountain lion sniffing around the area. Dan saw him down by Big Thompson River one morning and one of my ranch hands found his tracks circling around the chicken coop. He was a big sucker too. Easily 200 pounds. We were all on high alert. I didn't go anywhere without my rifle for weeks.

Except that one morning. Isn't that always the case? The one time you really need something is the one time you don't have it with you. It was a clear cold mountain morning and I was coming down the hill from my ranch to see if I could bum a cup of coffee from Jocelyn. I had run out. Seems like we always have all the weed and wine we need, but never enough coffee.

Sarah Joy saw me coming down the path and ran out the front door to meet me. She came running up to give me a big hug, when I heard that deep growl. It was unworldly, like nothing else I had ever heard before. Made all the little hairs on the back of my neck stand straight up.

I was still holding Sarah and I turned around and there was that huge lion staring straight at us, tail weaving back and forth, back and forth. A tawny killing machine. Nothing but muscle, claws, teeth, and raw desire. Before I knew what was what, he was down in a crouch and ready to rush us. It was like time froze there for a second or two. I could see my life and Sarah Joy's life reflecting back at us in those black deadly eyes. What could I do? I wrapped my arms around Sarah Joy as tightly as I could and braced for the attack.

But the lion never reached us. Just as he sprang at us with teeth and claws bared and ready to shred, someone appeared out of nowhere right in the lion's path.

Guess who, Nate. Go on guess. Nah, you'll never.

At first the big brown figure was just a blur. A blur who took the entire brunt of the attack. The lion slashed him really good. Right across the face. Then, he was bear hugging that thing and wrestling it to the ground and punching it in the head over and over again with all his might. I mean, who wrestles a lion, right?

Sarah Joy was screaming and I picked her up and started to back away. I thought to myself, 'Oh my God, it's Dan and he is getting absolutely destroyed. His daughter is going to watch him die.' The lion's jaw was latched onto his shoulder and his hind legs were ripping and tearing at Dan's belly but the big man never stopped fighting back. Just punching and punching as if he felt no pain. They death rolled to the left and then they death rolled to the right, and then Dan was giving that beast everything he had but his own blood and chunks of his skin were just being flayed off of him by those vicious claws.

And then the lion was on top of him avoiding his punches, jaws agape and ready to strike. I remember thinking, 'Dammit, it's going to tear his face clean off.' And I was completely frozen. There was nothing I could do to help him. Not a damn thing.

I don't know who was screaming louder, Sarah Joy or me, but we were raising high hell and, who the hell was just getting mauled by that mountain lion down there in the dirt and the blood and the mud?

I know now it was one of those damn clones! I don't know where he came from or why he was alone. He must have been coming down from one of the greenhouses, but usually those big dopey clones always stick together.

But just as that mountain lion was about to end him, one clean shot rang out in the clear morning air. The report overpowered our screams, and that lion flopped down, still, on top of a bloody clone. They both lay there like dead weight and I could see half of the lion's head was gone.

Sarah Joy was latched onto me tight and I held her face into my shoulder so she couldn't see that horrific scene. I finally looked up and around to see who had taken the shot. It wasn't Dan and it wasn't Russel. It was Jocelyn standing on the porch holding Dan's rifle. Smoke was still curling out of the barrel as the report rolled out across our little valley and then echoed back to us like thunder off of Deer Mountain.

Little Jocelyn! Who would have thought she had it in her? Or that she would be such a good shot? She missed the clone entirely and hit that lion in the eye with one bullet! Then she dropped the rifle sobbing and ran straight over to us to cradle Sarah Joy in her arms. That's when Dan finally ran up, pistol in hand and breathing heavily. He kicked the already dead lion off of his torn and bloody clone who wasn't moving at all.

I have to admit, Nate, I kinda collapsed. I just sat down there in the dirt with the shock washing over me.

That clone was really badly cut up. He was in sorry shape. His brothers were there by then, gathered around him making that weird cooing noise they make and then they were helping Dan carry the scarred clone back to the house.

He almost died that night. He had lost a lot of blood and there was no clone doctor to call. Dan had to bandage him up the best he could and pray over him. That was the best anyone could do.

But Dan's prayers worked, and he recovered. A few days later he was trying to get up to go help his brothers on the farm. Jocelyn was so impressed with his saving little Sarah Joy and me, that she kept him at the house and waited on him hand and foot for a week. She cared for his wounds and made sure he stayed in bed resting. She even baked him a peach pie all for himself. You should've seen Scar eat that pie. That was the happiest I have ever seen him (if you can call a clone happy). Ha ha.

They started calling him Scar because that lion left him with a nasty scar across his face. He seems fine now, and because of that scar he always seems different from his brothers. He sticks out from the pack.

Now here is my big question, Nate, Why did he do it? If you had asked me before any of this happened, I would have said all five of those clones are probably consumed with selfish thoughts like an animal. 'How can I be more comfortable? Where can I get something else to eat? What can I do to please my master?' Certainly nothing more complicated than that.

But in that one instant, when a 200-pound mountain lion was rushing toward his master's daughter, that clone must have been thinking something. Something rather unselfish it would seem to me. The strangest thing to me is that while he was wrestling that beast, rolling around in the dirt with its teeth buried in his shoulder and him punching it over and over in the side of its head, he looked so different. I never saw him look so much like Dan before. In that instant, I wouldn't have been able to tell them apart. In fact, I thought it *was* Dan down there fighting that lion. I think I thought that right up until the real Dan ran up with his pistol.

And ever since then, Dan and Jocelyn have been a little kinder and more loving toward the Five. They upgraded their living quarters from that little feed shed next to the house to the loft in the big barn on the east side of the property. It's pretty far from the house, and up a steep hill, but they are more comfortable out there and the roof doesn't leak. Dan even built them bunk beds. They clothe them better too, and make sure they get bathed at least once a week. That's in everyone's best interests, to be honest. Those big boys can get pretty ripe.

Point is, those clones are a part of the family now. They started out as big dumb slavish brutes, but now they are more like Dan's mentally handicapped brothers. Especially Scar.

Lately, Dan, Jocelyn, and Sarah Joy have been feeling like family to me. I guess that means Scar and the other clones are family too. Is that weird or what?

Well, that's it for today, Nate. You come back in a few weeks and we will finish up.

Yeah, I am going to ride down the hill to talk to Russell and Dan before it gets too dark. There are only a few hours of daylight left, but I am worried about the river.

The rainy season has hit us hard these last few weeks. It has hardly let up from raining for almost 10 days now. This isn't your normal rain either. This is monsoon weather.

The good news is we got all the weed harvested and hanging in the dry sheds just in time. The bad news is that the Big Thompson River is getting bigger and bigger by the day and she is spreading out towards my vineyards pretty quick.

Dan's been busy because Scar and two other clones are pretty sick right now and holed up in the barn. I saw real worry in Dan's eyes when he told me. They are running a high fever and he's scared its pneumonia. That idiot doctor in town won't even look at them. He called the clones "unhuman abhorrent abortions of science." Idiot. Anyway, Dan's got no one to take them to. He has been tending to them himself.

I've been staying indoors mostly. I'm too old to be out in all that wet. But I still gotta get out for a quick ride today to check on the river and talk to Dan. The Big Thompson's got me worried. She was three feet higher yesterday, and if she bursts her banks, she could flood the whole valley. We could lose everything.

FORTY SIX

MARY WAS GLAD TO leave Trevor and his newfound family behind. They had definitely started to creep her out. She kneaded her wounded thigh and stretched and flexed the leg out as Dan drove the old truck away, the sunrise at their backs. The leg was still sore and stiff but was feeling better each day. Mary could feel the fight coming and she wanted to be ready.

Dan had not spoken for hours. The guy was usually pretty quiet, but today he was even less communicative than normal. He kept glancing at the rearview mirror. At first, she thought he was making sure they weren't being tailed, but he wasn't looking at the road behind them. He had the mirror focused on the back of the truck and the Five. Dan was probably just worried about his cargo, and what he might be able to get for them as they neared their destination. But Mary couldn't shake the feeling that he was expecting them to do something. She glanced over her should to where the clones slept in the back of the truck. All except Scar, whose eyes met her own in a stone, emotionless stare. Creepy.

Mary shuddered and tried to shake off the chill that swept over her. "It feels good to be back in California." She gazed out the window as the mountains disappeared and the suburbs of Sacramento started to form around them. She was talking just to talk. Dan did not reply.

In some areas acres and acres had been scorched by wildfires, then they would pass through other neighborhoods that were pristine and untouched.

"Before Calexit, I was a United States Marshall," she said and waited a moment to see if her partner would respond. Dan remained silent as a stone. "S.O.G. Special Operations Group. We chased terrorists and eliminated them. It was my job to execute people. Take 'em out. Don't get me wrong, these were real bad guys... I just..." Her voice faded away. Dan remained silent. The truck cruised past bulldozers tearing down the charred remains of a strip mall. An army of construction workers were putting up new frames for houses, rebuilding an entire neighborhood that had burned down.

"Then when California left the United States I had to decide between the New Federal Union and the Republic. It was an easy choice for me. All the Nationalist rhetoric and hate speech... California seemed so peaceful, so forward thinking. We didn't realize how hard it would be... The fires, the earthquake... We've had a tough couple of years."

They were nearing the remains of downtown Sacramento now, which had once been the capital of the State of California. The California Independent Republic's capital was Los Angeles now. Sacramento had been nearly obliterated by fire several years ago but the cleanup and rebuilding effort was in full swing. Everywhere Mary looked there were either new buildings going up or old charred ones coming down.

Mary checked her device again. Still no contact from Dr. Timm. She gave up trying to engage Dan in conversation.

It was so quiet for the next hour that she was shocked when Dan finally whispered, "How'd you get hooked up with the California Counterterrorism Agency?"

"CIRCA? They recruited me. Showed up at my door in San Diego right after Calexit." The rebirth of downtown Sacramento had already sped by. West of the city there were still ash heaps everywhere and the sky was a dull brown. Here and there shanty villages made of pallets and cardboard boxes had sprung up, but there was little sign of life.

"CIRCA gave me a good sales pitch. 'California is going to be a world leader and usher in a new era of peace! The New Fed's old rhetoric of closed borders and catering to the rich while screwing over the poor will get them nowhere! California is the future!' I bought it hook line and sinker."

"Doesn't sound like you're still buying it," Dan rasped.

"They needed me. I had already had special training as a spook, as Trevor put it. 10 months of Counter Assault Team paramilitary training changes a person. I was... I am a capable agent, that's exactly what CIRCA wanted. But California can't maintain the moral high ground without spooks like me doing the dirty work for them. I have done some jobs for California that I am not proud of, just like I did for U.S. Marshalls..."

Dan glanced sideways at Mary for the first time that day, she looked over and met his eyes with hers.

"I've got blood on my hands. Someone has to do the dirty work. That's what I was doing in Nevada when we met. Very dirty work. That's how I got assigned to this job."

Dan shook his head with a quick and subtle movement that Mary would have missed if she hadn't been trained to catch microexpressions.

"If this Abraha guy is so important, why didn't they send more agents?" Dan's voice sounded like old car tires rolling on gravel.

"Pffff." Mary exhaled sarcastically. "There are no other agents like me. No one does what I do. I'm the best."

They drove on in silence again, into the rich agricultural fields of the San Joaquin Valley. The sky cleared and became blue again. Mary rolled down her window to smell the green vegetation all around them.

"This is where I grew up," said Dan hoarsely. "Close by here. In Stockton. It's been almost three years, since I was last here."

"Stockton. That's where you said you were headed."

Dan nodded. "Before I got sidetracked with you."

"Why are you helping me? For the money?"

Dan paused, it seemed to Mary that he was searching for an answer and couldn't find one.

"Seemed like the right thing to do."

FORTY SEVEN

AS DAN'S OLD TRUCK RUMBLED on down Interstate 5 through the green fields of the San Joaquin Valley, Mary edged her thin frame toward the passenger door and rested her head against the glass window. Dan was silent as a stone again.

Tired from all the madness of the last few days, Mary drifted off toward sleep, but her mind was replaying old memories for her. Memories she had done her best to submerge and forget...

Ø Ø Ø

She was pressed against a row of lockers in a dark elementary school hallway. She could hear school children crying weakly through an open door at the end of the hall. The lights were out, but sunlight filtered through a high window above the rafters and reflected dully off of the cheap linoleum flooring at her feet. She wore black tactical body armor with the United States Marshalls star emblazoned over her pounding heart. She held a .40 caliber Glock in both hands, ready at her shoulder, pointed at the ceiling.

Across the hall, her partner Andrew grinned back at her. He was dressed identically in fatigues and armor. There was a boyish quality to his gleaming smile this morning. His long brown bangs covered his forehead and hung almost to his eyes. Her attraction to him was becoming a distraction.

They had been partners for almost a year, but had slept together for the first time the week before. It had been a drunken mistake, but also something that they had both needed to have happen. "Us hooking up was inescapable," he had told her confidently flashing that white smile. "I'm surprised you resisted my charm for as long as you did." Two attractive young people working so closely together. It happened.

And, today was their first active mission together since that night. They had been surveilling Mohammed Al Kahn for over a month. The Afghani bomb maker had reportedly designed a new bomb visually identical to a small cell phone. The device worked like a normal smart-phone, you could binge-watch Hulu on it, yet it remained powerful enough to blow an 8-foot round hole in the side of an airplane. Undetectable to airport security, the cell phone bomb was a game changer.

They had been closing in on Al Kahn on a busy Arlington street, but Mary had gotten too close and he had made her. Possibly he had seen her side arm under her jacket. In any event, before she was aware that her cover had been blown, Al Kahn had walked straight into the local public school. Now he was barricaded in a George Washington Elementary second grade classroom with 17 seven and eight-year-old children, a handgun, and a very powerful little bomb. Mary blamed herself.

The local swat team had arrived in force. Streets were blocked off, the rest of the school evacuated, and then it was a standoff. As the senior agent on the scene, Andrew had made the call, "You and I are going in Mary. We will take out the target. There is no other way." He was already strapping into his body armor.

"What about the kids?"

He just nodded. "Our primary objective is to eliminate the target as quickly as possible." When his eyes met hers, she looked away.

And now, he was silently signaling her in the hallway to

prepare to charge the classroom. She would take the hallway door and he would enter through the adjoining classroom that connected through a janitor's closet.

Mary took a deep breath and edged her way closer to the open door. She heard radio chatter from the police outside. She could still hear the children's stifled sobs. In her head she counted to three before swinging her body into the open doorway gun at the ready.

In the corner of the room stood Mohammed Al Kahn. He was surrounded by small unhappy children. He had strapped them all together in a ragtag web of red plastic ribbon. The ribbon had white lettering printed on it. "D.A.R.E TO BE DRUG FREE" over and over again. It was wrapped and tied around the children's necks and waists tightly, keeping them all pressed up against him.

Clutched to his chest the terrorist held a normal looking black cell phone in his right hand. Mary had her Glock aimed directly at his head. The head that Al Kahn was steadily shaking back and forth at her. He had a British accent, his voice a whisper, "Dead man's switch. If I drop this phone all these children die. Put your gun down."

Mary calculated the situation for a fraction of a second before releasing her handgun and placing it carefully on a small desk in front of her. "Let's talk about this," she said her voice calm and soft, as her training dictated. "No one needs to die today." The children whimpered. She could smell their fear and it smelled of stale urine. At least one of them had wet their pants.

Al Kahn pulled his left hand from his jacket pointing a pistol at her. "Allah Akbar," he whispered.

Just as his finger tightened on the trigger, the door to the janitor's closet burst open and Andrew Eldritch stormed the room firing directly into the crowded group of children. The side of Al Kahn's head dissolved into a red mist with a direct hit. Mary reached out her hand and screamed as the cellphone slipped from the dead man's grasp and the entire room exploded...

∅ ∅ ∅

Mary pulled herself up from the floor of the hallway where the explosion had thrown her. She could hear nothing but a dull ringing that vibrated her skull from within. Mary wiped at the dark matter splattered on her face, brain matter. A child's brain matter. A small piece of a tiny finger stuck to her body armor. Mary brushed it away and staggered back into the smoking classroom. Small dismembered bodies were everywhere. A little girl tried to crawl toward her but kept falling forward. She only had one arm. Several other children writhed on the floor. Dying.

Eldritch grabbed her arm and shook her. Shouting something she could not hear. Mary looked into his dark eyes. The boyish smile was gone. A bloody piece of red ribbon clung to the back of his hand. "D.A.R.E...."

Mary pulled away from his grasp, and stumbled back out into a hallway that was filling up with rushing police and paramedics. Eldritch grabbed her again. Mary spun around to meet him and punched him in the face with every ounce of energy she had left.

FORTY EIGHT

MARY AWOKE SWEATY and panting, immediately grasping the weapon under her jacket. She unsheathed the heavy pistol, aimed it at the floor and checked the load in the chamber before returning it to its hidden holster. Dan watched this from the corner of his eye but said nothing.

When the San Francisco Bay appeared before them, Dan broke his silence with an audible gasp. He hadn't seen the sea in years. He shook his head trying not to remember the deluge that had consumed his family. *All that water...*

Then, they were pulling into Berkeley. The sun was just going down over the Bay. In the distance San Francisco still smoldered, sending up faint trails of smoke from broken and crippled structures. The air in Berkeley, California was fresh and clear though. Stars began to appear overhead.

Mary was checking her device for the hundredth time that day. "Still no contact from Derek Timm. Got me concerned..." she wasn't really talking to Dan, but there was no one else there. "I hadn't planned on meeting him at his family home, but at this point there seems to be no other option..."

As Mary directed Dan to turn the old truck off of the freeway and into Dr. Timm's neighborhood, Dan immediately knew something was wrong. There was a police barricade and several fire trucks on the Timm's street. Helicopters swarmed overhead.

Dan's voice was heavy in his own ears. "This is no good."

They pulled up to the barricade where Mary flashed her device at the State Police Officer in charge. His face instantly registered his respect for the credentials of a high ranking CIR-

CA operative that he saw on her screen.

"What happened?" She asked.

"Car exploded. Two fatalities."

Mary ordered the Statie to let them through and as they circled around to the Timm residence. There, they found firefighters still spraying water on a fuming shell that had once been a car. A car that had been parked right in front of Dr. Derek Timm's home.

Mary hopped out of the truck, had a short conversation with another police officer and then limped up to the front door of the Timm house. She was back in the truck in a matter of moments.

"Dr. Timm is gone. The house was tossed. He's been taken."

"You sure he wasn't in there?" Dan nodded at the smoldering wreckage where firefighters had pulled out one charred body and were covering it with a sheet.

"Those were the CIRCA agents assigned to protect Timm," Mary was typing quickly into her device as she spoke.

"They did not do a good job," Dan responded.

"One of the neighbors swore she heard a drone. It was a missile attack."

Dan thought about this. "How do you fight drones?"

"The trick is to see them first. These agents probably didn't even know there was a drone in the area. The best strategy is to draw a drone's fire first, so you can triangulate their position and take them out."

"That didn't work for these guys."

"No, it didn't." Mary was still working at her small black tablet. "Dr. Timm had an encrypted device that he used to contact Dr. Tadese and me as well. Whoever grabbed him up must have taken it. He was probably still waiting for Dr. Tadese to contact him and set up a meeting place. The last time he contacted me he reported that Tadese was in Nebraska. That would put Tadese in California... tomorrow morning? The device is powered down right now. Once they turn it back on we should be able to locate it and find Derek Timm. Hopefully, that means Tadese as well."

"Then there is going to be a fight?" Dan checked the load in his pistol and placed it on the dashboard.

"Yes. There is going to be a fight in the morning. Let's find a place to get some rest for the night."

In the back of the truck, the clones waited silently.

FORTY NINE

SHIN HAD TAKEN OVER the wheel of the old station wagon while Abraha slept in the back seat. The two doctors had been driving for almost 48 hours straight. Shin's eyes were bloodshot and he could no longer find a comfortable position to sit in no matter how much he shifted around in the tight cab. The good news was that they had met with zero resistance as they neared the California Independent Republic.

CIRCA had provided them directions via the encrypted tablet through a series of back roads and old highways. A slower route but a safer one. Tonight, they were attempting to enter California far south of the Reno blockade on an unmarked road over Mammoth Mountain.

Shin was moving the Mercedes at a crawl over a gravel path that was barely a road. It was a clear night with a bright half moon and stars hanging overhead. The moon's rays filtered through the black, like beams of light rippling through deep, dark water. Shin felt like he was swimming for his life, again.

Abraha screamed and sat bolt upright in the back seat. Shin slammed on the brakes causing the old car to slide in the gravel and come to a dusty stop in the middle of the darkness. He turned to find his friend panting, sweating, and staring back at him with hollow eyes. There was not another soul around for miles.

"Bad dream?" Shin asked.

Abraha could only nod his head in the affirmative. He seemed unable to speak, as if he couldn't summon the strength.

Illumination filled the interior of the car as the CIRCA

tablet lit up.

...

...

Incoming call...

...

...

The clock in the corner showed that the time was 3:03 AM. Shin shut off the engine, and the black night was still all around them.

"I thought we were supposed to initiate the next contact," Shin reflected. "Should I answer it?"

Abraha nodded again, still breathing heavily.

When he did, the face that filled the screen was not that of Derek Timm. It was a thin cruel face crowned with a short black cowboy hat.

"Dr. Abraha Tadese I presume?" The face twisted into a false emotionless smile, but stared only at the torn roof liner of the Mercedes as Shin held the device so it would not view their faces. He looked to Ab who nodded at him.

"Where is Dr. Timm?"

The brow under the hat furrowed, "You don't sound like Dr. Tadese."

"Where is Dr. Timm?" Shin repeated.

"He is here with me. Waiting for Dr. Tadese. He sends his regards."

The screen moved from the thin dispassionate face to that of Derek Timm's. He had been severely beaten. One of his eyes was purple and swollen shut. Blood was caked about his nose and mouth. He grunted a murmur despite what appeared to be a leather belt strapped tightly through his open mouth.

The face of Andrew Eldritch reappeared. "Where is Dr. Tadese?"

Shin looked back to Abraha who finally spoke, though his voice was shaky, "I'm here. Please don't hurt Derek. We will do as you say."

The cruel smile returned on the screen. "I certainly hope you will, for your friend's sake. We are in the city of Stockton, California waiting for you, Doctor. I will send the coordinates. I imagine we will be seeing you in a few hours. Drive safely gentlemen."

The tablet went dark.

FIFTY

MARY AND DAN PULLED the truck in behind an abandoned building that had once been a Starbucks. Real coffee had become such an expensive commodity after Calexit that Republic citizens could not afford the extravagance of a Frappuccino anymore.

"Don't you have a field office with a couch, or a Republic credit card for a hotel room?" Dan was not relishing passing the night in a dark alley.

"Shush. We are flying dark. If Eldritch powers up Dr. Timm's device one more time, I will be able to triangulate his location. We may need to be on the road at a moment's notice." Mary remained intent on her tablet.

Dan let himself out of the cab of the truck to check on the Five crouched in the back. The alley they had stopped in had recently been shelter to a group of homeless refugees, probably from the city. The remains of a cardboard shelter sagged, propped up between two overfilled dumpsters. The pungent smell of urine was everywhere.

Dan opened the tailgate and sat down heavily. His clones scurried out of the bed of the truck to stretch their legs and look about curiously. All but one.

Scar sat down next to Dan on the tailgate with a sigh.

Dan stared at his scarred twin sitting next to him in disbelief. The stories, they had to have been dreams right? *Scar isn't sentient. He isn't capable of rational thought...* His mouth fell open a bit.

Scar spoke in a whisper so that Mary, busy inside the cab, was unable to hear, "Dan, Dan, Dan. Let's take a short walk OK?"

The other four clones, who were milling about, suddenly looked back and forth at each other and nodded in unison that this was a very good idea.

Dan punched himself hard in the leg to assure himself of the reality of his surroundings. This all certainly seemed real.

"I'm going to walk these guys around the block," he found himself shouting hoarsely in Mary's direction.

"Don't go far," she replied. "We need to be on the road at a moment's notice."

As the six tall identical figures walked through the cool Berkeley night no one spoke. They were in what had once been a retail shopping area, but most of the stores were boarded up and abandoned now.

Scar spoke in Dan's voice. All Dan could do was walk slowly down the sidewalk with the Five and listen.

Scar said, "Dan, I have one last story for you, and it is one you already know. It is a story of great sacrifice and greater love.

"Dan, it was not so long ago that we were all working together on the farm in Colorado. All seven of us, until there were only six, side by side, growing and harvesting medicine."

Dan could only nod as the strange group plodded slowly along the deserted street together.

"To what end, Dan? Why did we toil day after day? You know why, Dan. It was because of love. Our love. Our love for Jocelyn and Sarah Joy. You would have given anything for them. We would have too."

The other four nodded silently. A single tear slid down Dan's brown cheek.

"And why have I been telling you these stories at night Dan? Stories about selfish men who wanted to buy love and came to bad ends. Men who chased what they couldn't or shouldn't have because of their greed."

The other four shook their heads in unison.

"Do you remember the day the mountain lion attacked Johnny and Sarah?" Scar's voice was rough with impossible emotion. Thick with the pain that they all felt together. "Do you remember when I fought the lion for them? I fought it for as long as I could until Jocelyn came and shot it. Remember? I saved Sarah Joy, and Jocelyn saved me. That's love.

"The day of the flood Dan…" Scar broke off overcome with emotion, then took a deep breath and continued on.

"The day of the flood you were helping we Five. I was sick, nearly dying, so were these two." Two of the hulking clones lifted their chins silently in recognition.

"You stayed with us in the barn, when you could have been with your family. You were helping us and it was storming and… there were all those cases of wine in the barn from Johnny's vineyard… You were drinking Dan and you didn't want Jocelyn to know. You could have gone home to your family that night but you passed out, taking care of us and drinking and… and you hate yourself for that. You hate us for that."

Dan had given up trying to hold back his tears. He shook his head in denial of Scar's words, but his heart accepted them and their truth.

"Dan, it's not your fault. If you had been with Johnny and Jocelyn and Sarah on the day of the flood, you would have been trapped in that attic too. You'd be dead too, Dan! There was nothing you could have done. Yes, you made a mistake and you got drunk, but you're not one of those evil men chasing after what you can't have. You are a good man, Dan.

"Let me tell you one more story, Dan. One more. It's not a story you're going to want to hear, but it's one you need to hear, Dan."

FIFTY ONE

SCAR SPOKE SOFTLY AND steadily as the darkness of the deserted street corner gathered around the six separate souls who were one.

Johnny Depp said goodbye to his old buddy Nate and waved as his car rambled off into the rain. Then he saddled up Ol' Tessie. She wasn't too happy about heading out into all that rain and was moving pretty slow. By the time he got to the bottom of the hill the road that lay between Russell's property and his own was a river four or five feet deep and eight feet across. It was growing by the minute.

A lot of people don't know that monsoons happen in Colorado but they do. Big ones, too. It was raining so hard that Johnny couldn't see where he was going from up in the saddle. He had to get down and lead Tessie across the flooded road. They almost didn't make it. Johnny took a slip in the middle of that deluge. He would have lost his footing and been swept away if he hadn't been holding fast to Tessie's reins. And that was just trying to cross the road.

But all that rain wasn't just pouring down on Johnny and Tessie. It was pouring down into the mountains above them too. All that water had to go somewhere and the valley was filling up quick.

When he got to Russell's ranch house, Johnny coaxed Tessie right up the stairs and onto the covered deck that wrapped around the house. She wasn't too excited about it, but they were both soaked and she was content to be out of the rain for the moment. The muddy water was already swirling over the road and into the front yard of the house.

Johnny shook the water off the best he could and went in the front door. It was dark inside, but he found Jocelyn and Sarah Joy right away. They were wrapped up in each other's arms and a big wooly blanket on the couch. The old man could tell right away that Jocelyn was scared, but she was trying to make out like she wasn't for Sarah Joy's sake.

"Where're your Uncle Russell and Dan?" was the first thing he asked.

"Russell took the truck into Loveland looking for antibiotics. The Five are pretty sick. Dan is up there at the barn with them now. How bad is it out there Johnny?"

"It's fine, it's fine," he told her trying to sound sure of himself. "Just a bad storm. Nothing to worry about. Why don't you have a fire lit?"

"Water came down the chimney and it's a wet soupy mess in there. I couldn't get anything to light."

Johnny moved over to the fireplace where he could smell the damp cold ashes. Water was still coming down the chimney in a thin stream and black ashy water had started trickling down from the hearth and onto the hardwood of the living room floor.

On the dining room table, he found an oil lamp and some matches to light it with so he could see better. Jocelyn had baked a cake the day before and there was still a piece on a clear glass stand with a glass dome over it. They had promised to save him some.

Johnny held the lantern up high and stuck his tongue out at Sarah Joy trying to lighten the mood. She smiled from under the blanket, but just a bit.

"Uncle Johnny, is it gonna stop raining?" she asked in her quizzically intelligent little voice.

"Of course, Sweetheart. And if it doesn't you don't have to worry 'cause Uncle Johnny is going to build you an ark."

"What's an ark?"

He didn't have the chance to answer her because Tessie was braying loudly and making a fuss out on the deck. Johnny took the lantern out with him to check on her. The sun was probably still up at that time, but you never would have known it. The sky was a black ocean pouring itself down.

Right away he could see what was making Tessie nervous. The water had risen at least four or five feet just in the few minutes he had been inside. The swirling black torrent had buried the steps up to the house and was lapping at the boardwalks of the deck where the old horse stood.

Johnny moved to pat Tessie's head and try to calm her, but he could see the water moving along the porch toward them inch by inch. Suddenly the black was split in half by a white hot flash of lightening. A second later thunder rumbled out across the valley, echoed against Deer Mountain and then rumbled back. Inside the house he could hear Sarah Joy starting to cry.

"Good luck old girl," Johnny told Tessie while untying her from the railing and unstrapping her saddle. He wanted desperately to do something for her, but he had Jocelyn and Sarah Joy to worry about. He knew you were out at the barn, Dan, and there was no way you could make it back to the house through the deluge. The barn was too far from the house. The water had risen too high. The barn was on higher ground so he was hoping you would be alright there. He even said to himself, 'Don't worry Dan. I will watch after your family.' He did.

But, Tessie was neighing nervously again as he reentered the house, and Jocelyn was trying to calm Sarah Joy down.

"I think it's best that we move up to the attic," he told them trying to sound calm. "We'll be safe up there."

Jocelyn moved to the hallway and pulled at the chain that released the folding steps that led up to the attic. They could all see the water pouring into the house from under the front door now. Not slowly either. Johnny couldn't hear Tessie anymore. The only thing any of them could hear was the torrential downpour of water breaking against the roof.

"Let's get up!" Johnny shouted to the frightened girls.

Sarah Joy climbed slowly and carefully up first with her Mama right behind her reassuring her loudly over the storm. "It's alright, Baby. It's alright. One step at a time. There you go."

Dirty brown water had started swirling around Johnny's ankles. He could see papers from Uncle Russell's desk floating in the murky waves by the light of the lantern he held up for the girls. He never had any idea water could rise that fast. It seemed like all the water in the world was coming down in one place at one time.

The attic was small, cramped, and windowless. They crouched there, unable to stand, with shoulders rubbing against the rough wooden beams. Over those beams, the only thing protecting them from the storm was a layer of plywood and then a layer of wooden shingles. It was dry up there, but musty and confined.

Confined. It was there stooping amidst the old dusty boxes marked "Christmas Ornaments- HO HO HO" that Johnny realized his mistake. A huge mistake Johnny! He realized, if the water kept rising, there would be no escape from this room. No windows. No doors besides the one they had just crawled up through.

Johnny went back to the trap door and held the lantern down into the hallway of the flooded house. The water was half way up the folding stairs. He waited and watched counting slowly to thirty. The water had climbed about six inches in thirty seconds. It was rising a foot a minute.

Jocelyn and Sarah Joy were hunkered down by a stack of boxes all similarly marked "JD's Records". They had brought the blanket up with them and were wrapped tightly inside together with only their faces poking out. Johnny didn't know what to say.

"Well at least we are dry up here!" He was trying to sound cheery, but a reverberating crack of thunder elicited another scream from Sarah Joy followed by more sobbing.

"Hush, Baby, hush." Jocelyn did her best to comfort the scared child but the fear in her own voice was audible.

Then, he became aware of another soft sound underneath the onslaught of the rain on the roof all around them. A muffled churning was becoming louder. A quiet repercussion that sounded almost like a boat nearby!

Jocelyn and Johnny looked at each other eyes bright with hope for a moment.

Then, he held the lamp down to the floor. They both realized there was no boat. What they were hearing was the sound of the water beating against the floorboards of the attic. They could then feel the swells against the boards under their feet. Jocelyn shook her head and buried her face into Sarah Joy's hair.

They were both crying softly now, and Johnny had no words of comfort left. The space around them suddenly seemed suffocating. The air was vanishing around them as water started to leak through the cracks in the attic flooring.

And as the water swirled around his feet, Johnny took the sobbing Sarah Joy in his arms and stood where the roofing was tallest, at its peak. Jocelyn moved in tightly against him holding the lantern. The cold dark water was reaching shin level.

"Johnny, what are we going to do? Oh, Dan, where's Dan?"

"We're OK!" He shouted over the storm. "Everything's OK!"

Johnny began punching at the plywood between two beams.

BAM. BAM. BAM.

He kept punching and punching with bloody knuckles. Johnny always had been a fighter. That's one thing they always said about Johnny Depp. Love him or hate him, the guy was a fighter. The water was almost to his waist.

BAM. BAM. BAM. CRACK!

The pain shot all the way from his knuckles to the soles of his soaked boots. Johnny had broken his hand.

He shifted the sobbing Sarah Joy from one arm to the other holding her tightly against his chest with his broken right hand. Then he started punching the wood again with his left.

BAM. BAM. BAM. More bloody knuckles. The water had risen to chest level.

"Johnny, what are we going to do?" He could barely hear Jocelyn anymore. She sounded far away.

Johnny held Sarah Joy close to his heart as the water continued to rise.

BAM. BAM. BAM. A fighter, they said.

FIFTY TWO

DAN WAS OPENLY SOBBING now as were two of the other four. Only Scar kept his composure as he continued on with his story.

"And you won't forgive yourself, Dan, because you were passed out drunk in the barn loft. But listen to me, Dan! The drinking doesn't matter. If you had been sober, it wouldn't have made a bit of difference. We still couldn't have made it to the house. And we had no idea they were in trouble. We were trapped up in that barn with you for four days, Dan. Surrounded by water, starving hungry. No idea where Jocelyn and Sarah Joy were or if they were safe or not. Those were hard days, but not the hardest.

"Because when the rain finally stopped, and when the water finally receded enough so that we could get out of that barn, we were with you, Dan. We didn't care about our empty bellies, or your empty bottles. We didn't think about ourselves; we all only thought about Jocelyn and Sarah Joy.

"But they weren't in the house," Scar's voice grew hoarse and thick again. "The house was practically destroyed, full of mud. They weren't at Johnny's house. The flood trashed his place too. No one thought to look in the attic until that afternoon. Do you remember?

"It's hard to remember. It's hard to think about. They had already been gone for days, their physical forms floating in that dirty water for days. And we never found little Sarah Joy. She was..." Scar looked away from the others toward the sky. "Only Johnny and Jocelyn were left after the flood. Johnny, with two broken hands. Now you know why.

"And who carried them down? Who covered their remains and laid them out? We did. All six of us. The ground was still too soaked with water to dig graves. We sat in the house with them for two more days until the wood dried out enough for a funeral pyre. We six, just sitting and waiting, with Johnny, and Jocelyn, and little Sarah Joy's white dress. That was all we had left of her. Then we sat in silence for two days. Those were the hardest days, Dan. The hardest."

The six stood close together in the darkness. Dan and the other four were weeping and covering their faces with their hands in a manner that was all too similar. Scar reached out and put a hand on Dan's shoulder.

"It wasn't your fault, Dan. You need to lay this burden down now. You have carried it long enough. We Five love you. We are you, and you are us. We all loved our family. We are heartbroken as one in their passing, but there is nothing we could have done. Man does not control his fate, Dan. A man's character is his fate."

Through the blur of his tears, Dan thought he saw a little blonde girl in a white dress padding barefoot down the sidewalk away from them. He raised a hand to try and stop her, but she was gone...

All six came together then. For the first time in their existence the six hugged each other. Each sobbing in the loss of love. Each sobbing in sacrifice, and in the love of one another.

After a soft quiet moment, they came apart again each wiping at eyes and noses and gulping back the communal tears. Dan glanced from one to another of the Five in the realization that this was actually happening. As unbelievable as it was, he was immersed in reality.

Scar spoke once more. "Now, the time has come for me to make a sacrifice for you, Dan. It's not hard for me to do. I love you. I want to do it. The hard part is going to be you letting me to do it. I need you to let me do it, Dan. Can you do that for me? Can you do it for Jocelyn and Sarah Joy? Promise me that you will."

Dan could only nod.

And Scar, satisfied with his final story, nodded back. Then he never said another word ever again.

Suddenly, Mary was bounding around the corner. 'They activated the device! We need to move! They're in Stockton!"

Stockton? The name of Dan's hometown reverberated in his mind.

"Let's go! Come on, Dan! It's time for you to go home!"

FIFTY THREE

AS ALWAYS, Eldritch knew well in advance the perfect place for his final showdown with Mary. An hour outside of Berkeley was the city of Stockton. Downtown Stockton, once a bustling business community, was now mostly abandoned.

The city was built at the edge of the freshwater delta, and the Port Of Stockton had once been a busy harbor for ships from all over the world. Now mostly unused and desolate, downtown Stockton was a ghost town.

In the deserted heart of the inner-city was what had one time been a shining jewel of a destination. The Stockton Children's Museum.

Set in a refurbished warehouse in the industrial district near the Port, the Children's Museum now sat dusty and empty. Its entrance was guarded by two tin soldiers who stood over thirty feet tall in blue and red uniforms, now sun-scorched and fading from grandeur. One of the giant toys held a once golden bugle to its lips, the other was a drummer. Both wore tall cylindrical hats which were flat at the top. The perfect place to park an armed drone.

It was 2:00 in the morning when Eldritch cut the power to the building and broke in through a rear entrance. It seemed no one had been inside the building for years. The air was stale and dank, devoid of all movement save for the rustling of rats up in the rafters.

Eldritch opened the back of his van where Derek Timm lay bound, gagged, and bleeding. Though Derek was not a small man, Eldritch easily hefted him into a fireman's carry. Derek moaned softly as his solar plexus hit Eldritch's sharp shoulder. Eldritch punched him hard in the head, cursed him and told him to be quiet. Then, he grabbed an electric lantern with his free hand and carried his prisoner inside the old building.

The interior of the museum was a maze of grimy attractions that had probably once been very exciting to the children of Stockton. There was a police car, a helicopter, a fire engine, and a mock supermarket where kids could fill carts with plastic fruit. Heavy tin cans lined the dusty shelves marked with now fading labels that read, "Whole Sweet Corn".

Eldritch worked quickly and concisely, wasting no time. He carried the half-conscious Derek to the helicopter. Derek's hands and feet were bound with plastic zip ties so tightly they cut into his flesh and his hands were turning purple. A belt was bound tightly around his skull leaving his mouth open, and his teeth and tongue pressed against the leather.

As Eldritch dropped him into the front seat of the helicopter, he moaned softly again. Eldritch leaned back and viciously kicked Derek twice in his side eliciting soft sobs from his bloody victim.

"I don't want to hear a sound from you. You get me? Not a sound. If I hear you breathe, I will stop your breathing. You get me?"

Derek managed a slight nod and Eldritch strapped him into the pilot's seat with its dusty heavy safety belt buckles.

$\varnothing \varnothing \varnothing$

Eldritch placed the lantern on a large plastic table in what had once been the Children's Reading Room. All the bookshelves were empty now and the patterned purple and yellow carpet was musty and moldy.

He turned and strode back to the van at the back of the building, his black duster brushing against his long legs. From the back of the van he retrieved two heavy black plastic suitcases which he placed inside next to his lantern, then returned once more to the van for his short barreled assault rifle and another flashlight before locking it shut and barricading the back door of the museum.

It was 3:03 A.M. and he powered up the encrypted device he had stolen along with Derek. He held the device up to Derek's thumb and it unlocked itself instantly. There was only one contact listed, AT, Abraha Tadese.

"I'm going to leave this on, Dr. Timm. I know you're in deep with CIRCA. Agent 'Sister Mary' will be coming for you. They call her that, on account of her *morals*, you know." Eldritch scoffed at the word. "But let me tell you something. Her morality is just a front. She has done some ugly, and quite frankly, wicked work in the name of her beloved California.

"She should be zeroing in on your device right now from Berkeley which gives us about an hour or two...

"I have an old score to settle with her, and with a little luck she will be arriving at the same time as your friend Dr. Tadese. She probably won't even ask for backup. She will want to take me out herself. Oh, the arrogance of that woman. I know her well."

Derek's left eye was completely swollen shut, but Eldritch was aware that his captive was watching him through the right. He knew that Derek was waiting for him to make a mistake. *He doesn't realize, Andrew Eldritch doesn't make mistakes.*

"Watching me blow Mary and her Mexican friends into charred pieces of waste should put the fear of God into the good doctor. That way I can be sure I won't have any problems with him in the future."

Eldritch removed his long black duster to reveal equally black army fatigues. He dropped his hand down to check the automatic pistol that was strapped to his thigh, then thoughtfully caressed the long black knife that was sheathed at his chest. Both were secure and ready.

By the light of the lantern in the children's reading room, he opened his heavy black cases and started assembling the first of two Autonomous Hanwha Systems Unmanned Aerial Combat Vehicle MQ-9 Reapers. He mounted the four heavy Red-Widow missiles to the deadly machine before powering up the laptop that accompanied it.

Eldritch then moved with care and speed past the large defunct helicopter where Derek was secured, and toward the double front doors of the building. He kicked the doors open, sending a plume of dust out into the warm Stockton night. He glanced up at the towering tin soldiers above him before returning to his laptop.

"Operation of an autonomous drone couldn't be simpler, Dr. Timm. Just fire her up and the Reaper scans her own surroundings."

With a few taps at the keyboard the four rotors of the squat black helicopter engaged and it buzzed to life hovering a few inches above the surface of the colorful table and rotating a complete 360 degrees, sweeping the interior of the building with its high definition camera, infrared and thermal imaging scopes. Everything it registered appeared on the laptop screen before Eldritch.

"Now we scan me and register me as a friendly."

With a few more taps the drone turned its camera on Eldritch and the laptop screen flashed green.

"We don't want to accidentally blow ourselves up now, do we? The drone pivoted on its horizontal axis and began to scan

Eldritch's captive. "You on the other hand, Dr. Timm, well I wouldn't call you a friend. You're being registered as a non-vital entity. The drone won't seek you out for elimination, but it won't actively avoid killing you either. For lack of better words, it doesn't give a good goddam about you. Sorry."

A few more clicks and the drone buzzed up and into the darkness of the building to further scan its surroundings as it explored the maze of clutter and high raftered ceilings.

"I like this spot, because it is pretty well deserted. No one around for miles. Also, we have the water directly behind us, so there is only one way in and one way out. Your friend Sister Mary's partner grew up in this shithole town. I think that's another benefit for us, throw him off his game..."

A few more taps of the keyboard and the armed drone guided itself out of the open front doors of the building. Eldritch directed it straight up watching the uniform and then the face of the giant tin soldier spin down the laptop screen until the drone came to rest on the bugler's hat 35 feet above the empty parking lot. A crow's nest view of the museum entrance, as well as blocks and blocks of downtown Stockton were transmitted to Eldritch's screen.

"Now, let's test those motion detectors."

A few more taps and the drone's HD camera zoomed in on tree leaves blowing in the wind two blocks away then quickly to a small field mouse scurrying past a dumpster, registering movement in 18 separate places.

...

No threat detected

...

Flashed on the screen as the camera moved to focus on each detected movement.

"And we have our choice of several settings here..." Eldritch mused. "We can set Reaper One to recon, we can assign it a target, or my favorite, 'Havoc Mode' in which the Reaper just targets every life form in sight and causes as much destruction and chaos as it possibly can. Let's save that one for later shall we?"

Eldritch picked up his squat heavy assault rifle and moved back to Derek Timm. He popped the banana clip from his weapon and examined it to make sure it was fully loaded with shiny brass bullets. He then reinserted it and chambered a round before pressing the short barrel to the doctor's battered temple. Derek did not make a sound.

"Now we just sit back and wait for someone to show up. Pretty boring, Dr. Timm." He poked the gun at the side of Derek's head hard enough to draw another speck of blood. "What am I going to do to amuse myself in the meantime?"

Derek grimaced and braced himself for what would come next, when a soft buzzing from Eldritch's pocket stole his attention. The assassin removed his black device from his pocket.

"Well, well, well... Looks like the monetary offers on your friend Tadese are rolling in..." The soft glow from the tablet lit the assassin's sharp features as a wide toothy grin crossed his face.

"Dr. Tadese is in high demand..."

Eldritch watched as Derek Timm fought a losing battle with consciousness, then Eldritch shifted his focus to sending counteroffers to China, Iran, and the Russians.

Ø Ø Ø

Eldritch's laptop buzzed a warning sound as the screen blinked red. Dan's truck had just pulled into the parking lot.

"Here already?" Eldritch asked no one in particular.

Dan emerged alone from the truck with his pistol drawn. His digital thermal image was bright yellow and red on the laptop screen.

...

Engage target Y/N

...

"Shall we wait for dear Sister Mary?" Eldritch considered the second suitcase on the table.

"Why wait?" He tapped the Y key sending the Reaper into immediate motion. He then set the laptop down and began opening the second case in order to begin assembly of another drone.

FIFTY FOUR

AS ELDRITCH BOLTED THE rotors of Reaper Two into place, he kept one eye on the flashing laptop screen.

Reaper One had shot up from its perch on the hat of the tin toy colossus, and then quickly lowered itself down toward the museum parking lot. Dan's colorful thermal image stood its ground pistol in hand next to the truck.

Eldritch carefully removed a Red-Widow missile from its foam packaging at the top of the crate and mounted it to the rails at the side of the drone.

The first Reaper paused for only a second to thoroughly scan the truck and the rest of the parking lot for other movement or thermal images. Finding none, it centered back on its target.

Eldritch was carefully snapping the second missile into place when the explosion rocked the building shaking dust from the rafters. Plastic bananas rattled to the floor from their encrusted supermarket shelves.

Eldritch stopped to regard the laptop screen. The drone's thermal imager was focused broadly on a fiery red and orange ball of destruction where Dan and his truck had been a moment before.

. . .

Target eliminated

...

Outside, the fire blazed in the night illuminating the dirty deserted parking lot. A plume of smoke in the shape of a mushroom rose into the night sky. Dan's truck had been pushed over onto its side by the explosion, and all that was left was a sagging red-hot frame melting into the pavement.

Inside the museum Eldritch could hear the fire crackling and popping as he moved to finish assembling the second drone.

Then a sudden CRACK ripped through the night. The laptop screen blinked red.

...

Reaper One connection lost

...

There was a loud crash and a second explosion rocked the building throwing Eldritch to the ground.

Reaper One had fallen from the sky over the outdoor patio and play area where children had once eaten their lunches. The remaining three missiles, still mounted to the drone, exploded on impact with the ground, sending tremors throughout the whole neighborhood and leaving burning chunks of the west wall of the museum flying through the air. Fire was everywhere.

Eldritch pulled himself up and brushed the plaster dust from his fatigues. He checked on the second Reaper to make sure it was undamaged, then turned to the laptop to make sure it had established a connection with the second drone. Before he powered it up, Eldritch withdrew the long deadly knife sheathed at his chest with his left hand, while clasping the rifle in his right. He moved to the large helicopter where he unstrapped Derek Timm and cut the zip tie at his ankles before returning the knife to its sheath.

"Get up." He commanded the beaten and bruised man. Derek tried to rise but stumbled and fell; his feet dead with lack of circulation. Smoke was quickly filing the room. Eldritch pulled Derek to his feet and then briskly slapped him twice across the face.

"You will get up and you will walk."

Andrew Eldritch doesn't make mistakes.

FIFTY FIVE

DAN CREPT UP TO THE SIDE of the burning building with four of the Five following him from shadow to shadow. The sun was coming up. Fire flickered and popped from the two huge explosions that had rocked the entire city. Next to the abandoned Children's Museum, where the outdoor playground had been, there was a swirling tornado of heat and fire at least 20 feet tall.

The explosion had torn a huge hole in the side of the museum and knocked the fencing down. That's where Dan was heading. *Straight into a burning building. Great idea,* he thought to himself. The adrenaline pounding and pumping through his veins brought back the youthful memories of his skinhead days right here in Stockton. *Not too different from fighting Nazi Punks,* he thought. *Except Nazi Punks don't usually fight with military explosives.*

Dan was trying not to think about Scar or the explosion that had taken his life. Scar's sacrifice had been every bit as painful to watch as Dan knew it would be. The other four had made a sort of howling noise in unison the second the truck had exploded. He had never heard anything like it before. His clones had done many things he had never witnessed before in the past few days. Dan didn't have time to stop and consider how or why. Nor did he have time to mourn Scar.

Dan and the remaining four had been waiting down the block, and out of the line of sight from the museum, where Scar had dropped them off. The quintuplets had been crouched behind a dumpster as Scar had pulled the truck up into the Museum parking lot. They had already known what to expect.

Dan and his clones watched Scar exit the truck with Dan's pistol in hand. They had watched as he stood tall, firm, and brave waiting for his own destruction.

Ø Ø Ø

Mary had been positioned on the roof of the old court-house 400 meters to the North with a high-powered rifle wait-ing for Scar to draw the Reaper's fire. As Scar was being swal-lowed deep within his fiery demise she was locating the black drone in the dim morning light and sighting in on its position near the giant tin soldier. Mary quickly took out the left rear rotor with her first shot, sending the deadly little machine into a tailspin that ended in the huge explosion that tore the west side of the museum wide open.

Then, Mary was on her feet, limping down the fire escape at the side of the building as quickly as her wounded leg would allow her.

Ø Ø Ø

Dan rushed past the spinning vortex of fire and smoke, keeping as much distance between the inferno and himself as possible. Thick beads of sweat streamed from his brow and the heat rained down on him. His flannel shirt was soaked, but at least it was providing his flesh some protection from the abut-ting fire.

As he reached the building, he turned to peer into the gap-ing hole at the side of the blazing Children's Museum. Some-one opened fire from within, the quick burst of an automatic weapon. Dan ducked back out of the hole. One of the bullets passed so close to his ear that he paused to feel the side of his head and see if he was hit. No blood.

The remaining Four crowded close in with him. "You guys

go back," he commanded through the smoke, waving them away with his hand. "There is nothing you can do in there. This is my fight now."

The remaining four stared back at him as one from their crouched position, respectfully declining to go anywhere.

"Damn it. Just keep your heads down OK? I'm going in."

And with that, Dan charged into the dark smoky building, firing as he ran. The Glock Mary had given him felt a lot different than his old Colt, but it held 10 more rounds, and for that he was thankful.

He ducked behind a red fire truck with a mannequin firefighter standing next to it. Through the thick smoke behind him ran the remaining Four, still glued to his side despite his protests.

Suddenly the mannequin in the fireman's helmet shredded to pieces in a burst of gunfire. Dan wanted to find better cover, but in the midst of all the smoke and the sweat and the heat he had no idea where the shots were coming from. He didn't know where to hide.

He could see past the grocery store mock up to where the dual front doors of the museum still stood open, letting in the morning glow. Mary was now crouched there cradling the short barreled black shotgun that had once belonged to Papa Walt. Another burst of gunfire punched twenty holes through the fish mural just above her head.

Eldritch had them both pinned down.

Ø Ø Ø

As Abraha and Shin pulled up in front of the Stockton Children's museum it was burning savagely. The parking lot looked like a warzone of twisted metal and smoldering body parts. From inside the building they could hear the smash of rapid gunfire.

"This is not a place where we should be," Shin told his friend.

"Dear God, how am I always responsible for so much death and destruction?" Abraha breathed.

"Let's go, Ab. Get us out of here."

"I can't go," Abraha said doggedly. "My friend Derek Timm is in there. I have to get him out."

He then removed the small glass vial from his pocket, "Give me the tablet. I'm going to fire up my network and see if I can still reach those nanoautomatons in the Potomac."

∅ ∅ ∅

Dan attempted to peer around the fire truck again and through the smoke, drawing another hail of bullets. Mary had repositioned herself behind a six-foot catfish statue near the entrance. She sent a couple of shots out into the smoke, but could not locate a target.

Then, through the crackle of the fire and the soup of the smoke, Dan heard a high-pitched buzz as the second of Eldritch's lethal drones took flight within the burning building. He raised an arm to wave at Mary and warn her, but it was too late. There was a loud whoosh and one of the clones dove to cover his crouching master with his own body. Then the fire engine exploded into a rain of fire and brimstone. Dan and his clones were all thrown from their feet, landing in a bloody heap 10 feet away.

Dan's right arm was on fire and when he moved to pat it out, he found that his left arm would not work. A large piece of red shrapnel jutted from an ugly wound at his left shoulder. One of the remaining Four was laying on top of him and patted the fire out with his bare hands. Then, Dan was staring directly into his own dead eyes. Another one of his clones lay dead on the floor next to him, the one who had moved to cover Dan before the missile struck. His neck was cruelly and unnaturally twisted and his burned body was crumpled and flat.

The ringing in Dan's ears was so loud that he was barely aware of much else. He looked around briefly for his gun as the last Three helped him to his feet. They all shared various bleeding injuries, but Dan appeared to be the worse off with the gaping hole in his left shoulder and a piece of fire truck jutting out of it.

The quadruplets managed to shamble over to the helicopter that had previously held Derek Timm, then they collapsed again in a pile to examine their wounds. Dan could no longer hear the drone. He heard absolutely nothing. Dark blood was dripping down his left earlobe and soaking into his shirt.

$$\varnothing \varnothing \varnothing$$

The moment before the fire truck exploded, Mary had zeroed in on her target. Through the thick smoke she saw the gleam of Eldritch's laptop just 20 feet away. She pulled herself up and with all her strength she rushed toward the glowing screen and the thin hazy figure that held it.

Then, the massive explosion behind Mary threw her off of her feet, but the force of the explosion also propelled her directly toward her target. Her body flew with great momentum, but no control, directly into the tall thin figure in the cattleman's hat.

She hit Eldritch with enough force to send her rifle flying one way and his laptop the other. Mary found herself lying in a heap near a dusty old police car. She was stunned, but in one piece.

As she pushed herself up shaking her head to clear it, she found herself standing face to face with her adversary. Eldritch was braced into an aggressive position directly in front of her. In his right hand he held the long razor sharp tactical knife. His white teeth glinted into the familiar smile that she had once found handsome. Eldritch's ice blue eyes gazed through the smoke at her.

Mary's legs crouched into a fighting stance and she smiled back. It was time to do what she did best.

FIFTY SIH

THE BUILDING WAS ABLAZE all around them. The smoke was burning the back of Mary's throat but she kept her stance. Eldritch started maneuvering, circling to her right to bring the large black blade just a little closer to a point where he could slash at her throat.

"We always knew it would come to this, didn't we, Mary? One on one? A fair fight?"

"How fair was it when you ambushed my team in that slot canyon in Nevada, Eldritch?"

"Mary, Mary, Mary. That was no one's fault but your own." Eldritch feinted with the knife and Mary reacted as the two adversaries circled each other in the smoke.

"You fell for that trap like a rookie. Tadese was nowhere near Nevada that day. Once your friends were down the slot canyon, it was as easy as pouring piss out of a boot. I let you live though, Mary. I watched you climb out. I could have ended you right there and then, but I didn't. That's the second time I've saved your life. Because we have a history, Mary. We are a lot alike you and me."

Mary lunged forward bluffing with a left jab and then connecting a powerful right to the side of Eldritch's head. Eldritch slashed at her with the knife, tearing a deep gash into her leather jacket, missing her abdomen by a fraction of an inch. He recoiled from her blow but kept his eyes focused on hers.

"You taught me a lot, Eldritch, but you could never know what was in my heart. We are nothing alike."

Mary looked deep into the cold blue eyes of her opponent and then lashed out once again. The first roundhouse kick was only a feint with her left leg to bring Eldritch's body into the position she wanted before she hopped back to the wounded leg and swung a fully expressed second roundhouse directly striking her opponent's right hand with her boot and sending the big knife flying into the smoke. The attack sent a jolt of pain through her wounded leg but she ended it back in her fighting stance, as a surprised Eldritch grasped his now empty right hand with his left.

Eldritch took a step back but maintained his smile, "There is one thing that you forgot though, Sister. A lesson you should have learned from me but didn't. I don't fight fair."

Then she heard the high-pitched buzz of the drone as it floated a few feet directly above the black cattleman's hat, sighting in on her, missiles at the ready.

Suddenly, the killing machine was jolted sideways as a can of corn struck it from the side. Reaper Two began an evasive roll to the right when it was struck again by a second can which stunned it frozen in place as a third can narrowly missed and a fourth can smashed one of its front rotors, sending it spinning through the smoke.

From the mock supermarket, the last Three huffed at each other proudly as they continued to toss the cans from the dusty shelves at the drone.

"You fools! You'll kill us all!" Eldritch shouted, but it was too late, Reaper Two was already spinning out of control when another can struck the deadly machine with full force smashing its front sensor. With three Red-Widows still attached, the drone shot off at an odd angle through the smoke and out of sight.

Eldritch grabbed his rifle from the nearby reading table and then dove underneath for cover. The last Three ran to quickly gather up Dan who now lay unconscious under the inoperable helicopter. They began dragging him toward for the front doors of the museum; their footsteps falling in unison.

Mary ducked behind the police car searching the floor for her rifle and waiting for the explosion...

But it never came. The crippled Reaper Two careened harmlessly into a large pit filled with foam balls in front of a rotting trampoline. There it lay, damaged and useless.

Suddenly, there was another large crash as the flaming ceiling over the supermarket collapsed in a cloud of sparks and thick black smoke. Mary lost sight of Dan and the clones. She could only hope that they had not been crushed by the burning rubble as it rained down.

She was on all fours, face as close to the dingy carpet as she could get, coughing loudly, finding it hard to catch a breath. She crawled along, feeling on the floor for her rifle when she grasped the leg of someone lying next to her. She crept along perpendicular to the body until she was face to face with a bruised and battered Derek Timm who lay unconscious by the police car.

Mary grabbed the back of the collar of Derek's denim shirt and started scrabbling for the front door, dragging him behind her. Her lungs were convulsing spasmodically rejecting the foul air she was inhaling, but she continued, half-crawling, half-squirming but always pulling the unconscious doctor toward the door.

She was almost there, just ten feet away when Eldritch stepped out of the smoke and into the path directly in front of her. The smoke was so thick that she couldn't see his face as he towered over her. All she could see was the short-barreled assault rifle he brought to bear on her through the heat of the fire. Mary's eyes gazed down the barrel of the ugly weapon. *That's the last thing I am ever going to see.*

The edges of her vision were going dark and her head was pulsing from a lack of oxygen when the smoke cleared for a moment and she could once again see the gleaming teeth of Eldritch's smile as his finger tightened on the trigger.

"Goodbye, Mary."

Suddenly, Eldritch was bowled over. He went flying through the air ass over heels as he was struck by a stream of water that rushed through the building at a staggering rate of pressure. Mary heard several loud snaps as the force of the stream broke Eldritch's back, right arm, and probably several ribs, throwing him directly into the burning rubble that had once been the fire truck. Andrew Eldritch's thin frame disappeared into the flames.

The powerful and volatile stream of water passed above Mary and continued pulsing through the building. She thought for a second that it must be a fire hose but quickly focused back on the task at hand, pulling Derek Timm from the building.

When she finally dragged herself and the battered doctor through the front doors and into the sunlight, she collapsed on the ground gagging and vomiting up bile as her lungs gasped at the clean California air.

Mary looked up into the parking lot where a stout Asian man was holding what appeared to be a small tablet directly in front of him with both hands. His arms were extended and his legs were braced on the asphalt of the parking lot as a deluge of water sprang with such force from the surface of the tablet and into the burning museum that he was leaning and pushing forward with all his might in order to maintain his balance. The soles of his shoes were sliding backwards along the parking lot despite his best efforts to stay in place.

He was shouting at a shocked brown man who stood beside him, "TURN IT OFF! TURN IT OFF, AB!"

But Dr. Abraha Tadese could only gaze in wonder at the torrent arching nearly out of control with its fluid power sending four thousand gallons per minute directly into the heart of the already dying fire.

FIFTY SEVEN

DEREK TIMM WATCHED IN awe through his one open eye. The little man seemed to be barely in control of the raging torrent when suddenly, with no warning, the water completely stopped and he tumbled forward onto his face. The man, whom he guessed was Tadese's companion Dr. Shin, had been pushing against the force of the water with every ounce of strength he had.

The stout scientist immediately jumped up and brushed the soot from his face. Then he held both hands over his head in the thrill of victory, shouting words only he understood, in what sounded like Korean, at God and the heavens. The hand that held the black tablet rose up high and then spiked the device into the ashy asphalt like a football, sending slivers flying. Shin then proceeded to do a comic little dance in circles. Beside him, the tall brown man had seen Mary and Derek, and was rushing to their side.

Siren's wailed as firetrucks and police vehicles bounded into the parking lot. Shin and Abraha were carrying Derek away from the building and laying him down in a shady spot under a grove of gigantic oak trees which towered over the deep water channel nearby. Firemen and paramedics swarmed out of their vehicles.

Abraha hovered over Derek where he had knelt to check his various wounds. When their eyes met for the first time Abraha broke into tears and embraced his old friend sobbing, "I'm so sorry, Derek. I'm so sorry," over and over again into Derek's chest.

Derek found the strength to grasp Abraha's arms and push

him back up. With one eye swollen shut he contemplated the brown face that was responsible for what might be the greatest discovery since atomic energy. A discovery that would certainly save California if not the entire world. That sad, tired face was responsible for the deaths of almost 600 people at Adelphi, and for the death of Derek's wife.

Derek searched for the words to comfort his friend, who could not stop sobbing. Finally, with the paramedics approaching, Derek spoke through cracked and broken lips.

"Ab, look up above us into the trees." Abraha wiped at his eyes and turned his head toward the soaring limbs covered in thick alligator hide bark and thousands of green leaves.

"Do you know those trees Ab?" Derek's voice was a hoarse whisper. "Those are Valley oaks. The largest of the North American Oaks. They are probably 500 years old. Those trees were here before this city was. They were here before California was. They were here before the New Federal Union, before the United States of America, and they will still be here after we are gone…"

∅ ∅ ∅

Derek had a point to make but he passed out before he could clarify it. As the paramedics who had rushed up started to check his vital signs, Abraha pushed himself up from the ground and wiped at his wet face. He contemplated the trees and Derek's words for a moment, then turned back to his friend Shin, managing a slight smile.

As Derek was being placed into an ambulance on a stretcher, Abraha and Shin were whisked into a white van by several heavily armed CIRCA agents. Shin was excitedly chattering at Abraha about what exactly had gone right and shaking his hand over and over again, repeating in his thick accent, "We did it my friend, we did it!"

For the first time Abraha's new technology, the technology of Nanoinformatification had been used for its intended purpose: to put out fire and save life. The hint of a smile was beginning to expand on Dr. Abraha Tadese's exhausted face. *Despite all the negative consequences, perhaps sometimes the ends really do justify the means.*

∅ ∅ ∅

When Mary had first pulled herself out of the blaze, she could only lay on the pavement coughing and hacking and gasping for oxygen. She had sucked in a lot of smoke. Her teary eyes gazed in wonder at the little Asian man magically producing a cascading stream of water that rushed in a 3-foot-thick funnel at around 100 miles per hour seemingly straight from his bare hands which he held outstretched in front of him.

When the water stopped, Mary had started to control her breathing a bit better and she stumbled upright, desperate to find Dan and the clones. Had they gotten out? There was no sign of them. Mary pushed herself to her feet and saw that the two water wizards were tending to Derek Timm. She recognized Dr. Abraha Tadese, her primary quarry for the last several weeks, but at that moment, the fact that he was safe and close by was enough. She needed to find Dan.

Mary stumbled out into the parking lot still hacking dark rheum from her lungs. The sun was rising into the thick brown haze of smoke from the fire. It was already turning into a hot day. Mary covered her mouth with her torn jacket and wiped at her blurry eyes scanning the simmering wreckage for signs of life. Then, she heard a familiar huffing barely louder than a whisper.

"Huff Huff Huff, Ooh!"

She looked to her right where one of Dan's doppelgangers was making nodding motions at her, trying to get her attention from the other side of the parking lot.

She stumbled in his direction as he disappeared behind a small pump house which produced large pipes from its side that ran over the ground and out into the waters of the delta. Behind it, she found the last three clones crouching protectively around an unconscious and badly bleeding Dan.

"Medic!" she shouted as she rushed to his side.

Two of the clones were making worried cooing noises while the third was openly weeping and sobbing loudly from where he sat in the dirt by Dan's crumpled form.

Mary again barked, "Medic!" over her shoulder at the first fire engine to appear on the scene. She was again thrust into a fit of coughing and another one of the clones started howling hysterically like a huge dog. Mary looked at the grave wound at Dan's shoulder and at the thick dark blood oozing from it.

Sister Mary, agent of CIRCA, always cool confident and precise, started to panic in the realization that she didn't know what to do. "Medic!" she screamed again. And the third of Dan's clones also broke into uncontrollable sobs.

The final Three wailed turbulently as Mary did her best to pull, push, and herd them away from their master as paramedics rushed to try and save Dan's life.

Ø Ø Ø

An hour later, the previously abandoned industrial neighborhood in downtown Stockton, California was swarming with CIRCA agents and State Police. The fire had all but been out when the Fire Department arrived, so the firemen wandered through the smoldering wreckage with axes knocking down whatever charred debris hadn't fallen on its own. All that was left of the Stockton Children's Museum was a smoldering heap of ash with a helicopter in the middle of it.

It was one of these firemen who found a crumpled and broken Andrew Eldritch under the once purple table in what had been the reading room. He was burnt beyond recognition and his back was badly broken but he was still breathing. Barely.

Water was everywhere. Great black puddles gathered and poured down drains in the parking lot and at the corners of the charred frame of the building as the paramedics gathered up the scorched, yet still extant remains onto a stretcher.

"Gotta feel bad for this guy," one of the firefighters drawled. "He'd be better off dead."

And Andrew Eldritch's blackened lips pulled back into a smile revealing his perfect white teeth.

FIFTY EIGHT

STOCKTON, CA HAD ONCE BEEN the homicide capital of the United States. Then, the city had become the heart of the great recession at the center of the housing market collapse forcing the city into bankruptcy. After Calexit, downtown Stockton had been all but abandoned and it had become a hothouse of criminal activity. Gang murders, illegal narcotics trade, and prostitution had run rampant.

But Stockton's rebirth was imminent. The new economy was starting to catch on. The city was developing into a new community comprised of small peaceful family farms at the heart of one of the most fertile and productive agricultural areas in the California Independent Republic. Independent gardens and farms all around the delta community were breathing new life into the land and the people. Abandoned houses and strip malls were torn down to reclaim and repurpose the fertile land for horticulture. Hope bloomed in the San Joaquin Valley. Hope for all of California.

As the wreckage of the Children's Museum smoldered in the deserted city center, seeding, tilling, and harvesting continued at a rapid pace everywhere else in the area.

It was near one of these small family farms that Dan had found space in a tiny private graveyard to bury the remains of his lost clones. The last Three had done all the digging, the laying of the remains, and the interment, all without any hint of emotion. There was no sign that they were cognizant of the weight of their actions or of the contents of the bundles they buried. Mary stood by and watched as Dan gravely gave directions and encouragement from time to time.

Ø Ø Ø

"So, you're telling me you never taught Scar to drive your truck? Then how did he learn?" Mary asked.

"That's just it. I don't know. I never even heard him talk up until a few days ago. I didn't think he could, and I had him for years." It had taken Dan several days to recover after the battle. He had lost a lot of blood. Now, with his arm in a sling and his shoulder heavily bandaged, he was back on his feet.

"And did the other ones talk too?" Mary sounded confused.

"No, just Scar. But these others understood though. They seemed like they could communicate. Didn't you?" Dan half shouted at the last Three shoveling the remaining soil over their two lost brothers.

The eyes of Dan's clones remained glassy and emotionless, uncomprehending. One of them made his usual ignorant little huffing noises. "Huff Huff Huff, Ooh." Another one stopped for a moment to scratch an itch on his back that he couldn't reach, causing him to spin in place in a slow circular dance next to the grave.

"I think you imagined it," Mary said looking at the three dumb homunculuses before her.

"I didn't imagine Scar driving that truck," Dan said as he bent to pick up some of the loose dirt from the grave with his good hand. He then stood, absently tossing the dirt back to the ground little by little as he spoke.

"And what's more? It was his idea. Scar was special somehow. He saved my daughter, Sarah Joy's, life once a long time ago. I felt like I owed him a debt after that. Then, I took care of him when he was sick. I was trying to pay that debt, but I lost my whole family and farm in the process. And..." Dan paused.

"I was drunk the night they died.

"I blamed myself and I blamed them. That's why I thought I would sell him and the others. I thought I didn't need them anymore, but then Scar started telling me those crazy stories... I guess to show me that I was wrong." Dan's voice, usually a hoarse whisper, was strong and firm for the first time. He sounded, and felt, like a different man than the one who had met Mary out in the burning desert just a few days ago.

Dan continued, "My wife Jocelyn..." His voice trembled and he wiped at his eyes. "God rest her soul. She used to listen to this song that said, *I saw the crescent, but you saw the whole of the moon.* Have you ever heard that song?" He stopped again to rub his eyes before continuing on. Mary shook her head.

"I used to think it was the *hole* of the moon. You know, like H-O-L-E. I could see the crescent, but you only saw the hole, what couldn't be seen. But Jocelyn, she was super into music, she schooled me on that one. She said, 'It's about seeing the *whole* of the moon. W-H-O-L-E. Not just the crescent.'" He looked up from Scar's grave for the first time and into Mary's eyes. "I feel like I am seeing the whole of the moon now for the first time. You're the one who helped me to see it."

For a moment Mary was lost in the depth of Dan's moist brown eyes and they were both silent for a heartbeat. Two heart beats. Then, Mary came back to her senses and tore her own eyes away. She awkwardly pulled her device out of her pocket and pretended to busy herself with checking messages.

Dan turned from her and knelt in the grass by the fresh grave. He crossed himself and said a silent prayer for Scar and his other lost clone. When he finally arose, Mary was doing her best not to pay attention to him.

Without looking up she asked distractedly, "What now Dan? You still going to sell these final Three?"

"No." Dan didn't even have to think about it. "No, I'm not. My mom is still here in town somewhere. I'm going to find her and maybe buy a little patch of land on the delta. Try my hand at farming again. CIRCA paid me well for helping you out."

"I made sure of that," Mary responded. "Good time to be a farmer. Now that California, and only California has the digital water technology, nothing will ever be the same. The California Republic can choose to save the world with clean water, or drown it in a Biblical deluge."

Dan nodded as one of the last Three started chasing a butterfly through the grassy cemetery. The other two glanced questioningly at Dan for a second before following suit.

Dan watched them scamper off like enormous children. "I'm gonna have Trev come down and help me set up the farm, and then... I also want to find the other clones. You know, the other groups created by Bioserv. There are supposed to be at least five or six other groups that they completed before the lab was bombed. I want to know if they have had any similar experiences to ours. What the Bioserv lab created... Well, I just don't understand, and I want to."

"You'll have to cross back into the New Federal Union."

Dan shrugged. "Someday I will," he said.

The last Three half tackled, half tripped over each other and collapsed into the grass in a huffing pile of arms and legs, pushing and kicking at each other in a friendly tussle.

"What about you, Mary?" Dan looked to her eyes again and this time she did not look away. "You could stay here with me. Farming is a peaceful life."

Mary slowly shook her head. Dan had a sense that, for a brief second, she had actually considered his offer. "California needs me. We aren't out of the woods yet. CIRCA will still need someone to do their dirty work. That's always going to be me."

Dan placed his good hand on her shoulder and then pulled her thin frame to his thick chest in a warm embrace. Mary wrapped a pale muscular arm around Dan's large brown trunk and hugged him back.

Mary's device buzzed and she pulled away from him.

"Damn it," she cursed as she checked the black screen for new orders.

In Dan's head, he prayed silently,

Ave Maria

Gratia Plena

Dominus Tecum

Benedictus…

"This can't be right…" Mary looked confused.

From their pile on the ground the remaining Three looked up with just a hint of a smile on their identical faces.

"What is it, Mary?"

"Dan…it's your daughter, Dan. It's Sarah Joy. She's alive! She's in Colorado."

Dan's eyes grew wide as he collapsed heavily, unable to hold himself up for a moment. He sank into the dirt at Mary's feet.

"That can't be… How can it be possible?"

"Huff Huff Huff, Ooh!" the last Three cooed softly and happily to themselves.

THE END

3 CLONES

THE MONSOON'S RAINS POURED DOWN on the valley like an unstoppable avalanche filling the small wooden boat so quickly that Russel had to continuously bail water over the side with a small plastic bucket while steering and searching out into the darkness.

"Dan!" he screamed against the storm that roared all around him. "Jocelyn!" He could barely hear himself over the torrential downpour. The small Evinrude motor sputtered a moment as if it would die, but then kept on. Russel knew it was near to suicide taking the little skiff out into the storm like this, but he could only think the worst for his niece and her family.

He passed the top of an oak tree almost completely submerged in black dirty water. Could that be the tree by the greenhouses? Could he possibly be close to the house? He looked up but there was no sign of stars above him, only the unforgiving rain beating against his face with wet fists from the sky.

If he was near the greenhouses, then the ranch house might just be a few hundred feet away.

"Dan!" he screamed with all of his might. "Jocelyn!"

"Uncle Russel!" Came an unbelievably tiny reply through the rain. Surely, he was imagining things. But, then he heard it again. "Uncle Russel!" It was Sarah Joy's voice.

Where was it coming from? Lightening flashed again and from the corner of his eye, Russel could just see the tip of a white gable off to the right passing behind him. He sped the small boat into a loop and back to where the ridge of the roofline was just barely perceptible in the frothing flood as the thunder pealed out over his head making his ears ring.

Perched on top of the last few inches of visible roofline was a tiny figure, soaked to the bone. It was Sarah Joy! She was alive!

Russel pulled the skiff in close to her. Close enough to gather the drenched little girl in his arms, but she pulled away from him and out of his reach.

"No!" she screamed! "Mama! Johnny! They're still inside! They couldn't get out! The hole was too small!"

The boat was pulled by a swirling current past and away from the little girl and Russel had to swing around again against the wind. The ridgeline of the house was completely submerged now. Sarah Joy appeared to be standing on water, floating magically amongst the brown waves that lapped at her ankles. The last lightning strike had struck so close that electricity was crackling and dancing around her head in a halo of St. Elmo's fire.

Russell's boat was almost a third of the way filled with rainwater. If he didn't speed to higher ground now, he and Sarah would be drowned for sure. He gave the little motor all the gas it would take directly to the right of Sarah Joy, just missing her by inches. Without slowing down or giving her a second to object he grabbed the little girl and pulled her into the boat as he sped by.

"No!" She screamed. "Mama! Johnny!" Russel held her tightly as he looked back over his shoulder. There was no longer any sign that a house had ever existed in the middle of this ocean. His tears, like Sarah Joy's, mixed with the rain that poured down their faces.

"No!" Sarah Joy screamed again. And Russel held her tight as he gunned the little motorboat out, away, and into the rain and into the darkness.

ABOUT THE AUTHOR

Ed Bonilla is a teacher, writer, singer, husband, and father in his hometown of Stockton, California. Ed recently won the prestigious Kelly J. Abbott Short Story Contest for his short story "I won't tell..." which is also chapter 18 here in 5 Clones.